MAANA-FAAY
A novel

MAANA-FAAY

A novel

By
Maxamed Daahir Afrax

Translated from Somali
By
Ahmed Ismail Yusuf with Maggi Larson
Editor
Muna Afrah

Adonis & Abbey Publishers Ltd
24 Old Queen Street,
London SW1H 9HP
United Kingdom

Website: http://www.adonis-abbey.com
E-mail Address: editor@adonis-abbey.com

Nigeria:
Jimmy Carter Street,
Suites C3 – C6 J-Plus Plaza
Asokoro, Abuja, Nigeria
Tel: +234 (0) 7058078841/08052035034

British Library Cataloguing-in-Publication Data
A catalogue record for this book is available from the British Library.

ISBN: 9781913976101

Table of Content

Acknowledgments

Many people have supported the birth of this book in one way or another, and while I am indebted to them all, it is not possible to name everyone. First, I owe immense gratitude to President Ismail Omar Guelleh of Djibouti for providing wholehearted encouragement and support to the accomplishment of my work as an author and researcher, including this novel. President Guelleh is renowned for his genuine love of literature and culture and his unfailing support to the creative initiatives taken by writers, researchers and literary/cultural promoters, for which he deserves to be given credit. Sincere gratitude is due to Ahmed Ismail Yusuf, whose unparalleled commitment, unyielding determination, and unusual patience were the principal forces behind the accomplishment of this English version of *Maana-faay*. Over the years, Ahmed spent innumerable sleepless nights working on the translation of this novel, chapter by chapter, against all odds. I also thank the late Professor Virginia Lulling, who had inspired and taken the first initiative to translate this book from Somali to English. She had actually started the translation work; unfortunately, however Virginia's attempts were soon thwarted by her sudden illness and subsequent untimely death. I am indebted to Professor Lidwien Kapteijns of Wellesley College, who constantly supported my work on Somali literature and critically commented on it with invaluable insight. Ladan (as we, her friends, call her) had particularly made tremendous efforts on various occasions to promote the novel *Maana-faay*, provide a critical analysis of it, and translate a number of its chapters into English, as a labor of love. Special thanks go to Professor Ali Jimale Ahmed, who was the first to embrace *Maana-faay* when the story first came out in serial form in the Somali national daily of the time, *Xiddigta Octobar,* back in late 1979. He was the first to put pen on paper commenting on it and even translating the first episodes into English. His pioneering translation appeared in the weekly newspaper *Heegan.* More recently, Ali kindly read through the manuscript of the new English version, translated by Ahmed Ismail Yusuf, and offered invaluable comments. Moreover, he was kind enough to make unreserved efforts to support the publication of the newborn translation. I am grateful to the Africa Educational Trust and its former Director, Michael Brophy, for offering some initial support to the translation project. I also thank Maggi Larson, who was kind enough to voluntarily assist the translator, Ahmed Yusuf, in revising and polishing the translated text chapter by chapter. Special thanks are also due to Professor Christopher Winks for his impeccable copyediting. Last but not least, I sincerely thank Boodhari Warsame, Jill Bell, Muna Afrah and Ahmed Farah Salah, all of whom had volunteered to take part in the editing and/or proofreading process of the manuscript.

To them all I say *Mahadsanidin*.

Maxamed Daahir Afrax

Foreword

Lidwien Kapteijns

The Mogadishu of Maxamed Daahir Afrax's novel *Maana-faay* no longer exists– neither physically, as its buildings have been destroyed in war, nor socially, as so many Somalis have been forced into exile or killed. This makes Afrax's novel, written in Somali in the late 1970s, all the more important. In the Mogadishu of *Maana-faay,* the exuberant mood that accompanied the achievement of Somali flag independence in 1960 was slowly dying, as the moral and political corruption of the military regime of Maxamed Siyaad Barre, and its increasing violence against its perceived enemies, had begun to corrode the patina of national unity and the integrity of many who put their own interests first. The unique flourishing of literary creativity in the Somali language that had characterized the preceding two decades was gradually being undermined, as Somali artists were forced into political subservience, prison, or exile. This is the context of the love story of Maana-faay, the young Benadiri girl who gives the novel its name.

When it came out, *Maana-faay* was remarkably unique. First, prose writing in Somali was a brand-new phenomenon in this land of poets. Second, Afrax's ability to bring to life the conversational language of the youth of this time, and even, for his protagonist and her family, the Benadiri inflections of their language use, was (and remains) unequalled. This has also made the translation of the novel so challenging and explains why it has taken more than forty years before someone with the talent, skills, and courage of Ahmed Ismail Yusuf dared to take it on. Third, Afrax was able to bring to life the unique sense of place that characterized the centuries-old quarter of Hamarweyn, then still Mogadishu's ebullient, colorful, multi-cultural, and stunningly beautiful historical center.

Maana-faay tells the story of a young schoolgirl whose love for a young engineer is thwarted by her conservative parents, and who becomes trapped in the net spun for her by members of the new, corrupt and immoral state elite, out to get a taste of her young flesh. It shows the social costs of rigid, old-fashioned social customs that subordinated the rights and needs of young people to the interests of the kin-group and the sanction of elders, on the one hand, and, on the other, exposes the emerging political and moral bankruptcy, as well as the sexism and sexual exploitation of government officials and the newly rich.

Woven into this story are the many tensions and inequalities that marked this moment in Somali history: between the pillars of old-fashioned patriarchal authority and freedom-seeking youth, between the innocence of girls and the depravity of sexual predators, between rich and poor, between rural and urban ways, and between those who were complicit with corruption and those resisting it. Throughout, the novel resolutely takes the side of romantic love and of Mogadishu's urban youth, and this is what makes *Maana-faay* the quintessential (even if romanticized) expression of this unique moment of Mogadishu's modernity.

Having initially appeared in serialized form in the national daily *Xiddigta Oktoobar* ("The October Star") in 1979, *Maana-faay* was first published in book form in Moǧadishu in 1981, and then, after the author's exile in the early 1980s, reprinted in Stockholm (1993) and London (1997). To the translator and his collaborator, Maggie Larson, who made this jewel of the Somali national heritage available in English, we owe an enormous debt of gratitude.

Lidwien Kapteijns

Wellesley, 23 January 2021

Introduction

Ali Jimale Ahmed

The Somali novel is, by all accounts, of recent formation, and its emergence and development a recent phenomenon. Prior to the adoption of the Latin alphabet (1972), Somalia had a long tradition of excellence in poetry and prose, with both genres tightly linked to orature. Yet the orality of the language did not imply the absence of written literature. *Manaqib* stories, i.e., tales that extol a revered shaykh's virtuous traits and glorious deeds, whet the appetite of their readers, especially the disciples of the particular shaykh whose hagiographic tale was the topic of discussion. The manaqib, though, had their origins in the *sira*, where stories of the prophets (*qisas al-anbiya*), including the Prophet Muhammad, were placed at the disposal of the faithful. Since a majority of Somalis were illiterate, it became important to translate for the laity. Ironically, the preachers themselves were people who had only a smattering of Arabic. In Mogadishu, the Somali capital, and the scene of Maxamed Daahir Afrax's (Mohamed Dahir Afrah's) novel *Maana-faay*, the preachers' favorite sites were at bus terminals, where they entertained commuters waiting for their next ride. The preachers' sermons-cum-entertainment were never soporific or dull. The listeners engaged them and at times guided their sermons to respond to specific topics of interest to them. The shaykhs had to observe a delicate balance between what they wanted to address and what their audience wished to hear. The antiphonal logic of the Sufi sermon does not, however, mimic the traditional form of "call and response." Instead, "Responsive understanding is a fundamental force, one that participates in the formulation of discourse, and it is moreover an *active* understanding, one that discourse senses as resistance or support enriching the discourse" ("Discourse in the Novel" 280-1; emphasis in original).

The preachers also subliminally inspired budding writers and storytellers of all stripes. They unleashed imagination to set sail, and introduced their spectators to a cacophony of voices, as they themselves came from different fraternities and/or hailed from different linguistic backgrounds. Spectators were introduced to a kind of Bakhtinian polyglossia or "interanimation of languages." On a microcosmic level, the *sira* is both intended as a form of pedagogy and as epistemology. On the macrocosmic level, the *sira* brings to the fore the idiosyncratic intellectual and oratorical prowess of the Sufi storytellers. The maieutic intentions of the *sira* are instrumentalized through the rhetorical prowess of the individual preacher. Bakhtin argues that there is a close affinity and interaction between the novel genre and rhetorical forms. He writes: The novel, and artistic prose in general, has the closest genetic, family relationship to rhetorical forms. And throughout the entire development of the novel, its intimate interaction (both peaceful and hostile) with living rhetorical genres (journalistic, moral, philosophical and others) has never ceased; this interaction was perhaps no less intense than was the novel's interaction with the artistic genres (epic, dramatic, lyric) ("Discourse in the Novel," 269).

The rhetorician, like the novelist, uses language, and endeavors to populate it with his/her own intentions. Both novelist and rhetorician aim to engage their audience/readers consciously and subliminally. Generic interactions and relationships do not, however, imply that the novel loses its "qualitative uniqueness" and becomes one with rhetorical discourse (p.269). The novel in Somalia is no exception.

Once there was an agreed-upon system of writing for Somali, prospective writers emerged from all sections of society. The introduction of the Latin script heralded a new era where Somali consciousness was nudged towards a robust scribal culture. Two years after the introduction of the Latin script as the country's official orthography, Faarax M J Cawl (Farah M. J. 'Awl) published his novel, *Aqoondarro waa u nacab jacayl* (1974) (*Ignorance Is the Enemy of Love*, 1982). The Somali novel at its conception grappled with conceptual and practical categories that coterminously blossomed with the introduction of the genre: self-agency and individual responsibility, historical consciousness, and requisite social and political transformation. *Ignorance Is the Enemy of Love* is a case in point.

Ignorance is a historical novel, a story of true love recounted in fictionalized form, with a clear objective: to exhort people to learn the new Somali alphabet. As a realist romance, *Ignorance* investigates a historical event, using the "dervish" war as a framing arch. Calimaax ('Ali the seafarer"), the protagonist, is returning from a spy mission he has successfully carried out against the British in Aden, Yemen. Among the travelers on his return trip to Somalia is Cawrala, a young woman returning from a visit to a relative in Aden, where she had the opportunity to become literate in Arabic. They fall in love and agree to marry one day. But Cawrala is already betrothed, and the reader here senses the hurdles facing the couple. At the Dervish Headquarters, Calimaax briefs the Sayyid about an impending British attack on the Dervishes. The Sayyid and his high command are pleased with the report and "as a reward he was given a girl in marriage, and the wedding took place immediately" (*Ignorance,* 26). Soon after, Calimaax receives a letter from Cawrala reminding him of his promise to marry her. An illiterate, Calimaax asks his new father-in-law to read the letter for him. After reading the letter to himself, the old man refuses to read it for him. Assuming that his father-in-law's reluctance results from diminishing eyesight, he passes the letter to his brother-in-law, who is greatly offended. Eventually the brother-in-law reads the letter for him but admonishes him for his audacious ignorance.

The primer-like characteristics of the narrative encourage the author's contemporaries to spare themselves embarrassing moments at the hands of scribes/scriveners or, worse, in-laws. Thus, ignorance is not only an enemy of love, but also the enemy of self-esteem, as it compromises one's dignity by revealing a lack in one's life. The narrative construction and chronotope and its maieutic imperative leave no space or room for any flâneur, as Calimaax's predicament is reproduced as the requisite "concrete prehistory," to borrow from Lukács (*The Historical Novel,* 296), of the need for the author's contemporaries to attend literacy classes. The narrative also condenses time in such a way that time past, symbolized by the Dervish War of resistance to colonialism, is uncannily made relevant to an audience in the early stages of mastering a new alphabet. The learning process gains its impetus and relevance from the symbiotic relationship between the individual and the collective. The narrative's message and objective inaugurate the *raison d'être* of the novelistic imperative: the individual is the center of attention in that she/he assumes self-agency. But, as Brian Stock argues, "Literacy begins with the collective. The point of departure of reading is the individual. [...] To speak of literacy is therefore to shift the discussion towards the societal; to speak of reading is to shift it towards the individual" ("Historical Worlds, Literary History" 54). (Certainly, here Stock does not take into consideration other reading experiences where, as in the case of Ngugi's *Matigari*, a literate individual would read a book to a group of illiterate or semi-literate people.)

Ignorance, as a transitional novel, helped the indigenization of the novel genre. Stressing the importance of mastering literacy through a concrete example was an ingenious method to introduce readers to the new medium of writing. This also paved the way for other writers to foll ow suit. Slowly, and in less than eight years, the novel came to constitute a viable form capable of transmitting and aiding the spread of modernist ideas and sentiments. Modernism—literary, political and social— in the Somali case contains a paradox that could be described by its bifurcated intentions: first, its intention to challenge and supersede the hegemony of tradition, as revealed in its "commitment to innovation" and 'experimentalism" (Calinescu, 1987: 265); and second, its willingness to temper a tendency among some proponents of modernization to import (without installing sifting mechanisms) European Enlightenment ideas. The novel that best exemplifies this conception of modernism is Maxamed D. Afrax's *Maana-faay*, which ushers in a new form of storytelling, as it exhibits ingenious and conscious ways of using language to reflect the modus vivendi of its characters and their urban habitat. The eponymous heroine hails from a community of urban dwellers, the Hamari or Muqdishaawi, Hamar (Xamar) being the local name of the Somali capital. But as the capital of the nation, it is also the meeting ground of people from diverse backgrounds. The narrative accentuates the heteroglossic aspect of its characters through creative portrayal of "speech diversity." The narrative also delves into the protagonist's consciousness in ways hitherto not evidenced in the novels of the "transmuter" group of a decade earlier. In short, the novels that preceded *Maana-faay* retained structural, formal, semantic, and semiotic relations with the oral art form. Characteristic features of oral literature—characterization, speech patterns, plot infrastructure, including the privileging of action, etc.—abound in these early novels.

Afrax's novel and the characters that inhabit it, on the other hand, grapple with living in an urban environment. The novel opens *in medias res* with the protagonist meditating on her plight. The omniscient narrator furnishes a bird's-eye view of the room. The language is crisp, taut, poetic. The depiction is something we have not seen in earlier novels: "If you allowed your eyes to study her, you would see a white short-sleeved shirt with two newly grown breasts pushing up against it. You would have thought that they were protesting against the tightness of the shirt in which they were harshly confined. *Let them! Who is to be blamed; the breasts or the shirt buttons? Let them feel mistreated; who would mediate for them?*" (3; emphasis in original). The translators brilliantly capture the nuanced portrayal of the scene: unruly breasts, the shirt as a jailer of sorts, constricting and hampering the flourishing of the protagonist's tiny breasts. In such a beautiful and refined language, the narrator uses metaphors to metonymically refer to body parts abused and mistreated by shirt buttons. The novels of the transmuter group eschew any mention of body parts. The Hamari subculture is outside the agropastoral culture that dominates much of Somali imaginative literature. Also, the protagonist's plight finds voice in the novel genre, for the novel does not necessitate the assumption of a mantle inherited from the past. The characters respond to social, political and economic challenges created through human interactions in the present. The protagonist's narrative has its etymology in the private domain of the family. Needless to say, then, that such narrative has to forge its own requisite structure, style, and thematic innovation. Afrax's novel initiates a novelistic discussion of the experiences of Hamari families and their trials and tribulations. The Hamari subculture has in previous times been the subject of lyric songs and dramatic and performance pieces, but has never been a novelistic subject. Afrah gives the reader the flavor of urban living and of Hamari dialect as spoken by the protagonist and other characters in the novel. That did not come easy, as the novelist had to immerse himself in the study of the dialect and its intricate nuances. The rendition is admirably authentic.

That said, Afrah examines Maana-faay and other characters' existence in the midst of change initiated by a purportedly socialist government. "[E]xistence," writes Milan Kundera, "is not what has occurred, [rather, it is] the realm of human possibilities, everything that [a human being] can become, everything [they are] capable of." Thus, Maana-faay and her world "must be understood as possibilities" (Kundera, *The Art of the Novel*, 43). *Maana-faay* combines two elements that Kundera binarizes, namely, "the historical dimension of human existence" and "the illustration of a historical situation" (36). In this sense, *Maana-faay* both grapples with the dynamics and dialectics of a "novelized historiography,"while at the same time transcending temporal and spatial limitations. As a coming-of-age story, the protagonist's struggles against parental and societal injunctions link her anxiety and angst to the plight of other youngsters in a similar predicament. In other words, the sociocultural specificity of *Maana-faay* is not an impediment to the reception and understanding of the narrative across time and space. The narrative interferes with familial practices that thwart the desires of those in love, and, through this disruption, launches a parallel attack on the edifices of the patriarchal state. Here the writer juxtaposes the two institutions, while subtly remaining above the fray.

Afrax's *Maana faay* is a gendered narrative in that it brings to the fore the deep-rooted customs that deny women a voice in how they lead their lives. In her endeavor to chart her own path, the protagonist falls victim to a woman who runs a "brothel." The author here reveals the contradictions plaguing a regime that described itself as progressive and socialist. The narrative reveals the truth in Ileana Rodriguez's succinct observation: "It is obvious that the discussion of gender parallels the formation of the modern nation-state" (*House, Garden, Nation,* 86). The narrative also introduces new ways of representing contending forms of reality without employing a direct or linear form of narrating events, sentiments, and states of consciousness. Through taut and austere syntax, and dispensing with mediating descriptions, the reader is allowed a glimpse into the title character's subjective state of consciousness. Afrax's characterization in this novel approximates what Bakhtin calls "skaz," that is, "a technique or mode of narration that imitates the oral speech of an individualized narrator" (*Problems of Dostoevsky's Poetics,* 8, n. b). The title character's use of her Hamari dialect sustains the narrative's "double-voicedness, [astutely illuminated] by the intersection within it of two voices and two accents" that materialize in "a whole series of intonational, syntactic, and other *language* phenomena" (*Problems,* 192; emphasis in the original).

With *Maana Faay* the novel genre in the Somali language comes of age, both in terms of content and structure. *Maana-faay* was first serialized in the official government daily, *Xiddigta Oktoobar* (October Star). It was an instant hit, and to this day remains a rare event. The title became synonymous with modernization and urbanity. Parents began to name their newborn daughters after the title character. The name also became a popular place name, as shops and bars named "Maana-faay" cropped up all over Somalia — this while the regime showed apprehension over the novel's reach and popularity. This was a clear indication of the power of the written word, as the novel created a space for contumacy and dissension, thereby revealing the regime's frailty and vulnerability. Through elaborate and labyrinthine poetic language, the narrative accomplishes what conscientious citizens do to keep those in power honest. In the meantime, the novel, ironically, constructed a new national consciousness, a new sense of Somali-ness, a new dispensation.

It was clear that a new era in both gender relations and subjectivity was gradually taking root. Early in the narrative, the title character begins to interrogate the ethical and moral values of arranged marriages. Granted, this was not the first time that the institution/practice had been taken to task; even Cawrala in *Ignorance Is the Enemy of Love* had doubts about it. What was different this time, however, was the kind of questions flooding the protagonist's subconscious mind. She closes her eyes and a battle of ideas rages in her mind:

> Dadkaan qaf uula hadasho ma la waayey, oo runta u sheegto…Maxaa la ii khasbaa?! Ma rabi…ma rabi…ma rabi. […] Waalid-waalidaa la idinka badiyey…ammaan lee I siiya… Waalid oo ilmahiisa xaasad u eh maa la soo arkay?! Haddii aad iga naxaysiin wax dhibkeyga eh ma igu khasbi leheen. Qaftii aniga rabo ma ii diidi leheen. […] Nassib badanaa qaf xor eh … (*Maana-faay* 2).

> *Is there no one to come forward and tell the people in this house the truth? … Why are they forcing me into marriage with this man? I don't want him! I don't want him! I don't want him! I don't want him now or any other day! They say, 'Parents, parents, be obedient to your parents.' … How can parents be so cruel to their own child? If they cared about me and my distress, they would not be forcing me. They would let me choose.*
> *How lucky it must be to be free… (Maana-faay 2).*

Afrax's novel grapples partially with the new reality unfolding in 1980s Somalia. The military government by then had lost its freshness, charisma, and moral rectitude, but it had also impelled a great deal of social transformation. The Family Law statute (*Xeerka Qoyska*) of 1972 attempted to restructure gender power relations. Women generally supported the stipulations of a law that gave them quasi-equal footing with men in matters of inheritance and divorce. The clergy, on the other hand, castigated the regime for heresy and for introducing secular policies antithetical to Islamic teaching. The protagonist in Afrax's novel had at her disposal the full force of the Law. What her subconscious mind unleashes is also a summation of the newly created subjectivity that encounters the other in both language (Bakhtin) and in the psyche (Lacan). The regime was spearheading the creation of a new ideological grid for filial piety. Both language and the psyche, as pertinent sites for ideological battles, reflect the intense "labor of criticism" that precedes transformational periods in a nation's history. The heroine of the novel points to how the novelistic character "unsettles the patriarchal myth that there could be a language of truth transcending relations of power and desire" (Nancy Glazner, 1990:109; qtd. in Sue Vice, 1997:4). Yet the omniscient narrator credits her father with two crucial markers that the rest of his petty bourgeois friends are not endowed with, namely, his ability to understand "the changing times and the new social mores of the youth" ("isbaddelka casriga iyo dabeecadda dhallinyarada") (*Maana-faay*, 8). Needless to say, he gains this realization through a bitter experience when his sequestered eldest daughter, Iisha, falls victim to the chicanery of a procurer in the service of a *Shabeel Naagood*, a Don Juan. The title character, as we have seen before, also falls victim to the machinations of the procuress Beyydan. The narrative traces Beyydan's grievances to the colonial era, but does not absolve the postcolony of any guilt, for by choosing to become the appendage of the colonial government, the postcolony perpetuates Beyydan's cruel fate. She now becomes a sex worker, and only later becomes her own boss, procuring young, nubile girls for wealthy and influential older men. This is the first time that a Somali-language novel tackles the issue of human trafficking. The narrative deftly limns Beyydan's ability to live without moralizing about her experience or her profession. She does what she has to do without contemplating the moral issues or consequences involved in staying alive. Yet the narrative does not create unduly extenuating circumstances.

Afrax repeatedly ran afoul with the government of the day. The regime then in power had misgivings about the intent and drift of the novel. More than once, it was suggested that the government cease the serialization of the story in the pages of the *Xiddigta Oktoobar* (October Star). Afrax's other novel *Galti-Macruuf* ("A Rustic Putting on Airs"), partially serialized in the same newspaper, was not so fortunate: the censors banned its publication. Yet the writer's versatility and his artistic vision's boundless horizon allowed him to evade prison or overt harassment by the powers that be. Afrax is credited with initiating the first serious and extensive analysis of Somali plays. The above-mentioned official newspaper published the bulk of his articles dealing with Somali theater, which were later collected in a book called *Fan-Masraxeedka Soomaaliyeed* (1987; The Somali Theater). That his novels and ideas have thrived beyond the confines of Somalia is a clear indication of the brilliance of his works. It also attests to a simple fact that, as a character in Mikhail Bulgakov's *Master and Margarita* declared, "Manuscripts don't burn." Their writers could be harassed and forced into exile, but the work will never succumb to bullying. Afrax finally joined his work in exile, as he became *persona non grata*.

Maana-faay is one such manuscript that defied the odds and refused to be silenced. As a foundational text, it inspired and continues to inspire the imagination of a new generation of writers, some of whom are now writing in the diaspora. Yet because of its pioneering status and impeccable artistic quality, it still has (and will continue to have) a privileged position in the literary and social history of the Somali-language novel.

Works Cited

Afrax, Maxamed D. 1983 [2018; 4th ed.]. *Maana Faay*. Leicester, England: Loox[Looh] Press.

------------------. 1987. *Fan-Masraxeedka Soomaaliyeed*. Djibouti: Centre National de la   Promotion Culturelle et Artistique.

Andrzejewski, B. W. 1983. *Islamic Literature of Somalia*. Hans Wolff Memorial Lecture. Bloomington: Indiana University Press.

Faarax M. J. Cawl. 1974 [1982]. *Ignorance Is the Enemy of Love*. Trans. Andrzejewski. London: Zed Press.

Bakhtin, Mikhail. 1981. *The Dialogic Imagination: Four Essays*. Trans. Caryl Emerson and Michael Holquist. Austin: University of Texas Press.

--------- 1984. *Problems of Dostoevsky's Poetics*. Trans. Caryl Emerson. Minneapolis: University of Minnesota Press.

Brennan, Timothy. 1991. "The National Longing for Form." In *Nation and Narration*, edited by Homi Bhabha, 44-70. London: Routledge.

Calinescu, Matei. 1987. *Five Faces of Modernity*. Durham: Duke University Press.

Kundera, Milan. 1986. *The Art of the Novel*. NY: Grove Press.

Lukacs, Georg. 1983. *The Historical Novel*. Trans. Hannah Mitchell and Stanley Mitchell. Lincoln: University of Nebraska press.

Ngugi wa Thiong'o, *Matigari*. 1987. Trans. Wangui wa Goro. Nairobi: Heinemann.

Rodriquez, Ileana. 1994. *House, Garden, Nation: Space, Gender, and Ethnicity in Post-colonial Latin American Literatures by Women.* Trans. Robert Carr with the author. Durham: Duke University Press.

Stock, Brian. 1989. "Historical Worlds, Literary History." In *The Future of Literary Theory*, edited by Ralph Cohen, 44-57. NY: Routledge.

Vice, Sue. 1997. *Introducing Bakhtin.* Manchester: Manchester University Press.

Maana-faay's Migration from Somali to English Translators' Notes

Ahmed Ismaaciil Yusuf

The year was 1980 but the month could have been June or July. A group of us (teenagers) gathered at our favorite teashop when Sahal (not his real name) pulled out a crumpled page of a newspaper and proceeded to read. Sahal, a talented storyteller but mischievous in nature, made sure that we did not see what and where he was reading from the page. Whenever one of us tried to take a look, he either feigned leaving or put the paper back in his pocket, compelling us to beg and plead to pull it out and read on. With his tantalizing rendition, we could also clearly see *Xiddigta Oktoobar* (The October Star), which was the name of the most known Somali daily news, on top of the page. Below it, we could barely make out the words of *Maana-faay*. We were so hypnotized that when, true to himself, Sahal abruptly stopped reading, put the crumpled piece of golden paper back in his pocket, and walked off, none of us moved a muscle to rush to overtake him. We blamed *Maana-faay* and *October Star* on our gullibility that Sahal had used against us.

Did I mention that we were in my beloved hometown of Ceerigaabo, a city blessed with natural beauty, nestled in the tallest, most vegetated mountain (Surad) in Somalia and a few miles away from the pristine water of the Red Sea? But because we were 1100 miles away from the most cosmopolitan city in Somalia, Mogadishu in its prime, we thought Ceerigaabo failed us. It failed us because it was not the place where *Maana-faay* was available. With that, we also began to count our losses and noticed that it was not only *Maana-faay* that we were not privileged to peruse, but that the best Somali band, Waberi, refused to come to our city, and that we had no cinema theaters and no newspapers.

Now, I should remind the reader that *Maana-faay* was a novel serialized in *Xiddigta Oktoobar*. Apparently, the news that the story caught Mogadishu's attention, to the point where young and old would stand in line for the next instalment early in the morning, intensified our enchantment. We wanted to be part of the crowd in line. But the fact that we were not in Mogadishu, the capital, savoring the joy of reading *Maana-faay*, heightened our desire too. In other words, the book's serialized praises grew louder and louder from Mogadishu to Ceerigaabo, and from one teashop to another.

1981 arrived in Ceerigaabo but without *Maana-faay*. As luck would have it, though (or so I thought), I, like many, abandoned my hometown of Ceerigaabo for the capital. The urges to dive into my desires were many, but my first was to get hold of *Maana-faay*, now a book.

Alas, hardly had I set down my suitcase when the news that *Maana-faay*'s publication was banned and that the author was in exile, hit me like a ton of bricks. My dream of holding a copy of the book in my hand died there in Mogadishu but lived on in my heart.

Fast forward four decades. I was minding my own mundane business when, out of the blue one day, someone called me to tell me that Maxamed Daahir Afrax, the same Maxamed Daahir Afrax who wrote *Maana-faay*, was in town and that he wanted to see me. I should, however, alert the reader that I, along with many Somalis, had left Somalia and lived on the other side of the world, in Minneapolis, Minnesota, USA. Surprised that Maxamed even knew my name, but flattered, I went to see him. There, he made it clear that he wanted me to translate *Maana-faay* into English.

It was hard to believe that the same *Maana-faay* that I had the desire to read for thirty years or so had simply arrived at my doorstep.
A year or so later, a PDF copy of the complete *Maana-faay* manuscript was mine and mine alone. Now, much older, I nevertheless read the book with the same intensity and spirit that I would have when I was a teenager, but through a nostalgic adult lens. Reading it, I could neither believe how much of my motherland was frozen in time, nor could I measure the magnitude of its merit.

Once I began typing, every word of it became sacred, thus transferring that and more to English demanded delicate care, preferably a native speaker able to untangle the mystic nuance of this second language. Thus, Maggi Larson, a friend of mine, became a script companion. *Maana-faay* in translation would not have been possible without her competent hand and sharp mind.

So now we present you with Maana-faay, the book.

CHAPTER ONE

Without greeting anyone or even looking around, she rushed to her room and threw herself on the bed. She violently flung the books she had been carrying, hitting a nearby chest of drawers. Some fell to the floor. *Let them fall! Who cares about them! Who is going to pick them up anyway!* She could not even attend to her own legs. There she lay exhausted, one leg with the shoe still on swinging across the bed while the other dangled over the side. Her khaki school trousers were so tight it felt as though they were strangling her thighs. *Leave them as they wish; who cares to loosen them anyway! Who even feels the discomfort!*

If you allowed your eyes to study her, you would see a white short-sleeved shirt with two newly grown breasts pushing up against it. You would have thought they were protesting the tightness of the shirt in which they were harshly confined. *Let them! Who is to be blamed; the breasts or the shirt buttons? Whichever. Let either feel mistreated; who would mediate them!*

Anyone who came in would think that she had fainted or fallen asleep. Indeed, her eyes were closed but there was no question that she was not asleep. Sleep had not come to her for days. With effort, she took a deep breath and then let it out, as if she wanted to exhale the troubled thoughts that filled her mind. She felt as though she were carrying the weight of the world.

As soon as she closed her eyes, her thoughts ran wild. *Ah, how unhappy am I! How can I keep on like this? Oh God, what should I do? And this school adds to my misery! I hate it! I can't manage to learn anything while I am in this condition. I hate that teacher! He is cruel, and his math is incomprehensible. Why on earth did they replace the nice one we had? Did he say we'll have an exam on Saturday? Forget Saturday, bring it on today! I don't care anymore! I'm struggling against greater hurdles. Why don't they close this school altogether! Then I could breathe a bit. But there is no way to get any rest in this house either. It's worse than the school!*

I'm confused! Is there no one to come forward and tell the people in this house the truth? I certainly don't dare to. Why are they forcing me into marriage with this man? I don't want him! I don't want him! I don't want him! I don't want him now or any other day! They say, 'Parents, parents, be obedient to your parents.' I don't care! Give me a break! How can parents be so cruel to their own child? If they cared about me and my distress, they would not be forcing me. They would let me choose.How lucky it must be to be free, like Sahra Yuusuf! I wonder where Axmed is right now. Sitting in his office, maybe? Oh, why didn't I drop by earlier? I'll tell him tonight; he can say whatever he likes. I can't bear this misery alone. No, no! I can't tell him. It would create more troubles. Perhaps if...'

Her endless flow of thoughts was interrupted by a sound outside her door. She heard heavy footsteps, and her bedroom door opened. But she kept her eyes shut, pretending that she was still alone. She couldn't bear having to face anyone. It would make her feel even worse.

"Maana-faay! What's the matter with you, daughter?"

She recognized the voice of her once-beloved mother, but she still did not open her eyes or move a finger, let alone spring to her feet to embrace her and kiss her on both cheeks, as she usually did when she returned home from school. Today she was not the usual Maana-faay. Concerned, her mother came closer, lowered her voice, and said gently:

"Get up, daughter. Change your clothes and eat your lunch before it gets cold."

"I don't want lunch, just let me be!" shouted Maana-faay. She immediately regretted the rude words that escaped from her mouth,yet did not bother to apologize.

Maana-faay could imagine her mother, standing in shock, staring at her daughter with her hand over her mouth in disappointment. Like a commander defeated in a battlefield. Her mother, Aay Caddeey, walked out of the room, dragging her feet in retreat. Aay Caddeey was overwhelmed with anxious thoughts and questions:

Such is life! As the proverb goes, there's nothing you won't see if you live long enough. Is this the same Maana-faay? Is it really my daughter, Maana, who has turned out this way? Where is the obedient, attentive Maana? Where is her laughter; her joy? Where is her lively and sweet conversation? Where is her modesty, caring for her honor? Where is her self-restraint and exemplary respect for her parents? Where is her golden character, held up as an example for all the daughters in Xamar-weyne district? Mothers in the neighbourhood, displeased with their daughters, would hold her up as an example. They would say repeatedly, *"If I had been lucky, I would have had a daughter like Maana-faay."*

Maana-faay's refusal of lunch and her sharp response were nothing new to Aay Caddeey. Her mother had ceased to be surprised by Maana-faay's behavior of late. Every word, harsh or sweet, from any member of the family seemed to infuriate her. She would take offense at whatever was said. Even an ordinary conversation between household members annoyed her. She would say to herself, "I wish someone would shut these people up!" Sometimes she would get up and lock herself in an isolated room, brooding.

She could not remember the last time she enjoyed a meal. She dreaded the approaching of dinnertime. If her mother forced her to eat, she would just pick at it. Sometimes she would hide so she would not be forced to eat. She had lost a lot of weight and was so skinny now that most of her clothing hung on her. At times she wonders: where was the beauty that mesmerized the hopeful eyes of many disappointed men? It had withered away like a spring flower, once growing on fertile ground, now stricken down by the merciless gusts in the dry season. There was no comparison between this gloomy-faced Maana-faay, too sad to change her clothes, and the Maana-Faay of five months ago, who had made every place she entered fill with joy and laughter.

II

See how she looks now and compare it with how she looked a few months ago, that morning when she had stood in front of Cinema Xamar, shining like a diamond. That was a memorable, historic day in Maana-faay's life. It was a day she would never forget. Over and over, she would recall the memory of turning away from one luxury car after another offering her a ride.

In her school uniform and carrying her books, while waiting for a taxi, she heard a vaguely familiar voice, calling her:

"Maana-faay. Allah, it's her!" Recognizing the voice, she turned and ran straight toward it, shouting:

"Hey, Sahra! How are you, sister?" They hugged and kissed each other on the cheeks.
"How are *you* doing my dear?" said Sahra enthusiastically, "Where have you disappeared to?"

Chapter 1 (23-29)

"Allah! When was the last time I saw you, Sahra? It's been a whole year, I think! Once you got a job, not a hello, not even to your friend Maana, hah?" reproached Maana teasingly.

"You are terrible, Maana. Why haven't you come to see me? You know where I live. I'm all by myself with no one else to disturb me."

"I'll come and see you this evening" said Maana-faay.

"Okay. Then we will have enough time to chat tonight. But for now, I am running to work and I see you're off to school. I will be expecting you this evening at seven."

"Okay, dear sister. See you then; *Ciao.*"

"Right, sweetheart; *ciao!*"

To Sahra this plan was no more than a polite chatter, but Maana-faay took it seriously and carried the excitement of her upcoming visit with her throughout the whole day.

III

Maana-faay was not the type of young woman who would freely roam about the town. Unlike her older sister, Iisha, she did not care much for going out. So her parents were not concerned about her whereabouts and her movements. Therefore, Xaaji Muumin, her father, had no qualms about excusing her from the tradition of being *mukhabiyad* (housebound) and enrolling her in school.

Xaaji Muumin had learnt a lesson when he lost his oldest daughter, Iisha, to the streets. At the expense of education, he had restricted her to the family compound and set about grooming her for marriage when she reached the age of nineteen.

The whole neighborhood used to talk about how beautiful, intelligent, and well-behaved Iisha was. Both her mother and father would beam with pride and brag about her to all who would listen. People who knew her well would praise the fortunate parents in public, while privately envying them. Her self-confident attitude and frugal behavior added to her allure. As she grew older, Iisha's frustration and yearning for freedom reached a breaking point. Then, one day, taking advantage of Iisha's situation, an experienced local procurer managed to arrange for her escape. She trapped her with a false invitation to a

Chapter One | Maxamed Daahir Afrax

26

wedding party and took her to her place, only to auction her off to one of her clients, a playboy, who quickly flung her aside after consuming her as a delicious dessert for a few nights.

Once outside the safety and security of the family compound, she became an easy target for the predators of society. She was soon snared into the web of another madam who eventually included her in the network of her street girls. Iisha had not been prepared for the evil challenges of trying to survive on the streets. But no matter what horrors she faced, she would not go back to the imprisonment of being *mukhabiya*. Even if she tried, she knew that she would be disowned by her family and bitterly banished. Thus, Iisha went on to lead a life of indignity, yet remained burdened by the guilt of the disgrace that she had brought to herself and her family.

At home, her family members would cringe with shame at the mention of her name. Her mother would react with furious anger and her father would turn his head away whenever her name was uttered. He avoided his friends and colleagues, fearing that someone would ask him about his daughter or say something about her. When she left, he had disowned her, written her off by performing a burial ceremony and receiving condolences. But he could not erase her memory. Each reminder of her added a painful wound to the scar on his soul.

Iisha's disgrace had left the family with an indelible mark of shame. His close friends would say to him, "That is what you wrought by denying her education and imprisoning her in your house." Whether he accepted responsibility for his daughter's indignity or not, one thing was quite clear: that no one was able to protect a young woman from herself. Realizing this, Xaaji Muumin tore the *shuko* (oversized black robes) from his younger daughters. He replaced the robes with school uniforms for his remaining two daughters, Leyla and Maana-faay. He also purchased textbooks for them and sent them off to pursue an education.

V

Leyla was three years older than Maana-faay and two years ahead of her in school. While Maana was graduating from middle school, Leyla was completing nurse's training. Leyla began working, and soon thereafter she fell in love with Ciise-dheere, a meteorologist four years older than her. When her parents refused to bless their requests to marry, Leyla and

Ciise-dheere eloped. Later, the parents and daughter reconciled only after Ciise-dheere's family members intervened with carefully negotiated tasks.

Xaaji Muumin was a small business owner. Unlike his peers, he lately believed in the value of education, especially after his failure in his ways of raising Iisha. He accepted the fact that getting government jobs and leaving the family home was progress. He also differed with his peers on how best one should raise his children. He also acquired better understanding of the nature of young people. Yet he remained tethered to some of the same ancient social prejudices that burdened most of his generation.

His friends had warned him against the danger that he would unleash by allowing his daughters to go to school without wearing *shuko*. They also preached against government jobs. Those same friends, however, later changed their minds each time Leyla was called in to care for an ailing neighbor. They now wanted Leyla's achievements for their own children, and they suspected that it was only a matter of time before Maana too would be similarly successful. So, it followed that many now wanted to take Xaaji Muumin's path and send their daughters to school.

VI

Maana-faay began to groom and prepare for her visit to Sahra long before sunset, as if someone had invited her to the party of a lifetime. With self-assured assertiveness, she stood before the mirror and examined herself from head to toe. She threw off several garments before finally settling on one, and made numerous adjustments to her makeup and jewelry. Finally, she was ready. Noting that the time was 6:45 p.m., she remarked aloud, "Oh, I'm late!" She grabbed her purse from the top of the dresser and went to the window. Looking out, she surveyed the neighborhood, wondering which road to take. Not once in her nineteen years had she ever ventured out of her Xamar-weyne neighborhood alone after sunset. Now she was going to Sahra Yuusuf's house, and although it was only a few feet away, located at the end of Via Roma, near the ancient buildings of Xamar-jajab, Maana was shaking with nervous anxiety.

She opened the other window in her room and looked at her mother who was busy in the kitchen. If only her mother would go to another room or be called to a neighbor's house, anything to get her out of the kitchen so that Maana could leave the house unseen.

Maana twisted and turned, thinking to herself: *oh why is she not getting up? When is she going to be done with washing dishes? Look, she's just sitting there forever!*

Anxiously, she kept looking at her mother, and then at her wristwatch. Finally, her mother stood up abruptly and left the kitchen. Maana made her move and quickly descended the stairs, her heart beating fast in her chest. Her fear and anxiety intensified when she reached the street as she walked quickly, eyes down, hoping to avoid any contact with those "hundreds of eyes" watching her in her mind.

She was aware that the family had been keeping a close eye on her as of late. The pressure had begun days earlier, when she was told that she was going to be married off to her cousin, Abuukar Aw-Mukhtaar, known by his nickname, Iikar. The news was not only confusing but burdensome. How could she be a wife to Iikar? She had grown up with him. He was her playmate and she considered him a brother, not different from her own brother Aweys. She felt no romantic interest in him whatsoever, but how on earth could she disobey her parents' decree?

Her mother, Aay-Caddeey, was not in full support of the betrothal plan either. The proposal was conceived by the two father-brothers who wanted to cement their family ties for another generation. Maana was to wed Iikar and her brother Aweys was to wed Iikar's sister Jiija. With these intermarriages, the inheritance that Xaaji Muumin shared with his brother, Aw-Mukhtaar, as well as the family ties, would remain intact. It was Aay Caddeey's responsibility to convey this plan to the children, but she had done it unwillingly. She did not hide the fact that she had not been consulted. In the past, she had also been known to complain about her husband's dictatorial disposition and his disregard for her views. He admired his wife, but believed he was the husband and that this alone granted him the power to determine all family matters.

The wedding plans soon followed. A date was set for after Maana's summer vacation. With no expense spared, the furniture for both future households was bought, and invitations were sent out to all the relatives and neighbors.

CHAPTER TWO

I

Sahra Yuusuf's residence was a single room in a two-story, four-room adobe house. The room was meticulously clean and well kept. Art, both original drawings and painting reproductions, decorated the walls. As you entered her room, your eyes flew straight to a bed covered with a beautiful bedspread. Next to it was a small two-shelf bookcase. The top shelf was covered with a delicately hand-crocheted cloth with a tape recorder on the far side. A historical photo taken from a newspaper sat on the lower shelf. A dresser stood in the opposite corner. One of the drawers was slightly open and women's clothing could be seen inside. A dressing table occupied a third corner of the room. It too, was covered with a hand-crocheted cloth on which stood several half empty bottles of perfume and women's toiletries. Finally, just to the left of the bed was a small seating area with four seats and a coffee table.

Sahra Yuusuf took the most comfortable seat facing the door. She relaxed into it, putting her head back and throwing one leg over the seat arm. Maana-faay seated herself in the chair facing Sahra. Sipping a bottle of cool Fanta, she let her legs stretch free while engaging Sahra in easy conversation. For both women, the ease of cheerful banter seemed to chase away any worries or woes.

Suddenly, a knock on the door forced them to cease the jabber.

"*Hoodi, Hoodi!*" a male voice boomed, catching them both off guard. Wondering who it was, Sahra righted herself and sat up straight. She gathered the loose ends of her *guntiino* and lifted it around herself. Maana was seized with fear. Like a defensive turtle, she gathered all four limbs into her lap, grabbed her *garbasaar* (shawl), covering herself up while turning her face away from the door. When they were both appropriately covered, Sahra stood up and, while opening the door, asked, "Who is it?"

"It's me, Axmed," the answer came.

"Come in," said Sahra and let him in.

A five-foot eleven-inch-tall chocolate brown man in his twenties entered.

"Congratulations," he let out, "you look and sound happy tonight, Sahra. You can be heard from far off in the neighborhood."

Regaining her composure and a bit excited, Sahra directed him to take over her seat and said,

"Hey Axmed, how are you? We missed you too. You have not been seen in quite a while, but with your better sense, you have come to say hello this evening!"

Ignoring Sahra and interrupting her, Axmed plopped down into the chair, turned to Maana, and said,

"Hello!"

Maana responded with a single nod.

"This is a friend of mine who stopped by, and we are having a cheerful chat," said Sahra.

"Good for you!" responded Axmed cheerfully.

"Axmed, let me introduce you to a dear friend of mine, Maana-faay. Maana, this is my cousin, Engineer Axmed Jaamac."

"Nice to meet you," said Maana, looking down to hide her nervousness while responding in a somewhat hoarse voice.

Intrigued with her, Axmed continued,

"Hello, Maana-faay, it's an honor to meet you." He covertly gazed at her with a lingering smile.

Axmed was captivated by the scale of her beauty and was tempted to tease her, but in a manner that would not add to her nervousness.

God is great! She is gorgeous! Does a girl like this live in Xamar? He thought to himself. *I can actually say that I have never seen anyone like her before,* he added. By now, he was ogling her glistening golden tan, her chiseled coffee-colored cheeks, her angelic eyes, and the bundle of partially uncovered ebony hair. *It looks like she may be a little short, though. But I have to wait for her to stand up.* he murmured to himself.

Axmed was lost in her beauty when his thoughts were interrupted by Sahra's voice again.

"Why are you so quiet, Axmed?"

Sahra knew Axmed well and could sense where his mind went. She gave him a look that sent him scurrying to find a cigarette in his jacket. Lighting up, he said,

"Well, Sahra, you're the host, why don't you take the lead?"

Sahra and Axmed were soon deep in chatter, although Axmed continued to feast his surreptitious eyes on Maana-faay. Maana grew to feel increasingly uneasy, and so she decided it was time to go. She glanced at her watch and stood up to leave, saying,

"I've got to leave."

Sahra also rose and walked Maana-faay to the door, kissed her cheeks, thanked her for the visit and sent her on her way. When Sahra returned to her seat, Axmed began with a rush of questions.

"Hey, Sahra, who was this angelic creature? Is she really a friend of yours?" he asked, trying to make it sound like he was joking, but he could hardly disguise the intense interest in his eyes.

"Well, we're not that close, but she's a neighbor. I met her here in Xamar-weyne," Sahra tried to slow him down.

Sahra and Axmed were raised in the same household. Being close in age, they had come to trust each other, confiding in each other and guarding each other's secrets. Sahra had been married off at a relatively young age. She could not tolerate her life as a young wife and so kept running away until her husband finally divorced her. Now she lived alone, outside her family's compound, and held a government job. Axmed and others knew that she was seeing a young man and that she was hoping to soon become engaged to marry. Thus, Sahra understood well the struggles of youth, especially the battle between modern dating and the tradition of *mukhabiyad* until parents could locate a suitable mate for their child.

II

Axmed asked Sahra to officially introduce him to Maana-faay. He wished he had met her a year ago, when he had just returned from studying abroad for seven years. He would not have hesitated to propose to her then. Now, however, after a year back home, working in Mogadishu, he was no longer in a hurry to find a wife. His ideas about a host of issues had changed – ideas such as work ethics, courting norms, and how people relate to one another in general.

When he was abroad, the weight of nostalgia for his motherland had been immeasurable. Once back home, his life plan was twofold: to find a good woman to marry and to find a career in his field of education.

After one year, no prospective bride had presented herself. He had met several eligible young women who initially impressed him, but they soon disappointed him. And although he had applied for numerous jobs, nothing had materialized, until he finally had to take up one he was not happy about. His spirits had been dampened and his hopes disillusioned.

His father, Jaamac-dhegey, and his mother, Cambaro Cali Dhoof, had both encouraged him to take a leap of faith and accept marriage to a respectable young woman, but Sahra Yuusuf advised caution. More than anyone else, she wanted to see him with his own family—a wife and children. She would have been especially thrilled if her new sister-in-law could be someone she knew and was close to. Yet, being an insider in the world of today's youth, she warned him against a rushed decision.

Luck smiled down on Sahra when Axmed asked her to officially introduce him to Maana-faay. Although she had warned him about making a hasty decision, her mind rushed to imagine Axmed and Maana together. It thrilled her to think of her cousin marrying a woman with a high school diploma and all the other attractive attributes of Maana-faay. As these pictures flashed in her mind, she responded to Axmed's request,

"I will be glad to do so, brother."

Then she suddenly hesitated. Something she remembered about him irritated her, and a bit of doubt crept in.

Men of today cannot be trusted, not even my own cousin, she whispered to herself. *What if I am successful in delivering this poor young lady to him, and then he deflowers her and moves on…? I would be responsible for helping to ruin her life.*

"Listen, Axmed," she began attentively.

"Go ahead," said Axmed.

"I am going to take on that responsibility under one condition, and one condition only."

"And what is that condition?" Axmed asked her.

"I want you to tell me what kind of relationship you have in mind. If it's the temporary type, don't count on me!"

Touching a nerve, she forced Axmed to examine his motivation silently. *Oh dear! She's talking to me like a traditional elder would. I just saw a beautiful lady to whom I'm attracted. What do I want from her? Am I considering a marriage proposal, or am I wanting a girlfriend – a young woman who will make me happy for a while? To be honest, I don't know, do I? I only know that I am attracted to her. So, I have to make sure that she is, first of all, in my hands, and then I will see what the future will bring and how it shapes the relationship. If she…*

"Why are you so quiet, Axmed? Answer my question," Sahra interrupted his thoughts.

"Will you leave those incriminating doubts alone and just introduce me to her?" he responded.

"If I do, and you deceive her, then I will carry the guilt of that crime with me for the rest of my life."

"Am I a pawn in a game that you are playing, Sahra?"

"No, it's the game you men play with women that worries me" she answered. "How many innocent young ladies have been lied to, deceived, damaged, and left disgraced and alone? That's a crime committed by men."

"These young ladies you mentioned aren't so innocent themselves either. How many men have they robbed of their shoes, throwing them out barefoot into the streets?"

"Please, you can't use that as a defense or an excuse for the crimes committed against young women," Sahra fumed.

"Frankly, sister, many of the young ladies of today behave like gangsters. And anybody who gets himself involved in a gang behaves just like them."

"You are so mistaken! Why do you think so poorly of women? Where does this prejudice come from?" Sahra asked.

"Why don't you tell me, for you must know a lot more than I do?" Axmed responded.

"If you dared to ask, I would tell you that men have been the cause of all social malfeasances. And if you philosophize…"

"Now, Sahra, it sounds like we have arrived at your military tribunal, where all men are indicted," Axmed softly interrupted her, smiling, trying to bring the topic back to its jovial stage, to cool it off and advance the conversation towards his own goal. But Sahra could not pass on an opportunity; she continued her fight against men,

"Deny it or not, you men are to be blamed. We are not going to let you get away with all the crimes you have committed against women. What gives you the right to lure a woman down the wrong path, then insult her with what you had taught her or persuaded her to do, and worse yet, discard her because of it? Who would execute such shameful acts and then brag about it? You men encourage and sometimes force girls to behave badly, and then discard them like yesterday's trash. This is disgusting! If every man mistreats a girl, how would his sister, his daughter, or his wife be safe? How are the women in your family going to be shielded from it all? How is it possible that you would sleep with a different young lady each night, and when it's time to marry one, you say 'I have to have a virgin?!'"

With his eyes wide open, Axmed asked,

"Are you crazy? How could a man marry a woman who used to sleep with other men?"

"Look at you; you still live back in the Stone Age! Why would she marry you when you have slept with countless other women already?"

"She can't behave like me. I'm a man!"

"What?" exclaimed Sahra flamboyantly. "I can't believe what you just said. I can't believe it," she said, looking at him straight in the face.

"Listen, Sahra, who entrusted you with the task to act as an advocate for all of womankind?" argued Axmed amusedly.

"I get enraged whenever I see innocent women being mistreated or prejudiced against by men like you"

"To be honest, I can't deny that there are some good women, but you also have to admit to the fact that there are some good men out there, too."

"No objection" Sahra agreed.

"Then, consider me as one of these good men and introduce me to Maana-faay."

"Then promise me that you have only one thing in mind: that you want to consider her as a potential wife and that you will treat her respectfully," she pleaded.

"I promise. But she needs to pass my test."

"I have to OK that test of yours."

"It's a man's secret, and you, as a woman, are not allowed to participate," he responded playfully.

"I'm not the one that you are testing."

"You are one of the students though."

"How am I one of them?"

"You are a young lady; thus, you should not know what a man's secret is."

"Aw, you are cursed; you have neither moral values nor integrity. It should be the other way around. You are supposed to let me, your own cousin, know about this secret, so that I can avoid any cabal you men cook up," she followed, in a similarly playful tone.

"I'm not going to share a secret that might be disclosed to other women, women I may be hunting. I will only let my sister know what is not likely to pose a threat to my own self-interest."

"Oh, come on, you selfish boy!" Said Sahra, smiling and keeping up her withering tease, "Don't you know that selfishness is doomed?"

"Would you please, Sahra, try not to derail me? I am well aware of your knowledge of history and philosophy, but I do *not* want you to take me far from what we were addressing. Don't try to make me forget about Maana-faay. Tonight, that is all I care about, so hold my hand and take me to the missing half of me, to the one who will share life with me?"

"Well, now you are saying the right words. Give me your hand on that," said Sahra, shaking his hand.

III

Axmed left Sahra's house pleased. He walked to Ceelgaab Taxi Stand and stood in the middle of a crowd that would rush collectively back and forth in an attempt to find a seat in an approaching taxi. People and taxis merged as they tried to make headway. It took a while, but Axmed finally forced himself into a taxi already occupied by three others. They took Hodan Road. As the taxi came to a halt, Axmed, who had not paid much attention to the other passengers, was startled to hear a woman's voice say,

"Brother, can you let me by so I can get off?"

"Yes, yes, Sister, welcome!" he responded as he jumped out of the cab. Once outside the taxi, he looked around and realized that he had passed his destination. Rather than get back into the cab, he put his hand into his pocket, scooped out some notes, and handed them over to the waiting taxi driver. He did not hang around for his change, but immediately walked away. He turned onto the road right before the Labor House, passing a warehouse and an abandoned building with faded paint three doors down. Continuing on, he passed a small house made of straw and adobe, then came to a white house. He climbed the four steps to the blue painted front door and knocked. The door was flung open, and he entered without acknowledging the young man inside. Facing a wall of three closed doors, Axmed pulled a key out of his pocket and unlocked the door in front of him. The room was dark. He shivered in quiet fear. He flipped the light switch, but nothing happened. Then he remembered that the light bulb had burned out the previous evening. He looked around in the small apartment for a candle.

Ever since Axmed left Sahra's place, thoughts ran through his mind. First his mind went wild with thoughts of Maana-faay. Second was the discussion he had with Sahra. It triggered a memory of a debate he had a year ago with his friend Kulmiye. Kulmiye was one of the people who had welcomed him back at the airport when Axmed returned from abroad. That day, Kulmiye had invited him to lunch. As they caught up with each other's past over lunch, he remembered Kulmiye saying,

"Axmed, you are going to be my guest for the whole day today. Once we're done eating, we're going to a *khat* party."

Axmed did not understand what he meant by *khat* party, but simply asked, "And where is this *khat* party?"

"We're going to the best brothel in all of Mogadishu, and we will partake in pleasures with the most tender of young ladies. You are luckier than me tonight, because you are new to the ladies of Mogadishu. So, tonight is your night to experience the delights of Xamar beauties."

Axmed understood that what his friend was saying was that they were going to chew *khat* with women! He had heard about *geerashayn*, where men and women chew the narcotic stimulant to get high and increase their sexual pleasure. But he had never been involved in such a party and he was not impressed with the invitation.

"Thanks for the invitation, Kulmiye, but I'm looking for a wife, a life partner and mother for my future children. I don't think I'll find her at this party."

"There are too many women around to choose from," Kulmiye said.

"Yes, there are too many women, but there are too many men also. If each of these men sleeps with a different woman every night, then leaves her, where will our future wives come from?"

"Why would you care about a wife, children and the likes, when you can sleep with a different beauty each night? When you don't have to deal with the everyday issues of 'the baby is sick,' or 'my uncle, the nomad, needs financial help…' It is pure stupidity to burden yourself with such responsibility when you can have so much fun, free of commitment." Kulmiye preached.

"So, you're saying that it's right to abandon the sanctity of marriage?" Axmed paused to see Kulmiye's reaction and waited for him to respond. When he realized how carefree Kulmiye was, and that he was not going to bother himself with a reply, Axmed went on to add, "It takes two to tango. It's not only the women who should be blamed, but it should be shared by those young men you are trying to vindicate!"

"Uncle," Kulmiye began sarcastically, "that is the moralistic illusion that you learned from your books when you were away at school. I have experience in these matters and if you ask me, I will tell you that the women of today are treacherous. They are always scheming about how to ruin your life. If you were on a dhow in the ocean in order to rescue them, they would make sure that you were capsized once they get saved!"

"My friend, you have the wrong idea about women. At least don't lump all of them together," warned Axmed.

"I'm not stopping you in your search for the perfect wife," Kulmiye said, laughing. "I'm going to leave you alone, but whatever lesson you learn, don't run back to me if it doesn't work out."

"If marriage is so awful, why has it endured since the beginning of time?" asked Axmed.

"The fact is that marriage is like aging and death. It will catch up and grab you sooner or later. Once you fall into its snare, you can't break loose," Kulmiye responded.

The discussion between the two lingered a while longer, but they remained a world apart.

Kulmiye, who was a little older and heavier than Axmed, had failed to pass the middle school centralized tests twice, before his father, a rich member of the parliament, managed to secure him a coveted scholarship to study in Italy. Once in Italy, Kulmiye joined the night-clubbing scene and paid no attention to learning. In Italy, the only connections that he had sustained were with a crowd of like-minded youth, both male and female, and, as in Somalia, he spent most evenings in one-night stands, accepting no responsibility for any ensuing consequences.

Six years later, Kulmiye was back in Mogadishu claiming that he had a degree in business. However, as a privileged child, he actually excelled only in the art and articulation of having "a good time."

Back in Mogadishu, Kulmiye began where he had left off. He would pick up women—some from respected families, married, students, and a few from the guarded *mukhabiyad* quarters. To justify his behavior, he talked about having once fallen in love with a young woman who had rejected him for another man, saying, "I will never trust another woman." No one ever knew how much of that was fact, but what was known was that he now chose to associate himself with women who used *khat* and alcohol, demanding very little of him.

Partying became Kulmiye's full-time job. He spent his entire time either being in one party or planning the next. He was always busy concocting one plot or another to seduce women. His life was fast but shallow. Relatives who had supported him in earlier days soon avoided contact with him altogether.

He believed that if he ever married, he would not be able to stop hunting other women, and this would drive his wife into a jealous rage. She too would cheat on him, and that would lead to family conflicts and marriage breakdown. That was the main reason why he did not have much faith in the institution of marriage and advised his friends, Axmed among them, against it.

However, Axmed did not take Kulmiye's counsel to heart. He rather thought it was an outright assault on women to nurse that kind of cynical view. None of his friends knew that when he was in Italy, he had dreamed of returning home to marry a Somali woman and having children with her. He even knew the number of the children he wanted to have and their names; Maxamed, Fatima, and Cali.

He loved to spend time with girls but, unlike his friend Kulmiye, he was not a playboy, and though he dated western women when he was abroad, he always dreamed about Somali women. Raised in a large family of meager means, he had a better perspective on women. Though his father, Jaamac-dhegey, was now a high-ranking government official, they had had a rough start when he was a child. As a matter of fact, when Axmed went abroad to further his education, his father was still a low-level government employee.

Lying in bed that night, Axmed Jaamac mulled over the discussions he had with Kulmiye, contrasting them with the one he had with his cousin Sahra tonight. He realized how far apart his thoughts of a year ago were from where his thinking was headed now. It occurred to him that the social knowledge he had gained since returning home had surpassed that which he had acquired during his college years. He remembered that when he was growing up he had lived a simple, sheltered life of going to school, coming home to eat and sleep. It also occurred to him that when he was sent abroad, he had met many other young people with different values and cultural norms, but none of them had changed his belief in the sanctity of marriage. He just had not yet found his true soulmate. In appearance, the Maana-faay he had seen tonight was close to the girl he had pictured in his mind and dreams, but it was too early for him to gauge what her other qualities might be.

CHAPTER THREE

I

*T*his neighborhood has not changed since the last time I visited, Sahra thought as she entered Xamar-weyne Area. The narrow alleys were lined by the same dilapidated houses, all of which looked to have been built by the same contractor, a contractor who neither owned the ability nor the knowledge of construction; one with neither the artistic taste nor the aptitude to address the need for roads. *How could people live here?* said Sahra to herself as she counted the windows in the front of the building facing her. *Wasn't this the turn into her home?* She thought. *Yes, yes, it is. That's the mosque near her house.* She stopped and looked up at the building in front of her with the sloppily painted large door. Carefully climbing the steep, crumbling concrete steps, she reached the third floor and knocked on the door. When she was let into the veranda, Maana-faay jumped up from her seat with glee and kissed her on both cheeks.

"Hello Sahra, how are you? You've traveled out of your comfort zone today just to say hello?" Again, they warmly greeted each other with kisses on the cheeks and went into Maana's room.

Immediately they fell into rapid conversation. Soon, Sahra who wanted to steer the chatter to what had brought her there, started talking about love and how it can bloom from an innocent encounter. Sahra wanted to cultivate this topic, and so she encouraged Maana to share her dreams about love.

"Have you ever been in love, Maana?" asked Sahra amusedly.

"No, never," said Maana-faay.

"If you happened to be told that a great young man, with a great job, a doctoral degree and a great personality has a crush on you, how would you react?" Sahra asked again with the same spirit.

"I would welcome him with open arms!" replied Maana jokingly.

"Well, I *do* know someone who has a major crush on you," said Sahra.

"Tell me about him. Who is it? Don't hold back!" answered Maana, thinking that Sahra was only teasing her. But when she realized that Sahra was serious, she abruptly changed her mind and said: "Wait, Sahra! Men and crushes are not on my agenda."

Sahra tried her best to keep Maana engaged in the topic. She continued by saying, "Could you at least ask me who he is?"

"No, Sahra, no! I don't want to know."

"Just see him once, and if he is not your type just tell him, so that he won't waste his time, yours or mine."

Sahra's plan was simply to bring the two together and let them take it from there. She wanted to persuade Maana by telling her what a great and exceptional man he was. She did not tell her that it was the same man, Axmed the engineer, whom she had met a few nights back. Rather, she went on about how life could be lonesome and meaningless if one remained single, and how an open mind always has a hand in finding love.

Maana refused to take the bait. Her whole demeanor seemed to have suddenly changed, and her excitement dissolved into apathy.

It would have been better for both of them if Maana had been honest and just told Sahra that she had already been promised in marriage to her cousin Iikar – that the wedding had been set for the summer vacation and that after the marriage they would move into their newly furnished home. She didn't bother to tell her this part of her affairs. She was not necessarily trying to hide it, but she hated thinking about it. The memory of the impending arranged marriage caused her too much anxiety and pain, so she tried to avoid the topic as best as she could. She secretly hoped that what Sahra was telling her was true, yet at the same time, she knew that she could not allow herself to have such a thought.

But by keeping all of this to herself, Maana was rejecting a potential ally in Sahra.

Had Sahra known that Maana would reject her efforts to reintroduce her to Axmed, she would not have begun her match-making efforts and would instead have persuaded her cousin against his pursuit. Embarrassed and disappointed, Sahra became quiet. Maana, too, had become silent and the initial excitement she had expressed was now gone from her eyes. Her look seemed to say, *is this what brought you here this afternoon, Sahra? Were you simply spying on me and my feelings?* Sahra felt guilty about the visit. But, at the same time, she also felt pressured by the promise she had made to Axmed. Then her guilt quickly turned into anger. She became furious with her cousin, Axmed. *Look how much embarrassment he has hung around my neck! I should have had better sense than to be his stooge. Why did I let myself get involved in this? If he were that serious about marriage, he would have been with a woman by now, and they would have even had children. How am I going to get my integrity back? What have I gotten myself into? Is Maana going to think of me as a meddling fool and talk about me to her family? None of this was my business in the first place. Axmed, I knew you were going to throw me off a cliff. What am I going to tell him now? Why did Maana's attitude change so abruptly? Why is she acting so childish?* All these conflicting thoughts waged a war inside Sahra's head.

Her mind went in circles as she searched for a way to regain her composure. She was startled by Maana's sudden loss of interest in the topic of love. She somehow needed to take all those words back that had so thoughtlessly escaped her lips. Finally, an idea flashed into her mind all of a sudden. Laughing aloud, she gently tapped Maana on the thigh and while looking at her said, "Maana, I got you, didn't I?"

"What? How?" Maana asked.

"I made him up – this regal man, this young guy with a good job, a doctoral degree, a great personality, whom I told you had a crush on you," she said in a mocking voice.

"Did you make the whole thing up or is there really such a man?" Maana asked.

Sahra laughed, put both of her hands on Maana's shoulders and rocked her like she would for a child and said, "You poor Maana!" When she stopped, she took her hands off, looked straight at Maana and asked,

"Do you really think that there is such a man in this world nowadays?"

"How would I know? You're the one who brought it up to begin with," said Maana, confused.

"You should have asked, 'What kind of angel is he?' A handsome young man with a good job, great personality, who has a crush on you! Where would anybody find someone like him?"

"Was this a joke then?" asked Maana again.

"I went to see an Indian movie last night," Sahra began a fictitious story, "In the movie, the actor is in love with a girl, but his fear of rejection prevents him from expressing it to her. She only finds out who he is and about his love for her much later."

"And what does she say when she finds out?" Maana asked.

"Just as he had predicted, she rejects him. The bad karma of rejection takes its ultimate revenge on her. She eventually does fall in love with him, but it's too late by then. He's moved on and married another woman," said Sahra.

"Was he still in love with her at this stage?" asked Maana.

"No, he was no longer in love with her and tells her so to her face."

"Oh, poor woman!" said Maana.

"Yes, poor girl! She reminded me of you. She even kind of looked like you, and so when I saw you today, I thought I could test you by retelling the story to see how you would react to such a situation. I guess you would have had the same reaction as the girl in the movie."

Showing a little more interest, Maana sat up straighter and looked at Sahra. Tapping her gently on the thigh, she said,

"You're cruel, Sahra. What happened to your compassion?"

Sahra laughed nervously and patted Maana back on her thigh. Maana laughed too, thinking that Sahra had been teasing her all this time with the tale of the perfect man waiting to woo her. She did not know that Sahra was laughing out of relief, because her quick thinking had saved her from embarrassment. *Whew!* Thought Sahra. *Well, that plot to connect these two didn't work, I'll have to try another.*

She could not abandon her original idea and she was now thinking about a way to return to her attempt to connect Maana with her cousin, Axmed. Suddenly, a light bulb switched on in her head. She knew that Maana had no access to city news and was hardly aware of what was happening outside of her family's walls. So, she began by making up a couple of stories, pretending that she had read them in the newspaper. She told Maana about a good play that had recently been advertised in the paper. She updated her on the latest women's fashions. She went on to ask Maana about her perfume, and then told her about a new cologne that could complement hers, even offering to bring a sample with her the next time they met.

Maana enjoyed the stories and shared some of hers just to extend the conversation.

Sahra looked at her watch and abruptly said, "Maana, I'm late. I have to leave, OK? So, what's the plan? When are we going to see each other again?"

"You can come to see me any time," Maana responded.

"That's fine, but I want to invite you out this Friday," Sahra said.

Maana said, "My sister, you know that I am not allowed to leave the house. I'm sorry but I'll have to decline your invitation."

"Sweetie, you won't be out long, all right! Please just stop by at sunset. We'll have a quick dinner, and I will bring you back home right after we eat," Sahra asserted.

Maana kept quiet for a while, and when Sahra insisted she whispered "OK," but felt nauseated with anxiety.

II

Sahra took two consecutive taxis to Axmed Jaamac's place and got off one block away from the Labor House. She walked quickly up the road, as though on an urgent call. In three minutes or so, she was able to see a painted white house on her right. From the outside stairway, she could see that the lights were on in a room to the right. She could make out Axmed lying on the bed, reading a newspaper. She had been worried that he would not be home and was quite relieved that he was there. She knocked softly on the door. The knock startled him as he was not expecting any visitors. The hesitant soft tapping obviously had a woman's touch. *Great,* he said to himself while putting on his shirt. *I need somebody to 'entertain' me before bedtime.* Eagerly, he opened the door. There stood his own cousin, Sahra, who marched right in, thus dimming his initial excitement.

Oh, she is the wrong one! This one is not going to offer much entertainment, he thought.

"Hello Sahra!" he greeted her rather icily.

"My friend, be ready on Friday!" she blurted.

Fully alert and excited now, he said,

"Give me the news. I knew I could count on you."

"'Cousin," she followed in a sarcastic tone, "Please don't try to stroke my ego. I have to tell you; she wasn't receptive to your overtures."

"Don't worry, it won't break my bones if she rejects me," Axmed said, while sitting down on the edge of the bed, clearly denying how much the words she had just thrown at him had stung.

Sahra grabbed a wooden chair from a nearby desk and pulled it closer to the bedside. She went on to tell him how Maana had refused to hear anything to do with courtship and men, but that she had eventually managed to get her to accept an invitation for dinner on Friday.

His feelings fluctuating, Axmed asked,

"So, what can I do to make an impression on her?"

"Assuming that she comes along," Sahra said, "I will try to put her at ease by 'breaking the ice.' From there, it's up to you to pull this off," said Sahra.

"Is that the best you can come up with?" asked Axmed.

"I'm planning to take her to Jungal for dinner. Maana thinks that it will be just the two of us, but it will actually be a double date with you and Cadinaasir," said Sahra, ignoring his question.

"Great! Your father was indeed a man of wisdom," responded Axmed enthusiastically, implying that she had inherited her father's abilities.

<h1 style="text-align:center">III</h1>

Maana-faay never expected that men would be involved in the dinner that Sahra had invited her to. It also never occurred to her that they would go for dinner outside of the city. But there was nothing she could do now that she had been caught in the trap. She felt she had been put into a situation from which she could not extricate herself. Such a feeling had overwhelmed her the moment Sahra opened the window of a waiting car, a white Volkswagen, and invited her to take the back seat, while Sahra herself happily got into the front next to a heavy-set guy sitting in the driver's seat. Maana had expected her friend to sit next to her. Her surprise intensified when a man got into the car and sat down next to her, saying confidently in a pleasant voice,

"Hi Maana!"

Maana-faay gave him a sideways glance and, just to be polite, let a cold "hello" pass through her lips. It was then that she realized that this was not an unknown man. This was the same lean fellow she had recently met at Sahra's house. He was talking to her as if they knew each other well, but Maana felt like a stranger, as if she was meeting him tonight for the first time. She remained quiet, reserved, and unresponsive. She felt nervous, and that surprised her. In a dreamlike state, she sensed her own discomfort and anxiety all at once, even when Sahra would look back at her joking and smiling pleasantly in an attempt to make Maana feel at ease and relaxed. Instead, Maana would respond with a stern glare as though saying with her eyes, *my friend, you have betrayed me tonight; you have breached my trust! Was your hidden agenda to put me into this kind of trap?*

Cadinaasir had continued driving the car with one hand on the wheel while Sahra coyly drummed her fingers on his other hand. Every once in a while, he would turn to the back seat trying to engage Maana and her companion into common conversation. Maana later came to understand that both Cabinaasir and Sahra shared the same cheerful nature and outgoing personality.

Axmed's chatter continued, as he tried to engage Maana, as if pulling out one key after another, in the attempt to unlock an unfamiliar door. *And so begins the play. I am the talented actor trying to entertain my audience,* he whispered inaudibly to himself.

Maana was very careful to avoid physical contact with the man, but she later became receptive to his tales and began to cast furtive glances at him, all the while making sure their eyes did not meet. She tried her best to hide the nervous anxiety that troubled her. But it was not an easy feat.

Axmed knew it too. He tried his best to put her at ease. Unaware of the nervous occupant in its belly, the Volkswagen Beetle leisurely cruised through the capital, winding its way through the busy city streets. Once on General Daa'uud's Road, they began driving straight north.

In Maana's mind, they had traveled a long distance. The buildings they passed were many and the city streets they were now cruising were much wider than the ones she had known. She had never been on a ride this long. She had never traveled this far from her family's home and had no idea that Mogadishu was this large. *Is Mogadishu this big, or are we in the Afgooye that I have heard about? Where do all these people come from?* She was in disbelief watching the throngs of people milling about in the streets.

She was careful not to lock eyes with anyone on the street, lest she be recognized or have fingers pointed at her or be laughed at. She felt as if every face stared back at her. She tried to avert her eyes. She felt more self-conscious whenever children ran by, thinking that they might run up to her and chant, *Hey! We're going to tell; we're going to tell!* She thought the adults too were giving her the evil eye and would soon be giving her a tongue-lashing. *Is this what you end up doing, Maana, going out with a man? Wait until we see your father, Xaaji Muumin, and your mother, Aay Caddeey.*

As the Beetle continued north, the crowds of people thinned; the stream of cars decreased; the streetlights dimmed, and the buildings shrank and then disappeared into the distance. Yet they kept on driving. *Where are they taking me? Are they lost or have they lost their minds?* These were the questions Maana was mulling over. She knew neither how far they had travelled nor where they were heading. She looked at her watch and was able to calculate that they had travelled a long distance. *Oh my gosh! We have gone too far! Now we're leaving the whole city behind.* She grew increasingly nervous and wanted to get Sahra's attention to ask her a question and let her know how uncomfortable she felt. When she raised her hand to tap Sahra on the shoulder, she realized they had reached the end of the road. Hoping they would be forced to turn back, she hesitated to follow through. The Beetle did not turn back but made a right turn and headed east along a straight road that came from the west.

Driving through the dark, deserted land, Maana's fear intensified and her heart beat faster and faster. A strange chill spread through her body. Her teeth were tightly clenched, making her unable to speak or whisper her fears to Sahra. Never in her lifetime had she left the illuminated city streets of Mogadishu. And the fact that this was the first time that she had ridden in a car which was not a taxi, with men she was not related to, added to her apprehension. Regardless of how many others were with her, she felt alone. *Get me out of here. Get me out of here!* she repeatedly protested in her mind.

Burdened by the knowledge that she was not only with unrelated men, but that she was on a date with one of the men, a cultural taboo, stirred up fear in Maana. She felt as though she were stranded on a boat in the middle of the ocean, with no ability to swim.

She recalled stories she had heard from girls in her neighborhood and some of her classmates about rides they had enjoyed with men. They would cruise in town, dine in restaurants, and go home with them. Somewhat intrigued with their rebellious attitude, Maana had listened to their stories, even asking them to report their adventures to her. At times, she had offered an opinion on how to plot against men. She shared her ideas on love as though she was the foremost authority among them. She would advise them against snares that men set and admonish them that carelessness and haste could creep into youth's decision-making. She was willing to participate in those conversations only because she knew that she was safe behind the comforting walls of her family home. She was amused by their audacity to thwart the cultural norms, while she wrestled with the fear of breaking those same norms yet envied their carefree lifestyle. At times, girls invited her to join them at the dinners which men had invited them to, but she always declined. But when she was alone, she used to blame herself, asking secretly: *What on earth makes me different from my age group?* She had never dreamed that she would be involved in an evening like the ones reported to her by her friends. She felt as though she were drowning in a deep blue sea.

As the Beetle moved through the pitch-dark, desolate place, Maana's confusion doubled. As the others' attempt to entertain her continued to fail, a faint light appeared in the distance, and then a large building with many lights came into view on the right, cleaving the darkness like an island in the middle of the ocean. Maana was relieved and spontaneously asked; "What is this town? Is it the one called Balcad?"

All three let out a synchronized chorus of laughter that robbed her of her relief. On top of that, they began to make fun of her trepidations. She regretted her question. That is what she had feared, that they would laugh at her if she said something. That is why she had remained quiet all evening. But it was not as she thought. Her companions liked her question, as it opened the door for the light banter they enjoyed. Still laughing, all three looked at her with mischievous interest. Cadinaasir was the first to take light-hearted potshots at her.

"What's the matter, Maana, you can't tell one city from the other? This isn't Balcad, it's Beledweyne!" he alleged jokingly.

"Have we been driving all night just to be in neighbouring Balcad?" said Sahra, finishing off her boyfriend's sentence. As the laugher intensified, Axmed said:

"No, no! It's neither Beledweyne nor Balcad. It's a city that was just built that hasn't been named yet. It's a city that is lucky enough to be about to be discovered by Maana. I suggest that we name it after you and call it 'Maana-faay!" he said playfully, and then, pretending to be at a meeting, he continued, "I request the esteemed committee gathered here tonight: please heed my plea and consent to my proposal. Tomorrow, the news of the new naming will make the headlines and reach everyone!"

"With unanimous consent, we say 'aye' to your motion," said Cadinaasir humorously, "This city is far more beautiful than those cluttered with streetlights and high-rises. It should therefore be named after the most beautiful of Somali girls."

"Who is the most beautiful Somali girl you're referring to?" asked Sahra slyly.

Keeping one hand on the steering wheel" as he drove, he lifted the other and pointing back to Maana, Cadinaasir said: Who else can it be but her? It's Maana, The-Radiant-One. Who can compete against her God-given beauty and her posture! Isn't that so, Maana?"

"All of this just because I wanted to know what city this is?" inquired Maana with a smile. It was as though all her worries and woes had faded with the light-hearted chatter and teasing.

Sahra, who was now trying to redirect the teasing, said: "You guys, stop feeding my friend from the bowl of your distorted reality. If there really is a new world or city as you claim, then I'm going to introduce

Maana to that world myself." Then, turning to Maana she asked: "Are you serious, Maana? Don't you really know where we are? It's the Macaroni Factory in the outskirts of Mogadishu."

"Oh, really?" said Maana, looking around.

She was still trying to make sense of where they were when the car made a left turn, left the asphalt, and drove into a forest along a narrow path. *Oh dear, what did I get myself into this evening?* thought Maana. As they drove along the deserted path, they came into an area of thick brush, and then on the right-hand side, small lights sparkled through their car windows. What kind of lights these were, lanterns or bulbs, was not clear. Maana had never seen lights like these, and she felt the tension return in full. Scary stories she was told when she was younger flashed through her mind. As they approached the lights, she could make out a short rectangular building with some people around. Before the car came to a halt, an opening in the side of the brush emerged. Right next to the opening, flames licked the wood of a small bonfire. A large dog appeared to be warming himself by the flames. But then again, perhaps the dog was simply waiting for a taste from a leftover meal. A nearby fence kept out several other sniffing dogs. As her eyes wandered past the fire and the twinkling lights, there was only darkness, dotted with the bright stars in the infinite sky. It was there in the darkness that Cadinaasir applied the brakes, bringing the Beetle to a halt.

"What is this?" Maana let out. With a halting voice and churning stomach, she again asked, "What is this, my dear? Where are we anyway?"

"Sweetie, this is the new Jungal restaurant," Sahra responded as though Maana knew the old Jungal.

Cadinaasir, who neither heard the question nor the response, was already engaged in conversation with a skinny, white-shirted attendant boy. The boy was holding the front passenger door open. He had run alongside the car before it had come to a complete stop. He was one of a group of young boys who had been standing right at the front of the building. These young men scrambled to earn a living by working as waiters and valets. And the fastest, most agile of them earned the best tips. With civility and deference, the young man talked to Cadinaasir in a soft, low voice and asked,

"Would you prefer indoor seating or mats spread under a tree?"

"We would like to be under the trees," said Cadinaasir, in the same tone of voice.

"Of course, Cadinaasir," said the young man, who it seemed knew him from past encounters in the same place.

Looking at him, Cadinaasir said, "It's Faarax-yare, isn't it?"

"Yes sir, it is," said the young waiter.

"Great," said Cadinaasir.

The young white-shirted waiter then quickly hopped in front of the Beetle and gestured for them to follow him to park the car. Cadinaasir knew the terrain and so he dimmed the headlights and slowly rolled forward like he was maneuvering an airplane into position. The agile youth trotted ahead of the Beetle, passed several already occupied trees, and then reached a vacant spot under a tree and waved them in. The tree, an acacia, with its low-hanging boughs hugging the fencing brush, looked like a man with his arms folded around his middle.

The young man ran back to the building and returned with two mats.

"Should I lay them next to each other or separate?" he asked.

"Lay them side by side, my friend, for there is no reason to separate us all," Sahra answered before Cadinaasir could. They had all heard him ask the question, and by keeping them all together she wanted to reassure Maana that there was nothing to fear and that she would not be alone with the guy. Faarax-yare unfurled the mats and shook out imaginary dust before laying them on the ground side by side. He then walked over to Cadinaasir who whispered something to him, and the young waiter took off, jogging.

While the other three eagerly hopped out of the car, Maana's heart jumped. Fearful, she remained glued to the car seat. Sahra, aware of her hesitation, opened the back door for her and with difficulty persuaded her to come out of the car. She took her by the hand and gently pulled her forward and over to the waiting mats on the ground. Before sitting down, Maana looked in all four directions. When she saw the frightening darkness in the surrounding bushes, a new fear gripped her. *So here we are!* She thought to herself. *Now I am totally trapped. What else can these mats laid out in the darkness mean?* She wondered. She was very suspicious of why she had been brought to a place like this!

"Welcome, Maana," said Axmed, trying to soothe her as he motioned to her to take a place on the mats. But Maana remained standing while the others positioned themselves on the mats.

"Maana, feel at home." Cadinaasir tried to disarm her while taking off his shoes. "I'm sorry that we crammed you into such a small car. Being in the open space now and stretching out on the mats are meant to help you loosen up and relax," he added. "What do you think about this for a change, Maana? Is it something that suits you?" he asked.

"It's nice, but why is it so dark here?" Maana asked, trying to sit down next to her girlfriend, Sahra.

"Why are there no lanterns here?" followed Sahra, in support.

"They could have brought some lanterns to us, but we didn't ask," Axmed teased. "I knew that Maana was enough light for all of us. She's telling us that it's dark out here, but we're all using her glow to provide us with all the light we need," he added amusingly.

Maana was flattered but could not find the right words to respond and simply said, "Thanks."

The teasing and bantering back and forth continued until Faarax-yare, now serving them as the waiter, returned carrying a stack of six large plates. One by one, he put them all on the edge of the mats: three empty plates and one laden with rice, one with veal and the other with salad. Cadinaasir struck a match and lit a piece of straw and a small candle so that they could see what was in front of them on the mats. The waiter ran back to get bottled water and some soap. Axmed poured a little water into Maana's hands and Cadinaasir did the same for Sahra so that they could wash before eating. The men followed suit, and they all began to feast, all except Maana, who seemed to show little appetite. Axmed tried his best to encourage her to eat. Close by, the meowing of hungry cats pestered them.

When they finished eating, the waiter returned with hand towels. Cadinaasir tried to move his mat and his girlfriend to the other side of the car, in order to leave the other two in privacy. He stood up, bent down, offered his hands to Sahra and with confidence said,

"Would you care to dance with me, Madam?" He was pretending they were at a party, enjoying an evening of music where he was cajoling a young lady he did not know to dance with him.

"No thank you, sir," she snapped, playfully shrugging her shoulders. Thinking that she did not understand his ruse, he held her hand and said, furthering his role-play, "Could you stand up so I can have a word with you? You are summoned to my court for your crime. But to read you your rights as well as to hear why you have been indicted, we have to be alone!"

Sahra was on to his game but was not willing to play along. She knew that Maana was not ready to be alone with Axmed. Axmed too was aware of Maana's apprehension, but he said nothing, not wanting to verbalize her fears.

Sahra, holding Cabdunnasir's arm, pulled him down and said,

"Sit down, my friend. There is no reason for us to be alone tonight."

He read her refusal to mean: *'Are you out of your mind? Are you trying to scare the poor young lady who has never been out of her house, let alone being out on a date?'*

He read the signal just fine, sat back down next to her and said aloud, so Maana could hear,

"Well, now that you have turned me down, let it be known that I am not the first man rejected and I will not be the last. So, I'm going to be patient." Looking at Maana, he added, "Isn't that right, Maana? Or should I not let your dear friend have her victory and consider this a permanent rejection?"

"It does not sound like a permanent rejection, so you should let her off this time," Maana replied, now joining the light-hearted banter.

"OK, it's for your sake tonight that I am going to withdraw my challenge," said Cadinaasir, looking at Maana.

"Thanks," Maana followed.

Sitting on the mats, the ladies were positioned in the middle with the two young men on either side of them. Conversation and jokes flew between them. At times, all would take part in the conversation, but other times each couple would carry on alone whispering to each other.

The lead instigator was Cadinaasir. He would stare at his girlfriend and coyly carry on with the courtship. This was his forte, and he was so good at it that other lovers could have taken lessons from him on how to woo and win over hearts.

Axmed was so impressed with Cadinaasir and Sahra's mutual ease and coziness that it made it easier for both him and Maana to forget about their anxiety. Whenever Sahra and Cadinaasir turned away, he interpreted this as a message to him saying, *seize the opportunity, you fool! We two have nothing new to tell each other but we are only giving you a space. Don't waste the golden opportunity that may never come around again if you don't seize it now! Secure the trap in which you will catch the tender heart of Maana-faay.*

Axmed was hard at work. On the one hand, he was trying his best to choose the words and stories that would please a girl like Maana and would leave traces in her heart. On the other, he was trying hard to show her that he was not a playboy, a vulgar skirt-chaser just looking for one-night stands. He wanted to give her the impression that he was a calm man not interested in anything she might resent. That evening, he changed his usual approach when dealing with girls. He usually treated them like children whom he would entertain without bothering with big words and weighty issues. He would present himself as an easygoing man, indifferent about everything, whatever might happen. He would rush into bringing down the wall of unfamiliarity separating him and a new girl. He would allow his hands the freedom to work over the girl's body. While amusing the girl with jokes, he would rush her so she would not realize what was happening to her. He would let his hands roam free. He would grope, grab, and fondle. His intrusive hands would start with soft touches on the arms. If the new young lady did not promptly pull away, he would proceed and pass on to parts that should have been off limits. If she did not stop him, he took this as a consent to go further. Holding her by her shoulders, he would gently turn her to face him and then guide her hands to embrace him, all the while looking into her eyes, before laying a kiss lightly on her lips. If all that was fine with her, he would repeat it until the passion of her responses matched his. Any cautious wall of fear would just melt like ice under the heat of the sun. Letting his lust lead the way, he would unleash shocks of electricity through her body, and with further explorations of her anatomy, rest in places he should never have been allowed.

Tonight, however, that same crassly-behaved man had become all but a perfect gentleman. With effort, he would search for the right words, tell charming tales, and keep his hands and arms to himself. The hands that had learned to explore fast were held in place. *Any act of assertiveness toward Maana tonight would destroy all my chances,* he warned himself. He believed a man could bring any woman to accept his advances if he could master the art of combining the right words with the right treatment. Axmed was a completely changed man that night. No one was more surprised than Axmed himself. *What has she done to me?* He thought. *How is she different from the others? Why am I being so caring and careful around her? When was the last time I behaved around a date like this?* He had shocked himself. He knew how he used to prey on women. He was in disbelief that he was in such awe of Maana. She was his queen, and he was her servant awaiting her command! Tonight, the game plan had been forsaken.

He tried his best to bring some sense of comfort to Maana. Though their conversation was mostly general, she was no longer nervous or scared. In fact, she was following what he had to say with keen interest and actively participating in the conversation, with her earlier fears fading away. But she suddenly appeared to panic. She looked at her watch and abruptly stood up with, "I am late. Are we not leaving?"

Axmed gently reassured her and guided her back down onto the mat. Maana was not able to settle back into the moment, and so Axmed spoke up on her behalf saying, "Maana is late, so we have to go."

IV

Maana ran up the stairs of her house. She did not turn on the light to see where her feet were landing but ran through the darkness. She lost more time than she was trying to save when she stumbled and almost fell. The higher she climbed, the faster her heart beat and the more light-headed she felt. The closer she came to the door, the more fearful she became.

At first, when she reached her neighborhood of Xamar-weyne, she had felt such relief. She was relieved because she had survived Jungal and a date. Now, safely back home, a new feeling of fright seized her soul. She looked at her watch hastily and became even more fearful when she realized that it was 10:00 p.m. She had never come home this late without a chaperone. *How are you going to defend your conduct and what are you going to say?* These thoughts kept running through her mind. *Who is going to believe me if I tell them that I am late because my classmate and I were studying at her place which took us longer than we had planned? For sure, both Mom and Dad are still awake at this time. I wish I could vanish like a ghost and reappear in my room. My Allah, if you save me tonight, I will never ever do this again. God please, temporarily blind my parents, just tonight, and mute them too, so they can't talk to me. Aw, what am I going to do? Is the door locked already?* she said to herself in a panic.

She tiptoed closer. She tried to slow her breathing and put her hands on her chest to keep her heart from bursting. She stopped and took a couple of deep breaths. She took one tentative step, then another. Closer now, she put her ear against the door. She heard nothing. She peeped through a small hole and saw that nobody was on the veranda. "Nice!" she said, and let out a sigh of relief. She held her arms up to heaven and thought to herself, *I am so lucky!*

Because of that bit of relief, she gathered a whiff of courage to ever so gently knock on the door with a shaking hand.

Her mother, who was still in the kitchen cleaning the dinner dishes, asked, "Who is it?"

Again, Maana's heart began to race. She was sure it was going to burst right through her ribs. Once more, she tried to keep it in place by putting her hand on her chest, unable to bring herself to say a word.

"Who is it?" repeated her mother.

"Mom, it's me," she managed to say in a feeble voice.

Her younger brother, Cumareey, who was standing next to their mom, ran to the door screaming, "Sister, Maana, sister, Maana!" He opened the door and threw his arms around her legs. Maana bent down to kiss him on both cheeks and whispered the question that had been burning inside of her, "Cumareey, is Dad here?"

"Sister, Sister, did you bring me candy?"

He is so innocent. He doesn't know anything about the trouble I might be in, she thought.

"Listen, Cumareey, I'll give you candy if you tell me whether or not Dad is here," she whispered to him.

Cumareey did not whisper back but yelled out in his excitement,

"Dad isn't here. He went to the Mosque."

She lifted him up, held him there and kissed him again on both cheeks. With his innocence, Cumareey had no idea that these were not just kisses of love from his sister but presents he had earned with the news that he delivered that their father was not home.

"Maanaaa!" her mother yelled from the kitchen.

"Ummaa!" Maana yelled back, putting Cumareey down and running toward the kitchen. But before she could reach the kitchen, her mother met her halfway.

"Do you know what time it is? What have you been doing out so late? Where have you been?"

Maana cowered, feeling like a feral cat caught in the light. She tried to find something to say,

"Mamma, I was studying with a classmate of mine. We have exams coming," she managed to squeak out.

"You have an exam? So, does that mean you can stay out this late, hah? And after this one, will there be more exams that will keep you out this late?" her mother asked.

"Mamma, today the teacher gave us difficult math, so tonight we had to study for a very hard math test."

Aay Caddeey knew that her daughter had never lied to her, nor had she ever brought a whiff of dishonor onto the family. She loved her for that. The evidence in support of her innocence and honesty was piled high. She had always been her mother's precious child, and at birth her mother had bestowed on her the name Maana-faay, combining Maana and Faay, meaning Fatima-the-blessed-one. High praise for such a small infant. Aay Caddeey quieted down, looked over Maana from top to toe as though she might spot some sign of what really had gone wrong tonight. Looking into her daughter's eyes, she guessed that she must be tired.

"Go ahead, change your clothes and come back to eat before your food gets colder," the mother relented.

"Ok Mommy," Maana said, relieved. She ran to her room, feeling light and elated, as though exonerated of all charges that would have been leveled against her. She could not believe she had gotten off with such ease tonight. She thought that there was no crime bigger than the one she had committed by going out on a date with a stranger. She could not believe that her lie had worked. Yet somewhere in the back of her mind, she remained suspicious that her mother had seen through her and knew where she had been and with whom.

Inside her room, she closed the door, quickly took off her clothes, and put on a light *guntiino* (a long shawl draped over the body and tied on the shoulder). She did so in a hurry, as she did not want to meet her father while still wearing high-heels and party clothes. Feeling safe in her lie for now, she began to ruminate on what she had been through tonight. These were thoughts to savor in the solitude of her room. Now her anxiety and fears had turned into warm, beautiful memories: *Oh, how delightful was the evening breeze; the twinkling lights; the music; all had seemed frightening when she was there. The tender mutton she gobbled up; the joking and humorous tales tastefully told, and the great group of friends—old and new. They were all great, both the guys and her friend Sahra,* she thought to herself.

As the night wore on, Axmed's face was the compelling image in her mind's eye. She was attentively attracted to his gentle manner and his way of speaking, retrieving the sweet words that touched her heart. She was aware that she had not had these feelings when she was with him but only now that she was home safe and sound. She sieved and sorted out word by word all that he had said. She tried to recall how she responded. Ruefully, she concluded that she had not been able to participate with equal sagacity. Now she had the right words and responses she should have used when they were together. She wished that she were back in time so that she could correct all her mistakes. She was thinking that she had acted so immaturely he might think her unsuitable for his civilized world. Rehashing all that had happened and the feelings that had been aroused, she eventually fell asleep.

CHAPTER FOUR

I

Everything was boiling hot as usual in the capital city of Mogadishu on that March day. The whole world outside was on fire under the glare of the subtropical sun. The heat it radiated penetrated the houses. Jaamac-dhegey, unable to sleep, got up from the bed on which he had been tossing about, his bare chest and upper body dripping with sweat. His wife, Cambaro Cali Dhoof, was lying on a mat in a place she believed to be slightly cooler, the verandah. Always anxious to please, she hurriedly lifted her heavy limbs as soon as she noticed her husband's movements. She brought his lounge chair out into the courtyard. It was the seat he preferred at times like these. It was made of a narrow strip of multi-colored striped canvas, with a frame and legs of red wood. She put it in the western corner of the courtyard, whereby late afternoon you have both shade and a soft, sweet breeze coming from behind the western wall. The trees planted outside were still small and provided little shade. They were planted only two years ago when the house was built. Wearing a *macawis* (a traditional waist-wrap) and with a small towel on his shoulder, Jaamac stretched out in the chair Cambaro had readied for him.

Cambaro was still busy preparing the things required by her husband. She put a small table next to him, gathered his cigarettes, matches, and ashtray. She placed all these together with a mini radio set on another small table which she set in front of him. Now all that was left was his late afternoon cup of tea. She entered the kitchen to prepare it.

The whole place was quiet, with no movement other than Cambaro's. The maid who worked for the family had gone out shopping. Now, while the rest of the household was taking their siesta, the poor maid took her shopping basket and went out into the afternoon heat. As always, after cleaning up from lunch, she would go out to purchase the fresh vegetables and meat for the evening meal. Resting and taking shelter from the heat were not for her. The children were all in their beds. Even if they could not sleep, they were not allowed to get up until four-thirty. This was the discipline laid down for them that they were not allowed to break, and fearing their father's wrath, they had never broken this routine. They would, however, speak in hushed tones and move about sneakily. In accordance with the old man's rules, there were specific times for everything: a time to sleep, a time to study, a time to have fun, and so forth. That was what their father had taught them with his strict, old-fashioned authoritarianism. However, when their father was away, they made as much noise as they wanted and paid little attention to the schedule. Although even then, the oldest child would warn the younger ones, frightening them with words like "I am going to tell Dad!" They felt far less constrained by the presence of their mother; they had no fear of her. Yet if she became angry, they would do what she told them. Perhaps it was their love for their mother and their permanent closeness to her that tempered the fear they might otherwise have felt for a parent. When their father was not around, only Engineer Axmed, the oldest son, could inspire some fear, especially after he had come back from abroad and grown into adulthood. They started treating him with special respect.

As his mind was soothed by the breeze and the fragrant tea his wife had brought him, Jaamac-dhegey suddenly remembered something. He instantly looked at his watch as though he had missed something important. *No, no, just relax!* He reassured himself. *It is still broad daylight; only a few minutes past four o'clock, and not even close to the time to get ready*, he thought, as he leaned back and relaxed again. His friend Cawaale would stop by at 5:30 p.m., as he had announced by phone that morning. While taken away by the thoughts of prospective pleasures, Jaamac was suddenly struck by two contrasting realities: his memory of the sinful subject of his telephone conversation with Cawaale that morning and the image of his wife, Cambaro, sitting innocently right in front of him. She had been sitting not far from him on a small mat, embroidering a small tablecloth, her needle followed by threads of many colors outlining the stem of a flower printed in blue ink. As she stitched, immersed in her work, he carefully observed her: her old, red diric dragging on the ground around her, and her body, shapeless and corpulent, with bulges of fat everywhere. He glanced at her face, which once upon a time had shone with youthful beauty. *May old age be damned! Look at the baggy and sagging skin of her temples and cheeks, once full and firm,* thought Jaamac. He looked at his wife with pity and studied her from head to toe as if she was someone he had once known but had not seen for ages. At this point, something that made him laugh flashed through his mind. He immediately caught himself and quickly glanced at Camaro's face, afraid that she would notice him and turn suspiciously in his direction. Having made sure that she was still fully engaged in her work, he leaned back again in his easy-chair and resumed his monologue:

Poor Cambaro! May Allah not punish me for what I am doing to you! What would you do if you knew what Cawaale and I were going to be up to tonight? What would you have said if you had picked up the phone when Cawaale called me and heard him say that tonight is my turn to organize our khat session with the girl escorts? What if you had been listening when he went through the list of the available brothels and asked for my advice about which one of them should be put in charge of tonight's program? Oh Cambaro, may Allah bless you! When Cawaale stops by shortly, you will welcome him cheerfully and warmly, as you always do. You will smile at him and he will laugh and joke with you, posing as a sincere family friend who wishes only the best for you! Only Allah can tell the difference between the words of the mouth and the intentions of the heart. What a difference between your smile and his! You're suspicious about me sometimes, but you are never suspicious of Cawaale. You have the evidence of me being away or coming home late, in addition to the gossip of some women. But you do not know that my guide, the one who led me along this new path, is none other than Cawaale, together with some of my other rich high-ranking friends. And you, because of their wealth and influence, welcome them respectfully whenever you see them, and you even boast that those powerful gentlemen are your husband's friends!

His thoughts of such a paradox prompted a sarcastic smile to break out, which he immediately managed to abort. Then he looked again at Cambaro to make sure that she was still too busy and innocent to notice his gestures.

But don't worry, my dear Cambaro, this is all insignificant. Cawaale has done no wrong and does not mean you any harm. When he takes me to certain places or encourages me to have a good time, his intention is not to wrong you or do you any harm. All he means is to please me, so that I will, in turn, please him on different accounts. Life is give-and-take. I do not like to violate your rights myself, but I have done you no wrong either, believe me. The love I feel for you and the way I value you as my wife have not changed a bit. You do not have to be afraid that I will think you have grown old and that as a result I am planning to replace you with a younger wife. No, it is not what I am up to. I have never done you any wrong, other than having fun with young girls every once in a while. No, no, I am not doing you wrong in any way, Cambaro. Allah forbid, my dear! Men of my age have many wives and are even then unfaithful! If you were intelligent, you would give me official permission to amuse myself and would not force me into the 'black market'! You have no reason to blame me, dear. It is that other sinful aspect, from a religious point of view, that is bothering me. May Allah forgive my sins in the hereafter. Forgive me O Allah, Allah, Allah! I am repentant. I am repentant.

As his thoughts turned in this direction, his expression changed; he hung his head. He remembered that it was time for afternoon prayer. He was suddenly struck with a bitter taste of guilt prompted by the sharp contrast between his thoughts of prayer and the sinful plans his mind was simultaneously engaged in. His moral sense started arguing with him inwardly.

How could Allah accept your prayer while you are already planning the great sin you intend to commit tonight? How could you dare to come before Allah to ask for forgiveness, while you are planning to break his commands in a few hours? Can you lie to Allah as you will lie to Cambaro, to whom you will say as you go out that you have been called to a long meeting tonight and will be late? No, no, forget about praying! Don't set yourself up for failure. Allah will not accept prayer from you...

But relax; don't punish yourself! Make use of the good times that have come your way. But... does that mean 'no paradise for you?' Why do you, at this age, allow indecent behavior to threaten what short time is left of your life? You are only reaping blame in this world and the next. Where is your good name, where is the respect in which you used to be held? In essence, this is the end of you. Who you really are is a far cry from what people think you are.

I repent, Allah! I repent! Cancel tonight's program. Let Cawaale and his party go to hell! But if you cancel tonight, will you go on with it some other night? Yes... No... Yes... No! That is a decision you have repeatedly failed to stick to. It really is a choice between two evils, either to be stuck forever with that old lady and lead a boring lifestyle or to party with budding young girls, drinking and chewing khat, and then having to endure eternal punishment. What to do, what to do? I really don't know! But enough of this! I will repent! To hell with Cawaale.

Consumed by his inner battle, Jaamac had neglected his tea, but now he grabbed it, finished it in one gulp, and took out a cigarette. His hairy chest, which initially dried in the breeze, was again wet with sweat. He wiped it off with his towel.

Although Jaamac was over sixty years old, he looked much younger. He felt surprisingly active and as strong as a young man, a feeling that had been reinforced over the last few years as he acquired wealth and achieved a great deal. As he relaxed in his easy chair, sipping a second cup of tea, he recalled how earlier in life he had experienced many hardships. Of his first twenty years in the world, he had spent all but one in the nomadic interior. He used to be a camel herder. He was the first to insult and pick a fight with other young camel herders. He had respect for no one. Other camel herders of his age used to be scared of him because of his assertiveness and physical fitness. He would order around and beat up younger boys if they talked back. One of those younger boys once became so angry with him that late one night, while Jaamac lay in the camel pen waiting for the evening milking session, he tried to split Jaamac's skull with an axe. Another boy who saw it happen came running and deflected the axe, which landed on Jaamac's ear, cutting off its lobe and wounding his neck. That is how he got the nickname Jaamac-dhegey (Jaamac, the cut ear).

When the nomadic life became too harsh, he moved to the city of Mogadishu looking for a better life. He was then nineteen. The years that followed were extremely hard. Totally on his own, he slept in the streets, tried anything new and dangerous, worked as a porter, and so forth. Later he tried his hand first as a peddler and then as a clerk for the government. But mostly he had worked as a low-level governmental employee, even though he had dreams of one day becoming a merchant. It was just a few years ago that he was suddenly promoted and became the executive director of a leading parastatal because he was related to the top leadership in the new Government.

It was then that Jaamac-dhegey began a new lifestyle. As his material circumstances changed, so did his moral principles. Along with his higher social status and increasing wealth came new friends who introduced him to a freewheeling lifestyle. In the past, he had struggled hard to raise his children. It was only recently that they had grown up —some had even started to work at his side. Now his income could be used to pursue his own personal pleasures, and so another door had opened and exposed him to a new way of life.

It took Jaamac-dhegey just the blink of an eye to review this long history of unexpected changes. He leaned back again in his easy chair and heaved a deep sigh, like someone tired from running. He then said with a voice audible to Cambaro this time,

"The weather is terribly hot today!" as if he wanted to utter anything to escape the endless chatter of the sickening internal dialogue. Cambaro, who always enjoyed conversing with her husband, took this opportunity and started commenting on Jaamac's passing remark.

"This is not just heat, this is hellfire!" she murmured. "They used to tell us that at the end of time the sun will move closer to us. I'm sure that it's now closer than usual. O Allah, make things easy on us!"

Jaamac did not pursue the idle chitchat further with his wife, but turned to his son Engineer Axmed. "Axmed, have you drawn up the design for Hagis's house?"

"No father, I'm sorry, but I had no time today," answered Axmed, who had just awakened from his afternoon siesta. And now, still dressed in a *macawis,* he went into the kitchen, poured himself a cup of tea, and joined his parents.

After lunch, Axmed did not go out into the heat of the day to take his siesta in his own apartment. Instead, he stayed on and slept in the bed of his younger brother, who was away at the time. He often felt quite comfortable with staying over and spending time at his parents' house. Here he felt relief from the reserved and sometimes pretentious formalities that weighed on his interactions with other people. At the family home, he enjoyed the uncensored freedom to say anything and move about at will and enter the kitchen, the bathroom, living room, children's rooms, and other bedrooms, all of which brought back childhood memories.

With the cup of tea in his hand, he pulled up a low stool and sat down between his father and mother. He was about to give a fuller answer to his father's question when his cousin Sahra Yuusuf arrived for her regular afternoon visit. Sahra had grown up in this household, just like any other child in the family, until reaching adulthood. After getting a job, she had moved into a place of her own. Greeting her uncle, she sat down on the mat next to Cambaro.

"Dad, I was planning to start designing the Hagi's house today," Axmed continued his report, trying to appease his father who looked angry. "But a lot of other responsibilities came up today. I will definitely draw up a design for him tomorrow."

"Why do you feel compelled to tell me a lie? If you are not going to do it, why not openly say so? Is anyone in a position to compel you? Every day you say, 'I will do it tomorrow.'"

"Father, I'm not being evasive, I just had too many things to do today."

"Too many other duties, too many other duties! You kill yourself over duties that do not benefit you, but for the work that is profitable for us you have no time. I don't know when you will wise up and know what is good for you. You are old enough to know better. I wish I had not relied on you and given a false promise to this gentleman."

Axmed used to shy away from arguing with his father. He tended to avoid talking back to him. When he was younger, he would never have contradicted his father, not even if he had told him to jump into the ocean. He always pretended to take his orders, whether he intended to obey them or not. But Axmed had matured while studying abroad, and upon his return to the family, his father had begun to treat him as an adult. He refrained from shooting sharp barbs and angry words at his son as he had when Axmed was a boy. Recently, Axmed had begun to converse with his father and on occasion even tried to propose an alternative opinion, although he was rarely successful. They were usually diametrically opposed to each other and unable to find common ground. The old man might have raised his family in the city and lived in an urban environment for a long time; he might have made an effort to educate himself and to learn a smattering of foreign languages, but his mindset had remained that of a typical nomad. He was often stunned by the opinions and manners of his children. When despite his best efforts he failed to change their ways, he would hold his head and say softly, "this is the end of time, these are children of the end of time!"

Axmed himself was quite aware that he could not change his father's mindset or convince him of anything. But what he was being blamed for this afternoon had come up once too often. Until now, he would just shake his head, trying to avoid an argument, but this afternoon he said to himself, *just try to explain your views to him a little bit.*

Looking down, he said,

"But Father, how can I go to design someone's private house and neglect my national duty?"

Jaamac looked at him calmly. Then he raised his eyebrows and said,

"I knew from the beginning that you were just putting me on and that you never really wanted to help that friend of mine. 'National duty… national duty…!' That is the extent of your intelligence!" Raising his voice, he added, "And how have you benefited from this work of 'national duty' which you have been pushing for more than a year? Are you killing yourself for this lousy salary that does not even cover your basic needs? Where are the fruits of all the effort and expense I have invested in you?

Today I cannot even prevail upon you to help a man who is my friend and is indispensable to our interests."

"Father, I am not opposed to helping him. I'm more than willing to help him, but only after I have fulfilled my duties. How can my salary be raised if I neglect the work that would generate more income? If our ancestors, like those of the developed countries, had made sacrifices and worked harder in the past, we would now be better off."

"Now look at what he is arguing!" said Jaamac, looking in the direction of Cambaro and pretending to be calm, but quietly boiling with anger. He was tempted to slap his son. That was how he forced Axmed to behave as a child whenever he made him as angry as he was making him now. However, he was well aware that Axmed was now different. He had to be careful not to criticize him too sharply, let alone slap him. He had to take into account that Axmed had grown up and could not be intimidated into correcting his mistakes. Calm advice would be more fruitful.

"Listen, Axmed, this is how they brainwash short-sighted people," he began his exhortations. "Of all these people you see, everyone is pursuing his own interest. This talk about nation and 'working to serve the national interest' is nothing but slogans. I am not telling you to quit your job as a government employee or to stop going to work regularly. You do not need to be an obvious do-nothing. It is wise to stay away from what may earn you blame and to try your best to advance yourself and win promotions. But at the same time, you must invest more time in quietly pursuing your personal interests. As things stand today, no one can make a living depending only on a governmental salary. You need to engage in outside activities to make money."

"For example," Jaamac continued his lecture after a pause, stretching back in his easy chair; "The reason I asked you to help the Hagi is not for nothing. Because of this favor he will be useful to you and to us all in the future."

"How so?" Axmed asked his father.

"Let me tell you," responded Jaamac, "he is a wealthy businessman, and you, since you work for the Government, are not allowed by law to engage in commerce. He, however, can import for you whatever you wish, and you can hide your money in his investments, and then share the profits with him. That is what clever Government officials do nowadays. He has promised me that on his next business trip he will import some profitable trucks for me in his name. In return, I promised him to use my influence to make his imports escape Government taxes. The money I saved from taxes will be enough to cover the cost of my share of the imports. That is one of the easy ways to make money if you are smart enough, you understand? When this man told me about the new villa he was planning to build, I told him that my son, the best architect around, would design it for him at minimal cost. But I realize now that you are going to fail me. You have been stalling for a whole week. This project should have been finished by now. Educating you has been a waste of my time, money and energy!"

Axmed listened with his head bowed and eyes focused on the ground as his father preached his long scathing sermon. Every word he heard made his skin crawl, and some of his father's ideas made his stomach turn. It was impossible to argue any further, although he would have liked to say, *I have no intention of either importing lorries nor hiding money, stop ordering me to design a new house for that Haji.* But he failed to summon up the courage to tell his father openly that he was not about to comply.

"Tomorrow Axmed will work on the design, won't you, son?" Cambaro intervened, trying to calm her husband while coming to her son's defense. There was no one on earth she loved more than her oldest son, and the slightest criticism of him upset her and made her rush to his aid.

"Yes Mother, definitely," he promised.

"Dear son," she added, softening her voice, "dearest, don't let this matter drag on beyond tomorrow. That Hagi is a gentleman and, as your father said, we have something to gain from him. We are counting on him to order and import the furniture and other household needs for your upcoming marriage."

"Your son does not even seem to be ready for marriage." Jaamac commented sarcastically. "This fellow has something else in mind. Only you and I are pursuing this matter, it is not on Axmed's agenda," he continued, trying to provoke his son and make him reveal his true intentions on the matter.

Cambaro was the one most concerned with Axmed's marriage. She kept encouraging her son to get married, and he, trying to avoid the topic, would answer 'give me a little more time.'

"Dear son," said Cambaro in a strong and concerned voice. "What is scaring you away from marriage, for god's sake? Something has given you an aversion to marriage. They are always after you with so much work, or you are sitting around reading. You are either running off to work or have your nose in a book. May Allah cure you of this unnatural aversion. This is caused by the evil eye, I think, and I'm afraid that it's the bad women said to be chasing you who have cast the evil eye on you! Just recently I asked Sheikh Maxamuud to make you an amulet, for there is something fishy here."

Axmed and Sahra glanced at each other. This was nothing new to them. They had heard the old lady speak like this before, but at the mention of the word "amulet," they could barely repress their laughter. They winked at each other and exchanged amused looks.

Then Sahra spoke up.

"But Mother, why are you pushing him? When he finds the right girl, he will bring her to you."

Sahra called Cambaro 'Mother' and valued her as such. Cambaro had raised her. When Sahra was only two years old, her father died. Her mother, Jaamac's sister, was pregnant with her second child. Both mother and daughter were welcomed into the family, but sadly, Sahra's mother died in childbirth, leaving the orphaned Sahra to be raised by her aunt and uncle. Cambaro had been good to Sahra, although she had spared her neither hard work, angry words, nor blows, especially when her uncle was absent.

Sahra had married and worked as a teacher. But the couple soon separated, leaving Sahra to fend for herself. Her bonds with the family, however, remained as strong as if they were still living under the same roof. Sahra had fulfilled all the obligations parents might expect from a daughter and even more, so her maternal uncle had always blessed her and sung her praises.

Jaamac picked up on Sahra's words, saying, "And when on earth will he find the right girl? Is she one who still needs to be born? Where will he find a better girl than the ones he has refused, girls from honorable families of known ancestry and descent, who have been decently confined to their homes? I would have been ready to ask the parents for their hands in marriage and to pay the required dowry."

At the mention of "ancestry" and "descent," Axmed and Sahra exchanged meaningful glances. These concepts were part of what astounded them in the old fellow's way of thinking. Yet they dared not openly express their own contrasting opinion: that the value of an individual only depends on oneself, and is neither positively not negatively affected by ancestry or descent.

When the two parents finished going back and forth about Axmed's marriage, they redirected their attacks toward Sahra, letting Axmed off the hook and giving him a new lease on life.

Cambaro threw her first spear at Sahra:

"What about you, Sahra? Is that matter between you and Cadinaasir taken care of yet?"

"They have no plans together either," added Jaamac sarcastically, trying indirectly to extract information from Sahra. He wanted to know if she and her boyfriend were planning to marry any time soon. "If I didn't know his father and was not friendly with the whole family, I would have lost confidence in that chubby fellow a long time ago." Jaamac continued. "He had a belly even as a boy. I don't like young men who become fat at an early age!"

"We are almost ready," answered Sahra succinctly, trying to avoid further questioning. However, she would not have gotten off the hook that easily had Cawaale not saved her. The latter knocked on the gate and entered immediately, without waiting for permission. He was his usual laughing and teasing self. He jokingly greeted everyone present, asked Cambaro about the household and her children, and then joined Jaamac, who had gone ahead to the sitting room. The two men reemerged ten minutes later, handsomely dressed and in a cloud of expensive perfume.

Without a word, they walked out and got into the green sedan parked just outside the door and drove off into the early evening, oblivious to Camaro's concern mumbled under her breath, "This government with its many meetings is killing my old man."

Doomed is the one who is left in the dark!

CHAPTER FIVE

I

The setting sun, round like a hunter's shield, cast its orange glow into space, enticing the daylight to fade away, bringing forth the darkness of night. Through an open window, Engineer Axmed Jaamac watched the scant evening clouds drift as they blended into the amber glow of the evening sun. Sitting on the edge of his golden painted bed with its ash-blonde headboard, he leaned over to massage his sculpted calves, put on his flip-flops, and set his feet on the floor. In sight of those tanned, well-shaped legs, Maana-faay Xaaji Muumin was seated in a chair close to the edge of the bed. Her skirt and his sarong made gentle contact. Uncertain of their intent, inch by inch, the two lovers closed the gap between them until their lips locked, planting a seed of passion.

And, though Axmed had not had his afternoon siesta that day, he was filled with energy. Simply being in the presence of Maana-faay brought an excitement to his being. In his normal setting, his afternoon siesta would have been a must. The only thing that would prevent it was if he had to work. But if there was a plan to meet with Maana, all would change. In that case, forget about a siesta, and even a work commitment was then not sealed with certainty. She would usually call him from her home in the morning to secure a time to meet in the afternoon, and for the next three hours following her call his time was filled with anxious preparation for her arrival. He did not glance at a single newspaper or book with which he otherwise would have been obsessed. Except for when he was sleeping, or when he had an important guest at his place, he would either have a book or newspaper in hand. But whenever he was waiting for Maana-faay, he would forget his love for reading and rush to tidy up the place, cleaning and lighting incense. He would bring in some games, buy drinks and anything that might bring pleasure to her. He would plan where she would sit and make sure that he himself was presentable.

Yet with all that was on his plate, he still would have had time left for a nap if he had wanted. But he did not. Why didn't he, one might dare to ask? Either he was either simply afraid that she might come in while he was asleep, or rather, the anticipation of her arrival was enough to clog the pathway to sleep. Before he met Maana-faay, he had never thought that a woman could take over his self-assured life and his heart and occupy his mind day and night.

From the first night he saw her, he was awestruck by the purity of her beauty. That was what had initially attracted him to her. That first night when he had taken her to Jungal he had not thought her much different from the other young women he had seen. Forces that he did not understand, however, kept pulling him towards her. What were these forces? Was it her beauty? Was it how shy she was, avoiding even looking directly at him? Was it her innocence and her apparent lack of information about the cunning ways women play with men's minds? Was it the easy, unassuming way she talked to him? He did not know why he was so enamored with her, or whether this feeling was love or lust. He only knew that she had overtaken his thoughts, and quite possibly that she had captured his heart.

The nightly visits to Sahra Yuusuf's place made it easier to see her, boosted his self-confidence, stretched his foresight, and sprouted thoughts of matrimony that he might soon add to the courtship conversation.

From the time they were introduced, the terrain of thought they were traveling on took them further and further toward their entwined destiny. Time was moving fast, a month had already passed, another came and went and the third was halfway over. A significant change had come over Maana-faay: she was drinking from the pool of passion when only a short time ago she had not even been able to look directly into Axmed's eyes.

II

It was not that easy for Maana-faay to arrive at this stage. She had taken many steps to get there. Ever since that first invitation the three friends offered her, she had been left with an indelible memory, full of compliments, praise, and deference, as they showed her a world within Mogadishu that she had not known. All of these were the things that elevated her sense of worth and raised her self-esteem while bringing wonder into her otherwise static world and a pulsing vibrancy into her heart.

From the first night, her dreams were filled with memories of the planned and often spontaneous rendezvous with the other three at Sahra's place. The conversations they shared erased any fear that might have been in her, easing her into membership with the group. She was not a stranger to Sahra to begin with and felt at ease around Cadinaasir, Sahra's boyfriend. She started teasing him soon after they were introduced. Her daydreams seemed to be occupied with thoughts of Axmed, yet she was timid when he was around. However, it did not take long for her to free herself from the shackles of her shyness.

Time after time, she would feel an invisible magnet pulling her closer to Axmed. She found herself thinking about him more and more. Whenever they were together, she would be enraptured, hanging on his every word. When they were apart, loneliness would overcome her, and even her favorite pastimes would be forgotten. She knew neither when nor how that happened!

Sensing that her family was growing suspicious of her changing behavior, and not wanting to continue to lie to her mother, she decided to cut the cord with her friends, stop going to Sahra's place, and return home at her usual curfew. Realizing that she was riding on a wave of infatuation, she told herself never to go back to Sahra's again. However, she would soon find herself running back to the same place, unable to stand by her decision. She could resist the temptation for a day or so, but she would feel miserable and lonely. The everyday desires of eating, sleeping, talking, and reading would all leave her. And she would somehow feel an itch spreading over her body and loathe all that surrounded her. Relief would come only with a rush to Sahra's place.

Finally, the fact that the two, Axmed and Maana-faay, had fallen in love with each other could no longer be hidden. The truth was revealed, and their love was exposed on stage. The first to take the lid off was Sahra, who gave herself the assignment of diagnosing her two friends. That they were both afflicted with the same symptoms brought her to a diagnosis of Lovesickness. Then she simply informed each of them about the other, encouraging them to admit and accept that love for one another. So Axmed took to the stage. No longer able to hide her own affliction, Maana-faay tentatively followed behind. Pulling the curtain apart, she abandoned her fortress of denial and placed her hand in Axmed's palm. Together they sang a duet of love. From that point on, they were no longer confined by their undeclared passion. Love, their love, led them to other new venues, and one of them was Axmed's apartment. Every time she had a chance to escape, she would come to see him there. "I am going to study with my girlfriend" or "I have a class tonight," were her chief excuses to take leave of absence from home.

III

It can happen that when lovers are enveloped in happiness, others around them may feel envy or resentment. Dusk descended and Maana-faay was still in her lover's home. *Let others say what they wish to say. Whoever frowns would also say it aloud,* she thought. Sitting next to Axmed made her forget about all the scolding and hardship that might head her way later. *I should disregard all who whisper about Axmed and me. Singles are maliciously suspicious anyway,* she thought. *People should leave me alone. I am keeping company with my medicine, Axmed. Where is Iikar Aw-Mukhtaar? I have no idea. I have no idea. May God take that cursed man away!* she whispered to herself. Once the thought of Iikar came to mind, she was startled. She glanced at Axmed and then quickly looked away. Suddenly she was seized by a dreadful thought. What if Axmed had discovered her dark secret—that she had been betrothed to her cousin Iikar! She studied his face, searching for a clue, wondering if she could see anger in his eyes. Yes, she thought she could see underlying anger veiled in his eyes. She turned her gaze away, fearful that he might be able to read her thoughts. Trying to stifle her apprehension, with the heat of fear rising in her neck and up to her cheeks, she could no longer hear his voice. He was in the middle of a sentence when she, fanning herself with her hands, surprised him with:

"Axmed, your house is so hot!" trying to hide the discomfort and anxiety caused by her thoughts. Axmed looked straight at her and expecting her to say more asked, "Is it that hot, sweetheart?" He looked about and rushed to reach for a fan. "Please forgive me, darling. I am not able to tell how hot it is. I am unable to notice anything but your beauty and your love when you are with me," he added in a soft voice. He began to fan her himself.

As she felt cooled, she gently took the fan away from him and said, "Thanks." He opened his mouth to say something, but before he could speak, he heard a knock on the door, followed by a man's voice asking for permission to enter. Axmed looked up and responded, "Come in!" Maana-faay who felt disturbed by this sudden and unexpected arrival, hastily covered her head, and moved away from Axmed. A dark, plump young man walked in, holding a cigarette between his middle and index fingers. In his other hand, he was casually waving a set of keys on an elongated chain. His eyes immediately locked onto the mesmerizing beauty seated next to Axmed. A magnet seemed to be holding his eyes to her. As he walked in, he dragged his feet. Enraptured by the stunning beauty of Maana-faay, his thoughts ran wild. *Wow! That is what they call beauty! How did this monkey get an angel like this? How have I not seen her when I have been cruising throughout every corner of this city?*

While these thoughts were roaming in his mind, he said, "Good afternoon!"

He had never greeted his friend Axmed in such a polite manner. Normally, he would start by teasing him. Today though, languorously gazing at Maana-faay, he searched for clever words as he moved slowly into the room, aloofly holding his cigarette. He did it all to seduce the woman sitting before him. It was his nature to lose himself whenever he met a female he wanted to impress. Standing directly in front of Maana-faay, he held out his hand with exaggerated aplomb and said, "Sister, I am Kulmiye."

Before Maana-faay could respond, Axmed said to Maana-faay, as though he felt duty-bound to introduce his friends, "Maana, Kulmiye is a close friend of mine. Be careful, he is your first friend-in-law." Then putting his hand on her shoulder but talking to Kulmiye, he went on, "This is the Maana-faay that you have heard me talking about. Her name is not new to you, I guess."

Oh yeah! *This is the woman whom he had been trying to keep away from my eyes all the time!* Kulmiye thought. *At last, I got her today! Now I understand the reason why he no longer has a roving eye for other women; he has this sweet raisin in his grasp.*

Trying to hide these thoughts with a smile, he shook hands with Maana once again. He continued to hold her hand in his palms and smiled as a thought crossed his mind, while saying, "So this is Maana-faay? I got it. Maana, Axmed is right; your name isn't new to me, but I have not had a face that goes with the name. Now I have the great fortune to do just that. Nice to meet you, dear."

"Nice to meet you," she echoed, pulling her hand away from his firm grasp, thinking, *would you just release my hand?*

"I am glad," he went on to say, pulling up a chair, "that I have now been introduced to my 'sister-in-law.' And although we have not met before, I feel like I have known you for quite some time. That was why I told

Axmed that the first time he introduces us I will take us all out. Luckily, it is tonight, and I am offering you an invitation you can't refuse. The dinner will be in your honor, Maana. A celebration welcoming you into the family. Isn't that the point?"

"Thanks, brother, but I don't have time tonight," she said smiling, trying to keep herself from laughing and acting as though he had said something interesting. The fact, however, was that she was laughing inside at how loud-mouthed yet clueless he was.
Axmed himself almost laughed aloud at Kulmiye's phony invitation to a feast. Hearing Kulmiye's sweet, exaggerated lie, he turned to the wall and said in his mind, *go ahead, man, with your hypocritical snare that you try on every woman!*

Kulmiye's invitation was a spontaneous and poorly articulated gesture. It was not out of generosity and respect to his friend, Axmed, and the "sister-in-law" who had just been introduced to him. Rather, his offer was prompted by his interest in Maana. He blurted it out as he was dazzled by Maana-faay's beauty and surprised to discover Axmed and her together. He had already arranged dinner dates with two other young women he had seen the night before, and was scheduled to meet a third later at his place. His original plan was that Axmed would consent to go with him on a "double date," leaving the minor hindrance of his third date that evening. Now that he had seen Maana-faay, he no longer had any interest in the others.

Kulmiye was a womanizer. He was flirtatious and beguiling. If he was unsuccessful upon his first encounter with an attractive woman, he would try again, tracing her through a phone number or an address for school or work. He would not trust giving her his own number alone or leave her to her promise to meet him another time. Maana-faay was a new challenge, since she was the girlfriend of his friend who was present. If dinner tonight was not an option, he had to leave her with a slight yearning for another time.

He could try his "magic touch with women" on her, but this one was his friend's girlfriend. His mind's inner voice argued with him: *Should he pursue her? No, absolutely not.* His "integrity" was bigger than that, he told himself. So why was he going out of his way to invite them? Why was he sacrificing his own plan for theirs? Why was he wasting time if he did not have to sit here with them? Why was he drawn to her? Why was he savoring her every word? Why was he giving her lingering stares? He did not know. *Allah may never test me with such a transgression upon my friend. Allah has provided many beautiful women, and I should not be tempted by the beauty of my best friend's girlfriend. How many young ladies are running after me? So many that I am unable to manage all of my dates. But this one is one of a kind. She is perfect. She isn't like the other friends-in-laws,* he whispered to himself.

My God! Is this a human being? Look at her dazzling beauty! Can anybody resist staring at her eyes? Look at her sweet gaze! May Allah forgive me. Cursed be Satan. Go away, temptation! Shame, shame! But maybe it won't work out between the two of them. They aren't married yet! Yes, why could it not be possible? Oh brother! Why doesn't he leave her alone? How can I make this happen? At any rate, you have to present yourself well. His mind twisted and turned in circles.

All these thoughts occurred to him while he was busying himself with lighting another cigarette. He again offered his invitation to Maana-faay, trying his best to persuade her to go for dinner, but she would not budge. She let herself off graciously by saying,

"Let's make it another time."

Axmed also came to her rescue by adding that she had been away from home longer than planned. He reminded Kulmiye that they needed to invite his girlfriend too, which was not possible at that moment. "And whoever we are inviting should be told ahead of time, right?" Axmed asked coyly, implying that Kulmiye's invitation was not convenient. He also knew that it was not an honest offer. He was reminding his friend that if he was going to invite Maana-faay to dinner, he should have told her days ago. They agreed that the invitation should be postponed.

"Maana reminds me," said Kulmiye, his eyes traveling over her body, "of the winner of last year's Miss Universe pageant in London, the woman who took the crown. You look like her. If you were from the same country, I would have thought that you must have been twins."

When Axmed heard him say that, he moved over to grab the books he had placed on the table for Maana-faay and began to ruffle through the pages of one as though he was not paying much attention to Kulmiye's nonsense. Of course, he was not reading but following the tasteless tales. He almost said, *you're not serious, are you? Would you please stop lying to my girlfriend?*

"Where did you see her?" Maana-faay asked.

"I was there in London. I was a tourist in England then, and I saw her later in Paris, too. She was staying in the same Hilton hotel I was in. I invited her out once and she reciprocated with the same offer. European women aren't like ours; they're much more modern. So, we became fast friends," he unabashedly stated.

Axmed listened to this performance and knowingly glanced up at Kulmiye, then went back to his book. Now Kulmiye understood what Axmed was telling him, *you have no shame in telling such a lie. When was the Miss Universe competition held in London? How did you get to London when you were with me all last year?*

Maana-faay, unaware of his fabrication, asked with genuine interest, "What were you in Paris for?"

Kulmiye straightened up, softened his voice, and attempting to cover his story, replied, "I was conducting an inventory on a French company in which I own some shares."

Axmed, who could no longer stand it, interrupted and said, looking at his watch, "Hey, Kulmiye, you're driving, right?"

"Yes, how could I be without a car?"

Axmed stood up, reached for his trousers from the hanger, put them on, and said, "Great! Let's drop Maana off on our way."

IV

Maana-faay was taken to Xamar-weyne. They dropped her off by the Slaughterhouse, outside the neighborhood. She did not want to be let out any closer than that to her house. She was afraid that someone who knew her might see her getting out of a car.

Once she left, Kulmiye turned to Axmed and said, "Gimme five!" Still holding Axmed's hand, he went on to say, "Congratulations! I am happy for you that you got yourself an incredible woman."

Axmed did not say a word but smiled.

After a while, Kulmiye continued, "But I am afraid that you are not taking advantage of a great opportunity."

"What do you mean, 'taking advantage of?'" asked Axmed.

"What can I tell you about taking advantage of a woman who is in your hands? To tell you the truth, I was not impressed with the way you were sitting with her when I came. I am guessing that you have been together for a while now. How many weeks have you known each other?"

"Almost three months."

"My God! Look at your stupidity! You have known each other for three months and she is sitting in a chair. What can happen between the two of you if she is sitting in a chair? Is she reading verses of the Quran to you to bless you?" Kulmiye scolded Axmed.

"Why? Where would you have her seated?"

"What about on the bed where you were so regally perched? Why not recline and induce her to join you in the bed!"

"Do you think that two people of the opposite sex cannot be together without being sexually involved?"

"What are you doing with her? Is she a statue to admire? Is she hanging with you to earn credit for herself in the Hereafter, or has she brought you a message from the Divine? Why are you wasting time? How can you claim to be a man when a beautiful woman has come to your home, sat in a chair, and you did not pull her close to you on your bed, while taking her clothes off and…? I should use the Somali proverb, 'Lost items lie next to one they do not belong to!'"

"You are wrong, my friend", Axmed rejected, "Another Somali saying goes, 'Trust not violated is a tool for life.' You are wrong if you think that is what manhood is about. Being a man isn't being like the predatory hyena, jumping onto every woman who comes your way. There are morals, gentle bed manners, and overall appropriate etiquette. Just because you have an urge doesn't mean that you can act on it," Axmed stated, looking into Kulmiye's eyes to see if he was paying any attention to his advice.

"You have been telling me that you believe there is a perfect woman out there," continued Axmed, "who is waiting to be your wife — your soulmate. If you want to find her, you have to walk a different life path, set different goals. That is what differentiates mankind from the animal kingdom. If your lust and urge are driving you so that you only live for today by dancing to the tune of how full your stomach is, then you are no better than the animals after all."

"OK, I guess it is now your time to preach. You, Sheikh go ahead and enlighten me further. You, the one with God-given wisdom, what brings a man and a woman together? Isn't it the joy of sex?" argued Kulmiye.

"I agree with you about the joy of sex, but love isn't exclusively about sex. Love has many facets and multiple layers. Plenty of other feelings come into play. It simply depends on the particular relationship between each couple! It is possible that the conversation shared between this young woman and me could bring both of us more joy than the total time that you or I have spent in bed with many," replied Axmed.

"What you're saying is that you are in love with this woman, although you have never been in love before!" Kulmiye said with laughter. "Sheikh, is your Holy Book telling you that you shouldn't sleep with the woman you are in love with?" he asked sarcastically. Then, calming down a little, he put his hand on Axmed's shoulder and continued to laugh, saying, "If that is what you call 'in love,' how do you measure it?! How do you know that it is love? Here is a man that love has conquered! There is no known medicine for such stupidity!" Laughing louder, and in sarcastic tone, he sang a well-known Somali song:

"'Hey, you, Love, you who killed Qays / that which gored Cilmi with a spear / how many times did you throw one of us off a cliff?'"

"You don't believe that Qays and Cilmi died for love, do you?" asked Axmed, not sharing Kulmiye's laughter. He was angry that Kulmiye was mocking love.

"It is like believing that the world is like an egg precariously balanced on the tip of a bull's horn. There is a fly on the bull's nostril, pestering it, and when it tries to shake it off, there goes the world, flying off the horn!" said Kulmiye, alluding to an ancient myth.

"I was once like you ignorant of Love's gentle breeze." Axmed responded.

"You of all people have the audacity to insinuate that I know little about love? Thank you, sir. You can't compete with me when it comes to love. There isn't a single night that I am not in love. I fall in love with every woman who accompanies me to a *khat* chewing party, prior to going to bed together! Don't you remember that night when we were both at a *khat* party? What love sounds was I making? Where were you when I was singing to the woman who was with me, 'Honey, sweetie. My love, my life, I am moaning because of your love. Give me your breasts to cure me of my pain of lust.' She offered herself to me because of love! This happens every night. If I take a woman out, she is easily seduced, and together we sing a duet of love songs," Kulmiye boasted.

"And you don't know each other the next morning, do you?" retorted Axmed.

"Why should we know each other in the morning? Were we prescribed to each other by a physician? Each of us moves on in search of the next lover. 'Love is with what is new.' Spending three months just talking with a beautiful girl, like you, is not the way to express or receive love. Don't kill this poor young lady with temptation and your dalliance. Teach her to smoke and to chew *khat* and do all the other things that are fun. Or else she is going to dump you, because she certainly isn't going to worship you," said Kulmiye in one breath.

"You are the one who is in need of counsel. But you refuse to listen to sound advice, Kulmiye."

"What advice would that be?" asked Kulmiye.

"I would have advised you to change the way you treat others as well as your perceptions," replied Axmed.

"Do you think it's a bad idea to have a good time while you are still young?" asked Kulmiye.

"Let me ask you: is it a good idea to spend money and time on drinking, chewing *khat*, and being with women who seem to care little about their own self-worth and reputation? To be hungover and sleepy all day, and not be able to go to work the next day? When are you going to work for your future if you spend your precious days of youth so uselessly?" Axmed asked.

"Who am I working for if it isn't for my own pleasure and enjoyment?" argued Kulmiye.

"That is like being employed by the devil! You should be working toward your future and for your future children, Sir," Axmed countered.

Kulmiye scoffed, "My future children? You are talking about children today, too? You should have stuck with your favorite topic, 'working for the common good.' What was the other one? Hmm, public affairs, public what-is-the-name. Have you had any luck in public affairs?"

"The words, 'public affairs' and 'society' are very nettlesome to you," Axmed challenged. "You hear them, and you itch all over because you know you are guilty of shunning your responsibility."

"There is no bigger crime than one that is committed against me," responded Kulmiye.

"That is how you see it?" Axmed said.

"No, it's a fact."

"Even if that were the case, would you be able to separate whoever is guilty of transgressing against you from whomever you are guilty of transgressing against?" asked Axmed.

"No, I am not going to separate the two. Each person is on his own. On whatever road my interests take me, whoever faults me for following that road…it is he who is wrong. And you are one of them!"

"But my friend, your life and actions affect others—your friends, your family, your community and the public in general. If you fail, you fail them too. You are not an island. You have been able to live your lifestyle only with the help of others. You have a responsibility to pay back some dues."

"You are a lost man whose brain is full of foam. Do you know that? Leave all this martyrdom alone; it will quickly age you. Enjoy your life while you are still young. Or else you will soon be psychotic, like our friend Qawdhan."

"Who is Qawdhan?" asked Axmed.

"You don't remember Qawdhan? Our poor classmate who stayed behind to attend a local college while we went abroad," responded Kulmiye.

Axmed cut off the conversation by changing the topic before Kulmiye made any insulting references to the man's clan. He recalled how older nomadic men would cloud everything with clannish remarks whenever they were trying to talk about someone. They had to start their story by identifying each person with his particular clan by saying "the one from clan so and so." He did not actually blame the elders for such comments but attributed it to their age. His father was one of those men. But he was shocked to hear that kind of talk from an urbane college-educated young man.

What happened to the modern world that Kulmiye claims to be part of? whispered Axmed to himself. This was not the first time he noted the retrograde behavior which his friend espoused. He tried many times to tell him to mend his ways but to no avail. Now he was giving up on him. He had finally decided to cut him loose to stop the constant bickering between the two of them. It occurred to him that though they were sitting next to each other, they were worlds apart. He could not see how he could bridge the gulf that had developed between them.

"Kulmiye, I think we shouldn't give each other a hard time, because we can't persuade each other of anything," said Axmed.

"I don't mind that at all, but I would advise you of one thing: don't ever trust women. Don't be fooled by their charade, because I have the scars to prove it. They would lay a banana peel in your path. They are not who they present themselves to be. Get what you want quickly and get away from them," Kulmiye preached again.

"I thank you for your 'valuable lecture'," responded Axmed, avoiding another argument.

Kulmiye, who had caught on to Axmed's ploy, smiled and asked but not intelligently, "Are you mad? If that is the case, this is not a new problem for you. It's hereditary. Just the other day, a man from your clan tried to fight me after I had teased him. Why didn't I leave him alone to begin with? His name was..."

"Listen, Kulmiye," Axmed interrupted with fatigue, "please take me back to my place, I need to rest."

Axmed went off to a sound sleep early that night, and Kulmiye disappeared into the city.

CHAPTER SIX

I

At the *Daljirka Dahsoon* monument, in the heart of Mogadishu, a white Mercedes passed through the roundabout, turned south, and slowly proceeded into Somalia Road. Cruising with ease and now parallel to the Central Bank, the sedan's headlights caught a young lady wearing an oversized colored *Dirac,* a greenish head cover, and high-heeled shoes. The corpulent man navigating the sedan was intrigued. He aimed the car in the girl's direction, dimmed the headlights, and slowed down to get a closer look at the young lady.

Perhaps disturbed by the headlights directed at her, the woman picked up her pace and turned right, away from the road.

She, Maana-faay, had alighted from a taxi at the Shabeelle area and was now heading to Xamar-weyne. She repeatedly darted furtive glances at her wristwatch. It was 8:00 p.m. Not yet too late to be getting home. But failing on her earlier afternoon plan, she wanted to go back home earlier than originally intended.

After lunch, she had tried to go to bed for the afternoon siesta, like the rest of the family, but sleep was held at bay by the images of Axmed that kept popping into her mind. After a bit of a tussle with herself, tossing and turning, she had decided to pay him a surprise visit. She got up, showered and dressed, sneaked out of the house, and purposefully traveled several miles to the middle of Hodan District. At the doorsteps of a white-painted building, she stopped. The door was padlocked, but she knocked anyway. When no one answered, Maana, disappointed, turned and began her walk back home. She regretted the risk she had taken and was worried that her parents were now up, as she realized that she had left on an unsupervised excursion. Thus, lost in thought, she was not paying attention to her surroundings: the crowded shops and streets swollen with people, and the noise of engines revving as cars roared by. She certainly was not aware of one specific car and a driver who followed closely behind her.

II

It was not easy to follow a single woman through the overcrowded Mogadishu streets. The corpulent sedan driver had to make several maneuvers with his vehicle in order to keep her in his sight. The sight of her sauntering in and out of the waves of people heightened his interest, while the discordant hum of the lives heaving on the city streets grated on his nerves.

He began debating with himself. *Too many people! Are they pouring out of a factory that produces them?! Too many cars. Where are they streaming out of? I wish they would let up a little! Not a chance to talk to this lady! What the hell? Who is going to look at me? I will do what I want! No, no, this is not the place to accost a young lady. I am a man of integrity. I am a well-known, high-ranking government official. This is when I don't like the title of 'government official.' It deprives me of my anonymity. How lucky is a man whom no one knows! He can do whatever he wants. But me, what can I do? Is it possible that among all these people around here someone might know who I am? Is it possible that one of my children or my employees may be among them? To heck with my children and all! To hell with being a government official! Look at the opportunity and this beauty that I may lose if I do nothing right now! What the hell, I am going to go for her even if the sky is going to fall on me. Men and women are made for one another. No, no, just wait. If I stop the car for the young woman and she refuses to hop in, I'll be laughed at and disgraced. That would be disastrous. Well, I should leave her alone. No, no, she is not one who should be left alone. OK, why don't I just continue to follow her until she is out of the crowd? Who knows where she is going? See, now she's walking right in front of Café Nazunale. If she turns into the intersection, there is no hope. She'll get away. The street is so crowded. But if she heads straight, that is good for me. Once she walks by the Curuba Hotel, she will leave the lighted streets and the crowds of people behind. I can easily follow her then. If I am lucky, she will walk straight ahead.*

Still laboring with his own thoughts, he stopped the car and got out, with an excuse to buy a pack of cigarettes. He didn't care much for cigarettes, but he was trying to have a closer look at the mystery woman with the flowing *dirac* who appeared to be about to cross the intersection. Oh, how he was wishing that she would walk straight ahead, and then he realized that was exactly what she was doing! Hastily he turned around, got into the car, and gunned the engine. Excited and anxious, he followed her.

Maana-faay passed by the National Museum when the white sedan braked right in her path. It was as if the car had aimed directly for her. It did not take long to have her suspicions proven right.

The driver rolled the window down and said, "Hey, young lady!"

She glanced at him but kept walking, wondering if he knew her from somewhere.

Trying to take advantage of the look she had thrown his way, he said, "My dear, could you come closer? I would like to ask you something."

Now that he had made his intentions clear, she increased her pace to avoid him. *Oh, dear, he is older than my dad, yet he has no shame. What is this world coming to? You can't walk on the streets of this city without being harassed by older men. Where IS it safe for a young lady in this town?* Maana wondered. The fact that this was an older man of about her father's age bothered her. What she did not know was that this man, who was aggressively trying to engage her, was none other than Axmed's father: the very man who could perhaps be her future father-in-law!

Embarrassed by how he was ignored, Jaamac-dhegey stayed in the car. His ego had been bruised, yet he was emboldened to continue. He had to get to the bottom of this rascally little lady's resistant attitude. He told himself that he was going to follow her anyway. If nothing else, he was going to find out where she lived. He would then ask his aides, who had been successful in the past in assisting him to seduce young ladies.

But first, he should exhaust his own efforts. He decided to change his wording and try once more. However, his attempted delivery was aborted when out of nowhere another young lady appeared. She greeted Maana warmly with kisses on the cheeks. As he looked on, he sensed something was familiar about the newly-arrived lady. Shocked and confused, his mind ran wild. *Am I daydreaming or is what I see true? My Allah, please make it a figment of my imagination! Whether you like it or not, it is true. It's no one other than Sahra Yuusuf, my niece! Shame, shame on me!* Recognizing the other young lady, Jaamac felt as though the sky were about to fall on him. *What kind of misfortune brought her here tonight?!*

His heart was in his throat, and blood boiled through his veins. He wished the ground beneath him would swallow him whole or careen him into the heavens. *Why is she here in Xamar-weyne at this hour of night?* he exclaimed.

He turned his face away from the two young ladies and floored the gas pedal, hoping to escape before being recognized, but it was too late. Having recognized him, Sahra was just about to say hello to her maternal uncle when he sped off. Maana, watching him, felt compelled to tell her friend what had just transpired between her and the driver of the sedan.

"Sahra, sister, you should have seen how that old man behaved tonight!"

"Which old man? What happened?" asked Sahra anxiously.

"My God! If I tell you, you will be disgusted!" said Maana.

"Please, tell me!"

"My dear, that man you saw in the white sedan..."

"Yes? What did he do, tell me?" asked Sahra, worriedly anticipating the bad news about her uncle.

"The man that drove by here just now," added Maana, thinking that Sahra might not know whom she was referring to.

"Dear, can you believe that a man of such an advanced age was harassing me?"

Sahra felt shocked and embarrassed. A light breeze of contempt ran through her entire body. She put her hands to her mouth, wishing away the fact that this man was her uncle. She wished she could erase what she had just heard. She repeatedly asked Maana unnecessary questions. She wished she were lying or had mistaken her uncle for someone else. *How could that possibly be my reputable uncle, Jaamac? He is well known to be a man of integrity! Isn't it he who lambasts older men hunting young ladies? Isn't he the same one who calls it "impure and dirty" when women jump into cars that pick them up off the street? And isn't it he who has been preaching to his son against this style of predatory dating, which is so far outside our religious and cultural norms?*

No, no, no! No way this man with such vile behavior could have been my uncle. Would my uncle pick up young girls from the streets? That is like the sun rising from the west or setting in the east! It's not possible. But Maana does not lie. Well, it's not a lie. Hey, that man was not my uncle. It was all in my imagination. But wait, why am I kidding myself? How is my uncle any different from the rest of the men in this town? That was him! I saw his big bald head and the shirt with the stripes that he put on this afternoon. This is very strange. I don't know, I don't know. All these thoughts had run through Sahra's mind in seconds of puzzled silence.

"Maana, bye; I have to run; I am so late," she said abruptly, trying to escape with her inner conflict.

III

After a tasty cappuccino at Juba Hotel, Engineer Axmed Jaamac walked out onto the street. Counting the hours of his last days off, he stopped.

Where am I going anyway? he asked himself. He remembered that tonight he had planned an important dinner out with Maana, who suggested that they should take Cadinaasir and Sahra with them. He had agreed. But there was one problem. He was short on cash.

Axmed knew one thing: Maana was different from most women; so different that she would not simply fold her hands in her lap waiting for her boyfriend to shoulder all the expenses. as though men farmed money or were court-ordered to feed their female partners. Maana would not let her date pay for it all. She would insist on shouldering her share of the expense. Axmed welcomed this social etiquette, but he was also aware that Maana had limited means. He would need a plan to spare her this expense and any embarrassment it might cause.

What should I do? I could go to my father, he whispered to himself. He knew that if all else failed he could ask his father for an advance on his allowance. But he hated to justify his needs to him. It looked, however, like there were no other viable choices today. He looked at his watch and thought 8:00 a.m. was a good time for a morning visit. He knew that this was the best time to catch his father in his office.

Axmed crossed the Jamhuuriya Road, turned the corner across from the pharmacy, and got on the Jubbada Sare Road heading north. At the cafeteria, Foolbaxsi, he was tempted to grab a Coca-Cola but decided against it and pushed on. Eastward, he turned onto the new Bakool Road. Passing the *sambusa* vendor and the kiosk attached to it, he came upon a sidewalk vendor. Sitting in the middle of it was a woman wearing an old *guntiino* and a worn-out shawl. She was holding a baby girl in her lap while two older, naked boys stood next to her. People of all ages were passing her by from both sides. Right in front of her was a basket full of sambusas and mandazi. He was disturbed by the army of flies hovering over the food and by the hungry cries of the baby in her lap. The mother did not bother herself to lull the baby, because she was busy securing pennies that could be used to keep all three of her children alive. He watched as she handed two pieces of mandazi to two different customers. One was a middle-aged man. His outfit indicated that he was a nomad. His *go'*, originally white, had turned tan with age. He was wearing flip-flops made of tire shreds for shoes. He stuck the end of his cane into the ground and then, squatting, straddled it like a horse. The other customer—a barefooted boy, wearing worn-out shorts and an old shirt, took the mandazi in one hand while holding a shoeshine box in the other. It was quite apparent that the two customers shared the same misery: hunger. Their emaciated bodies and stained clothes testified to their plight. Both patrons gobbled down the dry mandazi with the flies trying to claim their share.

Axmed recalled the excess of good food and the delicious aroma of the breakfast he had eaten that morning at home. He now wished he had managed to save a meager leftover to pass on to the poor.

That same leftover would have been enough for breakfast and lunch for these two, he whispered to himself. He sighed and looked around, then resumed his walk.

Look, comparing where I am now with where I was a few minutes ago, in my neighborhood with our big houses, and the surrounding verdure; what do the two neighbors really know about each other? What do the huts made of straw have in common with those big, decorated houses with fenced and manicured lawns, where roses and other flowers reach to the high heavens and the latest models of cars are parked in the garages? What does such an affluent lifestyle know about the lives lived by the mother with three poor babies, the hungry nomad and the shoe-shine boy? Look at the difference between those that I passed by at the bar, where some were drinking lattes and others were sipping ice cold drinks, full of themselves, sitting on comfortable chairs, whereas just a few feet away the haggard souls covered in dirt and dust were nibbling dry mandazi in competition with the flies, he reflected.

As though trying to rid himself of the discomfort aroused by the glaring dichotomy of that young mother desperately trying to save her children and his easy, comfortable, carefree lifestyle, he shook his head and kept walking. Passing landmarks that he knew along the way, he grew increasingly disturbed by such a disparity of lifestyle. To his right, he walked by the old machine repair garage where both the door and the wires that had held it in place had been pulled off. He realized that he had arrived at his destination. He looked up and saw the tall corner of the Meteorology Project building. In minutes, he was climbing the stairs to the fourth floor where his father's office was located. There in the stairway he met Ciise, rushing down the stairs, holding a file in his hand.

"Hey, Engineer Axmed, how are you? You're a long way out of your comfort zone. It has been a while." Ciise greeted him warmly.

"All is well, Ciise. How are you?"

"We are doing well here, too. How is the family?" asked Ciise.

"They are all well, thanks."

"Leyla sends her regards. She always says, 'Say hi to Axmed if you see him.'"

"Greetings received. She is fine, isn't she? And little Burhan as well?" asked Axmed.

"Yes. Our boy was sick a while back, but he's doing fine now. By the way, your father is here, if that's who you've come to see!"

"Sure. He is upstairs, right?"

"No, it's reorientation day today. He is the presenter," said Ciise.

"That's why I didn't see any employees. It's reorientation day," he repeated after Ciise.

"Yes, I was there with him, but was sent back to the office to get this file. I am a member of his labor committee. Why don't you come with me and listen while you're waiting? It won't be long," said Ciise.

"No, can you let me off? I'd rather wait here. Isn't it exclusive to your committee anyway?" asked Axmed.

"There is nothing exclusive about it. It's the usual re-education thing."

Conceding to Ciise's offer and arriving at the lecture hall, Axmed felt a little out of place, but was in no position to change his mind now. Entering the room, all one hundred-plus captive employees who had been listening to their executive director (his father) looked in his direction. Seated in the middle of a long table and resting his elbows on it, his father looked at him, then abruptly turned away and went on with his lecture without the slightest hint of acknowledgement.

Some of the other executives tried to beckon Axmed to join them up front at their table, which was facing the staff. Ciise too tried to push him forward, but Axmed declined. He went all the way back to the empty chairs. En route, the employees' eyes followed him to his seat. He chose to sit with the rank-and-file staff. Many knew that he was the son of their boss and that he was an engineer. Some nodded at him, some smiled, some greeted him, some gave him the evil eye, and some simply ignored him. To those in the last category, he was just his father's shadow. And those who were in disagreement with his father did not bother to hide their hostility toward the son.

Some of those who were smiling at him were loyal followers of his father who lauded and campaigned for him to keep his job. Others were obsequious just to keep their own jobs. But once he was out of earshot, they cooked him in the gossip oven and cut him into pieces. The ones giving the evil eye to the son hated the father and prayed for his transfer.

Various grievances brought about these animosities. Some employees disagreed with how raises, vocational opportunities, and promotions were allotted. Others accused his father of incompetence, which they thought paralyzed the current projects. Many argued and spread the word that he was using project funds for personal use and had allied himself with men of commercial means.

Ciise put the file on the table in front of the Executive Director and walked to the back of the room to sit with his guest Axmed. Once he took a seat, he was treated to the same evil eye stares that had been leveled at Axmed.

"Look at that hypocrite. He is cozying up to the son to get closer to his father," they whispered.

But their malignant interpretation of Ciise's intentions was utterly wrong. In fact, Ciise was simply trying to be a good host to his guest, a man for whom he had genuine respect based on two reasons. One, he admired Axmed's character and principles and thought they were similar to his. Two, when Ciise learned that Axmed was in love with Maana, he liked him more, thinking that it was a testament to Axmed's taste in women.

To be frank, Ciise did not like his boss, Axmed's father. He suspected him of misappropriating public funds but had been avoiding confrontation and did not want his friend Axmed to know of his misgivings about his father. Because he had remained silent, he knew that others were now accusing him of being part of the problem, taunting him with You are a loyal soldier for Jaamac.

Those types of accusations from the employees within his department started when he had become a member of the labor committee and had intensified when Ciise was facing the daunting financial burden of his marriage to Maana's sister. Leyla's family had been against the marriage, and Jaamac, the Executive Director, had assisted him with a generous grant, a loan, and a job promotion. All were interpreted as a sign that he was Jaamac's pet.

He was aware that "Jaamac has been helping you, then," was their moaning mantra.

IV

Jaamac went on with his long-winded speech, raising his voice with emotional vigor. "Comrades, we will never allow things like lazy work habits, malingering, gossip-crafting, or rumor-mongering and muttering under your breath. These behaviors will not be tolerated. I know some of you are itching to see clan favoritism, lies, corruption, embezzlement, double-faced duplicity, and all the other rotten things that were going on before the revolution. I am aware of people who are ready to bring it back. There are some who are putting their own self-interest before the general well-being. We will use the full force of the law against them. The revolution will not allow that to surface again. Never!" he ranted.

Every now and then, a quick round of thunderous applause would interrupt his speech. Axmed felt embarrassed and cast his eyes downward. *Strange*, he thought, *is this my father speaking about revolution? Who is he, shouting about self-interest and kleptocracy? Has he become a new man overnight? Or has he always been this self-contradictory soul preaching revolution at work while seeming to be a part of the old guard at home?*

"We will take the appropriate action against any who loaf about at work. We have to maintain discipline here at all times," his father went on.

He meant what he said about dallying and all. He was a strict disciplinarian. And yes, he was competent, and a hard worker, who did not like wasting time. But as of late, his greed and self-interest had taken precedence over public service. He did his best to maintain the appearance of a man properly guarding his assigned duty.

He was trying his best to hide the misuse of the project funds. Deploying his charisma, he had been able to keep his position secure, distracting any attention of concerns away from the project.

V

Once the session was over, Jaamac headed straight to his office, while Axmed was held back by some employees who knew him. Shortly he too headed to his father's spacious and artfully furnished office. Raising his head from the pile of paperwork on his desk, he greeted his son,

"Hi, Axmed, how are you?"

"All is well, Dad," Axmed replied.

Jaamac loved his children, particularly Axmed, his firstborn son. He tried his best to prepare him for the future and would normally yield to his requests. He even let him rent his own place, though he did not like it when Axmed said he was moving out because he "did not want to live in a crowded house." Axmed had surprised him with this sudden visit today. He knew there must be some reason for the unexpected visit. So, he was a bit anxious and worried that his son might be bringing bad news.

"Are you in trouble, or is there something new?" his father asked.

"No, Dad, there is no trouble at all. I just need your assistance."

"Hah, take a seat. Have you made a man out of yourself and moved on to the issue that we talked about?" his father asked, attempting to preempt the coming question.

"Are you again asking when or whether I am going to get married?" asked Axmed.

"Ha-ha, or you are still 'exploring', as has been the word you use?" his father asked.

"Yes, Dad, I am still exploring but now I'm closer to taking action."

"Well, I have told you that if you don't introduce a likely candidate to me this month, I will take over the quest and find a good woman for you myself," the father threatened.

"Thanks, Dad, but I am not going to trouble you with that."

"How are you going to save me if you have not lived up to your responsibility? I want to see your children before I am aged, and death comes after me! Now, what do you mean by 'I'm closer to taking an action?'"

"Well, I met someone," Axmed responded.

"Wow!" followed his father.

"We have been together for a while," Axmed continued.

"Who is she? Do you know her family?"

Axmed knew exactly what his father was asking, although he had disguised the real question, he was asking what clan she belongs to. But he answered in a short, deliberate way, avoiding a straight answer,

"She is a high school student."

"Do you know her family?"

"No, Dad, I have not met her parents yet."

"Are you going to marry a woman without meeting her family beforehand?" asked Jaamac, in a louder voice with a tinge of irritation.

"No, Dad, I would not proceed in that manner. I would like to talk with you first. My marriage decision is in your hands. You are the sole authority. So, I have not yet talked to her about marriage."

"And if the two of you have not talked about matrimony, what have you been talking about? And how do you know whether she would consent to it?"

"I know she is in love with me."

Jaamac laughed loudly and chanted derisively, "'She is in love with me; she is in love with me.' Look what this grownup man is saying! You are deluded. You demonstrate to me that you can't handle your responsibility of finding the one! Of all the followers of Maxamed in Somalia, you do not know to whom this woman belongs–a woman from whom you have secured no commitment, yet you are telling me that she is yours. You came here today to tell me that?"

Axmed paused, while unpleasant thoughts ran through his mind. *My goodness! All this scolding is about the fact that I did not say what clan she belongs to! Why would I care? Am I going to marry her or her clan? She knows me well, and I know her well. She loves me, and I love her. What else do we need? I can't reveal these thoughts to my father because he would not understand. Who is going to interpret for my father?* he wondered, looking down at the floor. Then he raised his head, looked at the wall, and said,

"Dad, this wasn't why I came to see you. I will come to you with this matter when I am ready, but I just thought that I should let you know. I wouldn't have told you anything about her if I did not have that confidence in her. I am quite certain that you are going to share that with me once you meet her. She is a beautiful girl with strong personal values and excellent character."

Jaamac quieted and calmed down before responding with,

"Are her father and mother around?"

"Yes, they are."

"What does her father do?"

"He runs a small business."

"What is his name?"

"His name is Xaaji Muumin."

"What neighborhood do they live in?"

"Xamar-weyne."

"You don't go to their house, do you?"

"No. I've wanted to for quite a while, but I know that her family would not allow her to bring a man into the family home unless betrothed. She would be disgraced."

"They are right, because it's crass to do otherwise," his father agreed.

Axmed disagreed with his father but did not want to sound discourteous. So, he went on as though he did not hear the last part of what his father said.

"The only appropriate time to see the parents is when we are ready to ask for their daughter's hand in marriage. And whoever is going to talk to them should keep that in mind."

"So, what's your plan?" Jaamac asked. "Are you going to let us see her? Bring her home, and I will get involved. If she meets our requirements, we will go to her father." He paused, looked up at his son and asked,

"What was the other matter that you came here for?"

"Well, Dad, this isn't a major issue, but I have an appointment that will cost me, and I am rather broke."

"When are you going to get out of this business of being broke?" asked his father, getting his wallet out of his back pants pocket. He pulled out a bundle of notes and, without counting, handed them to Axmed.

Light-hearted now with the knowledge that he would be able to take his friends out, Axmed ran down the stairs. Realizing that he was sweating hard, he thought of the weight that remained on his mind but was happy that he had achieved his immediate goal.

CHAPTER SEVEN

I

Maana was lying on the bed that day, still wearing her school clothes as usual, her breasts were pressing against the tight, short-sleeved school shirt she was wearing. Tired of trying to get her daughter to eat lunch, her mother, Aay Caddeey, left her alone. So, her mother had proceeded to feed the rest of her children. In the past, she would not have let Maana off that easily. She would have tried both coaxing and scolding to get her to yield to her command. Now she just gave up. Aay Caddeey knew that this was a serious matter, but she did not know what was causing it or what to do about it. For sure, it was a puzzle she was unable to piece together.

Maana slept and woke up in the same confused state of mind as when she had lain down. It had been five months ago when Axmed and Maana had first met at Sahra Yuusuf's apartment. Following that first meeting, Maana had gone through a drastic change that shook her faith. People who had known her were baffled by the change and wondered what had gotten into her. They did not know that it was love. A love that she had been unable to fend off and which had crept into her heart slowly, little by little, spreading through her entire being.

Wherever she was and whatever time of day it was, images of Axmed occupied her mind. She remembered his look, she recalled his words and heard his voice, paying no attention to anything else around her. Physically present but absent in mind, she would wander off while others were talking to her. His image arrived at her plate when she tried to eat and was there when she laid herself down in bed.

When she did fall asleep, she would be abruptly awakened by a recurring nightmare, robbing her of any chance of lulling herself back to sleep. In the nightmare, she would come upon a group of classmates crowded around a car accident. As she ran towards the accident, the classmates rushed to her, wailing, "It's Engineer Axmed Jaamac!"

"What happened?" she would ask in a frantic voice.

"He was run over by a car," they would answer.

"Aaa!" In the dream, she would fall down horrified. At this point, she would be awakened screaming and then would spring out of bed, as though bitten by a serpent.

Other nightmares also kept attacking her. Poor Maana is deserted in a no man's land. It is neither a rural setting nor a city. It is frighteningly dark. The landscape is a cliff towering over the edge of the sea. There seems to be a cave and tunnels. The trees are covered with thorns. She is standing barefoot on a precipice. Frightening sounds come from all around. She wants to run but cannot. With each step she tries to take, she is either stopped by a large rock, or she seems to walk off the cliff as a snake slithers towards her.

In another dream Axmed and Maana are sitting together on his bed. They are content, relaxing in the shade of the tree of love and sharing ripened fruit, so soothing for the soul. Swimming in a pool of excitement, they hear approaching footsteps. Suddenly, someone, a man bursts in. Iikar Aw-Mukhtaar charges into the dream, grabs Maana's arm, throws her to the floor. He begins beating her with a stick that was not visible when he entered. "You are the number one slut, who gave you permission to be alone with a man?" he cries. "You leave me alone. Leave me alone! I don't want you. I don't want you," she shouts back. Axmed, who can no longer keep himself out of the struggle, jumps in with both fists flying. Iikar responds with equal force. Axmed then pulls out what appears to be a pen, which immediately turns into a pistol, and in a flash Iikar is shot five times!

"My God, he's dead! My God, he's dead!" Maana screams.

Suddenly, like a flood, crowds of people rush into the picture, out of the blue. Two policemen, each of them the size of an elephant, enter. Each one grabs an arm, and Axmed is dragged off.

"If you are taking him to jail, you'll have to take me with him," Maana protests, with high-pitched cries, dashing after them. The crowds are shouting at her scornfully.

"Come back, you firebrand. You could have stopped the confrontation. It's you who instigated this war between the two men!" She was still running when she jumped out of her bed.

Those nightmares refused to give her respite. She rarely slept. The war of worries weakened her spirit. Iikar's name and the planned wedding with him pained her like a festering wound. She hated hearing the word "wedding," because it reminded her of him. From the day when she was told that she was going to be "married off to Iikar," her family loyalties and her affection for kin had slowly died. An invisible wall had been built between them. The impending marriage and thoughts of Iikar were burdens that she was not able to bear. Once she had met Axmed and fallen in love, Iikar became the mountain between her and her ideal future.

"God, why did you create us both?" she would lament.

Iikar, though, was not troubled by the whole matter at first. The arranged marriage did not put much weight on him. As a young man enjoying a laissez-faire lifestyle, he was neither worried nor had remorse. He was not the kind of person to bother himself with responsibility. He liked to follow the latest trends of his peers and wanted to emulate the way they walked, talked, entertained, and socialized. It was because of this that when he graduated from high school two years ago, his father put him to work as a tailor in the family shop, just to keep an eye on him. Iikar had agreed. He had agreed so that he could continue to party all night in music houses or, if his female partner objected to night clubs, he would take them to Indian movie theaters.

Iikar was a compulsive womanizer. Working in a shop selling clothes as a tailor gave him easy access to women. Time and time again, his father, Aw-Mukhtaar, had tried to wean him off such a carefree, irresponsible lifestyle. It worried the old man that his son was wasting his time. He also feared that his way of life was a threat to the family's financial well-being, a worry that Iikar did not share.

When his father told Iikar that he was going to be married off to his cousin Maana-faay, he did not show that he cared one way or the other. It did not matter much to him. He understood it as just a patriarchal order issued out of his father's sense of familial duty. He did not think that the marriage would actually happen. As time went on, however, it became clear to him that this was not just a vague threat, and he felt its irritating weight. Slowly, he realized that he was going to have to lose his carefree lifestyle. He had to accept the fact that his womanizing behavior would have to end or change.

Once the arranged marriage was official, Iikar's usual interactions with Maana had ceased. She was no longer his young cousin to tease as he would with his sister Jiija. If they ran into each other, they would exchange limited hellos but no more.

II

Normally, it was right after the afternoon siesta when Xaaji Muumin and his wife Aay Caddeey would talk about the most pressing family concerns. On this day, after his prayers, Xaaji Muumin relaxed on the rug, grabbed a nearby pillow, put his elbow on it, and began supplicating with his prayer beads. He waited for his wife to bring him his afternoon tea. The prayer rug rested on a mat atop a specially built pedestal that rose twenty inches from the ground and was secured to the wall. No one was allowed to sit there but Xaaji Muumin in his capacity as the leader of the family.

Xaaji Muumin and his family lived in a typical Mogadishu house. The interior walls of a large open space were aged, and the furnishings were representations of a past that had not changed. Two chairs with woven rope seats stood in a corner. A baby's shirt and an old shawl had been carelessly tossed on one chair, and a small towel lay across the other. To the left hung a small red cabinet. The cabinet contained a few drinking glasses and several plates. Beneath the cabinet was the dining table and two decrepit chairs—one stood precariously balanced on three legs, while the other was relatively safe from human abuse. Hanging from another wall and spread far apart from each other were family pictures: Xaaji Muumin wearing a Barawani hat, a young Aay Caddeey, Maana holding her younger brother Cumareey by the hand, one with the whole family, Aweys wearing eyeglasses, again Aweys but as a young boy playing football, Leyla and Iisha side by side, Maana in a green dress with another girl, and friends from the past, and some relatives.

The veranda was the heart of this house. It was here that young and old, relatives and friends gathered. The master bedroom was attached to the veranda, and two bedrooms for the older children were adjacent to it. Off the veranda was also a large kitchen furnished with mats and *Gambaro* (low stools.)

III

Dust all over him, his shorts and t-shirt covered in dirt, Cumareey ran into the house. Full of confidence, he jumped onto the mat with his father and snuggled in.

His father stopped thumb-rolling his prayer beads, patted Cumareey on the head, and said, "Hey, son, where have you been?"

"Outside, Dad."

"Doing what?"

"I was playing, Dad, what else? Dad, can I have an ice cream?"

"Well, is your mother here?" the father asked.

"Yes, she is."

"Go and ask her!"

As Cumareey jumped down, his mother appeared carrying a specially-made cup of afternoon tea in her right hand for her husband. In her left hand, she carried a *gambar* for herself. She handed the tea to her husband and put the *gambar* on the ground next to him. She sat down. Several issues were on her mind this afternoon. Some were just a minutia of family matters and a to-do-list, but there was one urgent issue on her mind that needed immediate attention. She did not know that her husband too had his own urgent case to address. He wanted to talk to his wife quickly and be done with it. He was going to inform her that a decision had been made without her input, although she was to be the one to execute it. As his wife sat down, he pulled half a Somali shilling out from under the pillow, put it into Cumareey's hand, and asked,

"Hey, Cumareey, didn't you say you wanted an ice cream?"

"Yeeeh, Dad!" screamed Cumareey, excited.

"Take this half a shilling and go get it!"

As Cumareey ran off, his mother yelled behind him,

"Cumareey, when you get back, son, tell your sister to help you with a shower!"

As soon as Cumareey was out of sight, his mother shut the door to the veranda so that the children would not hear them talking. Xaaji Muumin, now sitting upright, had the first word.

"Aay Caddeey, what's the news? And what took you so long? Were you away?" he asked.

"I was out getting feed for the cows. It made me so tired, and my feet are now bothering me."

"So, now let us talk; what is on your mind?" he asked.

"Well, I want to have a talk with you, and I guess that you wanted to talk to me too. These days you seem to be busying yourself with other matters and not much involved in family affairs. You haven't been concerned about us. Do you know that? Not only that, but I must tell you I am so worried about our daughter Maana-faay. She has been coming home late; she has not been sleeping well; she hasn't been eating; she has been in distress and depressed. She isn't telling me anything, and if I ask her, she doesn't want me to trouble her! It is all very worrying. If you take a look at her, you can see how much she has changed. I am quite concerned about her mysterious illness. Would you mind taking her to a Sheikh or bringing him here or taking her to a physician?" she asked anxiously.

And though Xaaji Muumin looked ill-informed, and his wife thought that she had kept the secret of their daughter from him, he knew enough to gauge the change in Maana. He was worried too. Thus, in consultation with his brother, Aw-Mukhtaar, he had come to a decision that had preceded this afternoon's meeting. Finishing his tea, he put the empty cup down and said,

"Caddeey, it's true. Our girl's behavior is troubling, so it is up to us, her parents, to do something about it. Aw-Mukhtaar has proposed a marriage union between his son and our daughter. He said to me, 'Brother, listen to me! My son, Iikar, has been causing me worry. He comes home around 3:00 or 4:00 a.m. when I am going to my morning prayer. A man who comes home at 3:00 a.m. is up to no good. Maana also has grown up. I suggest that the two should wed, and that we should not wait for the summer vacation. The wedding should take place this Friday, the fourteenth, which is a blessed day because it's the prophet Maxamed's, peace be upon him, birthday.'"

"I said it's a good idea and good news. It's even better news for both of them. And why do we have to do this, Caddeey? Because this girl has grown up. She is a young lady. We have no choice but to marry her off soon. No Sheikh will be able to cool her off, and no physician will be able to suppress her raging hormones, but marriage will. Isn't this a well-thought-out decision?" he asked his wife.

Aay Caddeey heaved herself up, leaned toward her husband, put a bit of force into her usually quiet voice, and asked, "You have already decided, haven't you?"

"Yes, we have. What is the matter?" He cut to the chase but looked hesitant and startled. If he had known that she was going to question him, he would have been better prepared.

This was the first time that Xaaji Muumin had told his wife about the decision he and his brother had made to speed up the date of the weddings and that they had reached their decision without her input and without their daughter's knowledge.

"There is nothing that has been decided," Aay Caddeey let out with an angry tone. "You are coming to me to tell me that you already made a decision about my child without consulting me? You did not ask me my opinion, and now you are presenting me with your decision? I will never accept that!" she fumed.

Keeping his composure so as not to sabotage his plan, Xaaji Muumin said,

"This isn't a recent decision. Did I not tell you during Ramadan that we, my brother and I, would like to swap our four kids, two from each father, to cross-marry?"

"Even then you just said, 'we would like to,' but did you ask my opinion?" responded Aay Caddeey.

"This matter is now a done deal. I am a man of his word, and I can't take it back. So please don't conjure up a problem, Caddeey!"

"My daughter is not going to be married off to that man, and she isn't going to be taken to that house! I don't want my daughter to be worse off. And let me tell you; your brother is married to a terrible woman. I know Soonto. She has a big mouth. I don't want to be in a war all the time. I don't have the energy. Rather, Maana is going to be married off to her maternal uncle's son, my nephew. She will marry Jiilaani Xaaji Macow. No one else will ask me for her hand," she fumed.

Xaaji Muumin, now looking at her with intense anger, said,

"Hah, Caddeey, I thought you had no hidden agenda, but it now comes out that you have been plotting against me. While I have been in consultation, you have been scheming on your own. I just figured you out, Caddeey. Now I know, now I know."

"I don't care whether you know or when you came to know," Aay Caddeey followed with the same angry tone.

Xaaji Muumin stood up, took his prayer beads with him, and said,

"You listen, Caddeey. I am her father, and what I say is what you are going to do. Maana is going to marry Iikar Aw-Mukhtaar. That is the end of it. You don't talk back to me," he said, walking off hastily.

"I am going to talk back to you," Aay Caddeey yelled after him. "I swear, if you are giving me an ultimatum, I would rather have you divorce me. No man will wed Maana but Jiilaani Xaaji Macow."

She stood up and stormed out. She began throwing household items around, yelled at her children, and struck out at them. She broke the wall cabinet, tearing the door off its hinges, and grabbed her *shuka* garment, put it on, and walked out of the house, muttering to herself.

By nature, Aay Caddeey was not a rabble-rouser; thus, it was rare to see her clash with her husband. But Maana's arranged marriage without her consultation touched a raw nerve. It was a concern that had been festering in her. Anticipation had been building in her. Each, both mother and father, had a plan.

When Xaaji Muumin had first talked to his wife about his plan for Maana's arranged marriage, he had not made himself clear, and Aay Caddeey had initially not revealed her true feelings either. He had heard her taking a few verbal shots at Iikar and at his mother Soonto. Yet he still had not thought that Aay Caddeey would so fervently oppose him.

Actually, Aay Caddeey was not decisively against the plan herself. She liked half of what her husband had hinted at: that Maana's brother, her own son Aweys, would be given in marriage to Jiija. But she did not want Iikar for Maana. It was members from her family who had persuaded her to save Maana for her maternal side of the family. They told her, "That young woman (Maana) should not leave the family," implying that someone from Aay Caddeey's family side should marry her. Now if Maana was not going to marry Iikar, it meant that Aweys would not be marrying Jiija either. She would need to start looking for a new match for her son.

IV

Maana, who failed to fall asleep for the family's usual afternoon siesta, rose and left the bed. She walked over to a box on the veranda and retrieved a bar of soap to wash her body. As she approached the door, she overheard an argument brewing between her father and mother. At first, they were speaking in hushed tones, trying not to draw the attention of their children. But it did not take long for their angry voices to rise. The secret was out. Maana stopped and heard it all.

'My daughter is not going to be married off to that man, and she isn't going to be taken to that house! My daughter isn't going to be made worse off. And let me tell you; your brother is married to a terrible woman. I know Soonto. She has a big mouth. I am not ready to be at war all the time. I don't have the energy. Maana is going to be married off to her maternal uncle's son, my nephew. She will marry Jiilaani Xaaji Macow. No one else will ask me for her hand!' she recalled.

Hearing the acrimonious brawl between her parents, Maana was alarmed. She put her hand on her chest as though she were holding her heart in place. It was beating so fast and pushing so hard against her ribs that she thought it would explode. She went back to the kitchen and stood in the middle of the room. She did not want anybody to know that she had heard them. There was a part of her that did not want to know that the sons of both of her uncles were in the middle of her parents' fight.

Why aren't they asking me who my choice is? Look at these people! They are arguing about which one of them gets to pick whom I will marry. I am here, and they are arguing about 'She isn't going to be married off and she is going to be married off,' but no one is asking me who I would like to marry. Is this fair? I don't care what they say; I am going to tell them who I love! I am going to tell them that the man I want is named Axmed. He is the man I love, and I am not going to marry anyone else. So, please don't exhaust yourselves!

No, you can't say that to them! An inner voice warned her.

When she realized what she had said to herself, she panicked, fearing that her parents had heard her saying it. Where would she find the courage to confront her father? she wondered. All the trouble she was in: the insomnia, loss of appetite, distress, fear, and the worst of it all was the war of words raging at home, threatening the family unity. The brewing conflict burned inside her.

Both her mother and father would in an instant bring back their daughter's cheerful nature, but they had no clue where to find the prescription. And if she told them what her "illness" was, it would have astounded them. Neither her father, Xaaji Muumin, nor her mother, Aay Caddeey, would believe that their daughter did not want either man that they had proposed for her. They would not understand that she was in love with a man, unknown to the family, who was in love with her.

To them, Maana was a good girl who guarded her womanhood and in so doing preserved the family's honor. In their world, she deserved an arranged marriage. Who could help Maana shoulder the weight of this burden and help her resolve this dilemma? On one side, the flames of love were licking at her; on the other, the conflict between her parents tortured her. Maana had no time to waste. The designated marriage date was closing in, though her mother was on a plan to stall the proceedings.

Maana knew she had to think of a way to rescue herself but felt hopelessly inadequate and lonely.

What should I do? she asked herself. *I need to find someone who can help me, she thought. But who? To whom may I be able to plead? Well, maybe I should put my hope and trust in my mother. Let all the story loose on her. She is more understandable and caring. She must be of help. No, no, she has her own agenda. She is going to tell me to marry Jiilaani Xaaji Macow. Well, yes! Tell Axmed everything and shift the burden on to him! I am done with keeping it a secret. No, no, it will get worse for me! Rather, I should comply with the wishes of my parents.*

As soon as the last option occurred in her mind, she felt terribly shocked. Finally, she felt relieved with an idea that sprang in her mind: *Wait! I know who can help me. Leyla! Yes, Leyla it will be. I am going to ask my sister, Leyla, to help me. I will plead with her.*

Leyla was the only person she could share her secret with. They were close in age and shared some of the same ideas, and though there had been a bit of sibling rivalry between them when they were young, their relationship had improved. When they were young, they would hurl insults at each other. They fought a lot, and many times their mother would be forced to separate them. However, once Leyla married and left the house, they became close. When Leyla became a nurse and started working, they grew even tighter. Leyla made sure that she cared for her younger sister.

Leyla's husband, Ciise-dheere, was attentive to Maana, and this too helped to strengthen their bond. The young, progressive man loved his wife and valued his sister-in-law. Whenever Maana paid a visit to them, they would end up chatting, teasing each other, and she would come back home cheerfully. When their son was born, Maana named him Burhan, and since then when she entered their home she greeted him first, tossing him up into the air, grabbing him tightly, and kissing him on the cheeks.

When her stress began to show, Maana's visits to her sister became more frequent. She was running away from her family's home and to her sister's home for comfort. Every time she felt pressured, she ran to Leyla's. On those nights when she was to meet with Axmed, she used her sister's house for a decoy. She would tell her family that she was going to Leyla's. If she were late, she also would stop by Leyla's. Leyla would then accompany her back home to tell their parents that she had been with her.

It was Axmed himself who had initially gained the cooperation from his friend Ciise-dheere. He entrusted him with the acknowledgement of his love for Maana and encouraged him to share the information with his wife. He was well aware that Maana needed an ally within her family.

At first, Leyla berated Maana for going out with Axmed while she was betrothed to a cousin. She frequently reminded her of the impending wedding. But as Maana kept crying with the emotional weight and afflicted pain, Leyla relented. She had really known that Maana was in love, even before Maana had uttered a word about it to her. And Maana made sure that she let her sister know that she had not sought out a relationship with Axmed. She told her that she was a victim of a magnet that kept pulling her to him. She informed Leyla that she was not able to dispossess herself of this magical feeling.

Leyla was so different from her parents. She paid much due deference to her sister's feelings, for she fully understood the nature of love. She knew that blaming the afflicted was not helpful. Leyla had herself walked in the same shoes of being in love and knew all about the pain. But what was not fresh in her memory was the struggle she had endured before she convinced the family to allow her to marry the man she loved, Ciise-dheere.

The morning after the acrimonious brawl between her parents, Maana rushed off to meet with her sister. She told her about what she had heard. Crying, she pleaded with Leyla to help rescue her. She asked her to tell their parents the truth about her love for Axmed, to argue on her behalf to break the arranged engagement and allow her to marry the man of her choice. Leyla felt sorry for her younger sister and promised that she would fight for her to the best of her ability.

V

Leaving the house, Aay Caddeey walked out and onto the road. She looked neither left nor right but fixed her gaze straight ahead. When neighbors greeted her in passing, she did not bother to raise a hand to say hello back. Whereas she used to saunter through the streets, now she sped through the alleys of Xamar-weyne, wondering when, if ever, she had felt this type of driving wind against her back!

Keeping up her brisk pace, she reached her brother Xaaji Macow's home. Her sister-in-law Aay-Batuulo and her sister Aay-Khayrto, who had come by for a visit, were the first to greet her. After she took a seat, she shared the story with them and told them about what she planned to do. She said she had fought with her husband over Maana's arranged marriage without her consent and that she was not agreeing to it. She told them how she wanted her daughter for her own nephew and how her husband wanted her for his nephew. She went on to say that she was going to figure out a way to see her plan succeed, not her husband's.

They welcomed her audacious act and congratulated her for her bravery in facing and opposing her husband and his family. But they were the ones who had lit the fire under her feet to begin with, berating her in the past for not standing up to her husband.

"You are just like a hung portrait. You are simply sitting silently while others make decisions for your daughter without your input. This is the baby you carried in your womb for nine months while suffering morning sickness and the pain of childbirth, the girl whom you raised to become a young woman. Don't you know that your brother has a son, too? A son who can marry Maana! Do you have no feelings for your own nephew?" they had scolded her.

In this way they had more than encouraged her to reject the plan that her husband and his brother had concocted without her consultation. They pushed her hard to reject Maana's arranged marriage to her paternal cousin and tried their best to save her for her maternal cousin Jiilaani. Jiilaani was two years younger than Maana, and although this proposed marital arrangement with him was not exactly in line with the cultural mores of the time, he was the only son of the maternal uncle. And these women were now hell-bent on wrestling Maana away from the paternal side of the family. To affirm her objection to her husband's announcement, Aay Caddeey decided that she would not return home but stay with her relatives.

When Xaaji Macow came to know that his sister was in his house and planned to stay, it did not please him a bit. Earlier in the day, her son Aweys had reported to him that his mother had stormed out of the home and was on her way to meet with her sister-in-law. He did not like the idea of a woman of his sister's age abandoning her family responsibilities simply because she was angry. Aweys was disappointed that his mother had left her house. He pleaded with his uncle to infuse some sense into her and bring her home, because he too had an agenda about this marriage-proposal fiasco. He had been promised Jiija in the deal in which Maana was promised to Iikar.

Aweys, however, was very different from his cousin Iikar. He was reasonable, frugal, and a bit more forward minded. When he heard that he was going to be married off to his cousin Jiija, he, unlike his sister Maana, was ecstatic about the prospect of the arranged marriage. He opened his heart to Jiija and committed himself. His feelings moved from loving his cousin to being in love with her as a fiancée.

Jiija was also receptive to the marriage proposal. She liked her cousin a lot but was too shy to show it.

These two were excited; the breeze of passion bathed them, and the good omen of love was goading them. They could not wait to make a home in the house that had been readied for them. Now with the battle between his parents stalling Maana and Iikar's marriage, Jiija and Aweys's was also in jeopardy. The cultural tradition that blessed them with opportunity was the same cultural tradition now holding them hostage. The fate of the two in love was inextricably tied to the fate of the two who were not. If Maana and Iikar's arranged marriage would not go ahead as planned, Jiija and Aweys's marriage was not going ahead either. There was another possible obstacle to their happiness. If Maana and Iikar should wed, but later break up, Jiija and Aweys would also have to divorce.

Xaaji Macaw was a decent man who would not meddle in other people's affairs. He had not paid much attention when he heard the rumor that a marriage proposal between Maana-faay and Jiilaani had been made. He suspected that his sister and his wife had colluded in the arrangement. Now he understood what had made his sister so angry. Although he would have Maana as his son's wife, he certainly did not want a conflict between him and his brother-in-law Xaaji Muumin. They had always had a close relationship. He could not let the wound of this conflict fester. It could bring about a lasting disharmony between all concerned, and so he decided to confront the problem head-on.

Coming home to face a posse of his female relatives, he immediately began to lecture them. For their part, the women tried to put up a fight. They argued against Maana and Iikar's union. Xaaji Macow refused to hear it. His command was that they should leave the whole matter alone. Reserving his harshest words for his sister, he scolded Aay Caddeey for leaving her house, a home in which she had invested thirty years of her life. He wanted her to understand how her plan would contaminate the family affinity, unity, and cohesion. Later that night, he consoled her and allowed her to stay. But the next morning, he took her back to her house, smoothed matters over, and cleared the air by talking to his brother-in-law.

VI

It was usually quiet in the Xaaji Muumin house in the early evenings. This evening, Aay-Caddeey and her daughter Leyla, who had come to visit them, were sitting on their *gambars* on the veranda. Maana was absent tonight, reporting that she was not feeling well. Cumareey and his friend Cali were playing with toy cars on the cement floor, and whenever they came close to the grown-ups, they were scolded and chased off. Leyla's visit to her family was normally seen as routine. But this evening, there was nothing routine about it. Her mother, though, could not tell the difference. Leyla was on a mission. She was either going to leave with the sweet taste of victory or the agony of defeat. To ease her plan into the conversation, Leyla nonchalantly told her mother that Maana was going to stay with her for a few days. Her mother fudged a bit but then said,

"I am glad she will. She should stay with you if she wants to live. Please get her to eat something. Her behavior of late has puzzled me. Not only has she not been eating, but she has not been sleeping, and she has seemed so preoccupied. She used to help me in the kitchen. No more of that. You have seen how she is. She looks like she has just come out of a hospital."

Taking advantage of that opening Leyla said, "Mom, do you know why Maana is so sick?"

"My child, I can't tell you. I am truly puzzled by it all. I even brought in a Sheikh and a talisman was prescribed. She was taken to a physician. She has been consoled, yet she continues to get worse. She might have been bewitched!" the mother said.

"Mom, it has nothing to do with being bewitched. This girl is sick because she does not want to marry Iikar. If you continue to insist on your plan, you are going to make her lose her mind. I don't think this wedding will benefit anyone," Leyla attested.

As though she were poked by a sharp object, Aay Caddeey perked up, turned around, and said,

"I swear, I didn't want that young man for her either, but her father gave her away. And if I had been consulted, I would have proposed a marriage to her maternal cousin."

"Mom, she does not want him either!"

Aay Caddeey put her hands on her face and said, "What does she want then? Who is the shining star?"

"She is in love with another young man called Axmed, Mom," said Leyla, dropping the bombshell she had been carrying with her.

"Axmed, Axmed, who is he?" asked Aay Caddeey with her hands still on her cheeks, eyes wide open.

"He is an engineer."

"Where did the engineer come from, and who is his family? Do you know his mother? Do you know his father? The proverb says, 'Wed someone you know, and you will beget an offspring you know,'"she said, taking her hand off her cheek.

"No, Mom. I don't know his family. But he is a nice young man, not the contemptible kind. And she is dying for him."

"So, you have known about this so-called love match? Did Maana put you up to this today? Instead of shunning that type of behavior, you are aiding her? Who introduced this unknown young man to her in the first place?" asked her mother.

"Mom, I am just telling you this is a serious matter. Don't force my sister into a marriage she doesn't want! If you refuse her the man she wants and force her to marry another, she may die, and she may commit suicide! That is the truth, Mom," Leyla warned.

"Well, you are going to tell your father. I cannot speak out loud about this abomination. Your father and I just had a quarrel about whom she is to marry, and your uncle had to come here to mediate. I am staying out of this one."

Just then, Xaaji Muumin walked in from the mosque. He heard the last part of his wife's sentence. When Leyla looked up onto his face, her confidence drained from her. Her plan to convince both of her parents to support Maana's love match was shattered

"What are you two talking about?" Neither mother nor daughter responded. Which one of them was going to say a thing now? Finally, with eyes downcast, Aay Caddeey turned toward her daughter and said,

"You brought it up. You tell him."

"Baaba, it's nothing major. It's a minor matter!" Leyla started hesitantly.

Realizing that she was at a point of no return, Leyla tried to put on a brave face and sheepishly began to speak. She repeated the same thing that she had told her mother but left out the part about Maana being in love with another man. She did not dare to reveal the love side of the story to her father but tried her best to voice her objection to Maana's forced marriage to Iikar.

Xaaji Muumin, whose face was flushed with anger, remained silent for a while. And then he started to respond in a powerful voice, strongly articulating each word with the intent to make himself clear:

"Leyla, you listen to me. Those meetings that have been taking place at your house are offensively disloyal. Maana is my daughter, not yours.

She isn't going to tell me what to do, but I will tell her! You cannot stop her wedding; she cannot marry anyone but Iikar. Iikar is going to wed her. He is the one she is going to marry." Looking angrier and angrier, he stood up, wagged his forefinger in Leyla's face, and added, "You cannot bring another man into it, and neither can she! Go home; I don't want to see your face!"

Defeated and dejected, Leyla hung her head low, grabbed her purse, and walked out. Her father continued his rage as he entered his room muttering irately, "How impudent and boorish she is, saying that she does not want to marry Iikar."

VII

Maana was in her sister's house, despairing and depressed. A cup of tea she had prepared for herself earlier in the afternoon sat untouched in front of her. She had forgotten it was hers. She was anxiously awaiting Leyla's return, wishing that she would bring a small kernel of hope. It was Leyla's idea that Maana should stay behind and far away from the minefield that she had planned to detonate.

Maana wondered what was taking Leyla so long. Every time she heard footsteps, her heart raced faster with worries of what the news was going to be a blessing or a plain curse? She was waiting for a word that meant life to her!

She was in agony. This war of waiting was not new, though there was not as much at stake as in the past. In the previous months, whenever she had arranged a meeting with Axmed she wanted to fast-forward the time. She would look at her wristwatch over and over as though to help hurry it. She did not like talking to people, thinking they were going to distract her from his impending arrival. If she made an appointment with him three days ahead, she would count the remaining hours each day until they were reunited. *I wish I could jump over the last day,* she would say to herself.

Why is Leyla not here yet? What has happened to her? I think I hear footsteps. Her heart palpitated. *Someone is entering. Aw, I hope it is Leyla.*

"Sister, Leyla!!"

Overflowing with excitement, Maana jumped from her chair. Hope soon evaporated when Leyla gave her a gloomy, uncertain look. Dragging her feet in dejection, her sister came in and without a word threw her purse and shawl to the side. Signs of defeat were all over her.

Bracing for the worst, Maana brought herself to ask, "Sister, tell me; what happened?"

Enraged by the depth of the situation into which her sister had plunged her, Leyla walked past and hurled bitter words at her:

"My sister, if you have been awaiting news from me, get ready. Your wedding is to take place next Friday. Tomorrow is your official *nikaax* night (engagement night)."

Before Leyla had finished her sentence, Maana dropped to the floor. The emotions which had remained bottled up in her erupted, and she shrieked like a psychotic soul.

"That is it, that is it. That is it! Please don't tell me the rest, just keep silent!" Maana burst out crying hysterically. "My God! I am doomed! Where can I hide? Is there anything that can save me now? Is there anywhere under this sky where I can hide?" Maana continued to wail.

She moaned, wailed, and cried so loud that the people outside in the streets could hear her. A small group converged in front of the house, but Maana did not care. She was no longer shielding herself from shame and embarrassment. It seemed like she no longer had a desire to live. Judgment had been leveled upon her, and her life would end on Friday, the day she was to be married to her cousin.

The people from the neighborhood tried to help and console her, but she paid them no heed. Maana was so distraught and despondent that she felt like throwing off the *guntiino* she was wearing. She didn't care anymore. Life and honor were no longer worth anything to her. She wished she had not been born and hoped that the ground beneath her would give way.

The louder she wailed, the more neighbors came out, trying to calm her. Her brother-in-law Ciise-dheere arrived and seated himself next to her. He took her chin in his hands and then put his arms around her shoulders. He begged and pleaded with her to calm down. She twisted away from his hands, stood up, and hurried over to her sister, wrapping herself around her waist, accelerating her hysterical cries.

"My sister, Leyla, please save me; please hide me; please kill me; please bury me! My sister, where can I go? Why did God bring me into this world?"

Leyla was no longer able to tolerate her sister's pain. She began to cry and curse as well. She blamed her father and her uncle and then moved on to the ancient, cruel, cultural curse — the so-called "arranged marriage" — before shifting the blame to Axmed and his "aimless love."

She finally dumped the blame on Maana's vulnerability and her faint heart. The gathered neighbors were puzzled by what had caused this terrible affliction. Maana's behavior was quite disturbing, and now Leyla was not in much better shape. Which of the two should be consoled? The younger one that started it all or the older one that followed suit?

As the crowd around them surged, Ciise-dheere's attempt to soothe Maana and control the scene failed. Dejected, he thought it better to leave her alone. Reluctantly, he walked back to where he had come from, to the bottom of the adobe and plywood building that his family shared with several others, including a taxi driver and his nephew.

With none of the gawking neighbors seemingly willing or able to take a step to quiet down the sisters, an elderly woman of about sixty moved forward and attached herself to Maana and Leyla. She ordered the crowd, the laughing children and the gossiping women, to disperse. She told them to take their noise with them.

This take-charge woman was Beyydan Shabeel. Although she arrived late at the scene, she worked quickly to help shoo the neighbors back to their homes and clear the area.

Beyydan Shabeel was a short, full-figured woman who appeared much younger than her age. She was a resident of Boondheere, and she was well acquainted with the neighborhood. She peddled women's clothes on the neighborhood streets, pretending to be a saleswoman of a legitimate business. Beyydan Shabeel traveled frequently to Saudi Arabia, where she purchased clothing to sell to the young women of the neighborhood. But the neighbors all knew that her peddling served as a decoy to cover up her main occupation. Like a shark swimming among a school of fish, she hunted beautiful young women. Getting into their homes to entice them with beautiful fabrics, she would evaluate each young woman. Later she would attempt to pair the young woman with a man willing to pay a good price for a beauty to have to his bounty.

This afternoon, Beyydan Shabeel was working across the street when she had been attracted by the commotion. She heard and saw the children and women gathered outside of Leyla's home and wanted to get a closer look.

As soon as she laid her eyes on the beautiful young Maana, she knew that this was a catch she wanted to snare. This was her profession. She recognized the opportunity and wanted to find out some sort of secret about this young lady. She approached another young neighbor, took hold of her hand, pulled her to a corner, and whispered to her:

"My daughter, what happened to the young lady?'

"Her father gave her away to a man she doesn't want," said the girl.

"Why is she crying like that? She must be in love with another!" asked the experienced Madam.

"Yes, she is."

"And what kind of man is he, sweetie? Is he a man of means, this man she is in love with?" Beyydan asked.

"He is an engineer," the young woman let her know.

"Is he from the Howlaha Guud (the infrastructure agency)?" she went on to ask, in an attempt to indirectly trace his whereabouts.

"No, he isn't."

"Aah…" ruminated Beyydan.

"He works at the Glass Factory," followed the young lady.

"Yes, I understand. He is a nice guy. Is his name Cabdi?" she asked, indirectly trying to get the right name out of the young lady.

"No, his name is Engineer Axmed Jaamac," she revealed innocently.

"Yes, yes, that's it. Axmed Jaamac. But my daughter, I have heard that he doesn't love her back."

"It has been said that he loves her as much. But she must be out of her mind to become so distraught over a man!"

"You are right as well as smart. One should not allow herself to be taken over by a man."

Suddenly, the girl's mother came on the scene. The mother, knowing Beyydan Shabeel and her tricks to trap young ladies, interrupted them. Cognizant of how close her daughter was to danger, she pulled her away.

Beyydan Shabeel politely greeted the mother and then walked over to Maana and Leyla. She began pouring out sweet words of advice onto them, pretending to be a goodwill messenger, all the while laying her trap. She found Leyla in a state of frustration, with the neighbors again beginning to crowd around them. Stepping close to Leyla, she asked a question that resonated with her,

"Why are these children and women interfering in your business?" She turned to whatever was left of the crowd and ordered them to leave. When the last one had turned to return to their home, she locked the door and directed her attention to the sisters. She succeeded in consoling them and got them to quiet down.

Leyla, whose lessening anger gave her an opportunity to collect herself, began to mentally examine what had just occurred. She searched her mind for the next best step to take to guide her sister out of this troubling maze. Though it was hard to see through the fog, she refused to despair. Just then she found a light of hope, an idea to share with her sister, and interrupting Beyydan Shabel's fermenting scheme, she took Maana aside.

Leyla advised Maana to go to Axmed and tell him the whole story. She told her that he should wrestle with the facts as a test of his will and commitment to her. He would come through for her because failure was not an option. If he sincerely wanted her, he would come up with a solution to release Maana from the unbearable burden. She should ask him to officially propose to her tomorrow night, right before the arranged marriage was to take place!

"Or else he isn't sincere about the whole thing. He is just playing a game with you," Leyla asserted. "And if that is the case, then you have to move on and accept the blessing of our parents' choice," she counseled her.

Maana took that advice to heart. She needed that validation, for she had thought about it too and had arrived at the same conclusion. Now hope had returned and awakened a spirit in her, urging her to act on her sister's advice. At dawn she would go to see Axmed, she decided. They would elope and let fate wrestle with the rest. Of course, she was of the belief that Axmed was going to agree with her. With a sigh of relief, she waited for day to break.

CHAPTER EIGHT

I

A rooster crowed. Dawn had arrived with one note. Another rooster responded in kind and the Sheikh acknowledged that daybreak was near as the muezzin made the call for Morning Prayer. A cacophony of other roosters, muezzins, neighing donkeys, and crying babies joined in. The city had awakened and now was silent no more. Inside their houses, mothers tried their best to lull their babies back to sleep. Guilty was the rooster that had started it all. The rest should not be blamed, for they could not help but respond in choral conformity. It was the day that two diverging roads were going to dare Maana-faay to choose one: a damning defeat or a dazzling victory. There was no third option!

As a Somali proverb states, "Two people who slept apart at night could not be privy to the other's decision."

It was the thirteenth of the month of *Mawlid* as daybreak saluted the souls in Mogadishu. In Boondheere, inside Ciise and Leyla's house, where Maana had sought refuge, the residents were melancholy and worried. The night had come and gone without much sleep under the weight of a windfall of anxiety. In the houses of Xamar-weyne, however, Xaaji Muumin's and Aw-Mukhtaar's families were ready. Not only ready but excited. Excited about the double *nikaax* (engagement) and the weddings planned for that very night.

Aweys was the happiest of all that morning. He was hoping that he would return home tonight with his bride, cousin Jiija, close the door, and finally be alone with her. No one was going to fault him for that, in particular those in his community who had accepted and encouraged this wedding ritual, although some still frowned upon it. He was thinking ahead about what he was going to do! Every image that came to mind heightened his anticipation. Forgetting that he was alone, he laughed aloud! When he realized he was by himself, he looked around to see whether anybody had heard him. He was apprehensive about the tests awaiting him and wondered whether he was going to pass them. He, like his melancholy sister Maana-faay, did not sleep much that night. Unlike his sister, though, his lack of sleep was due to a different reason. He was too excited.

Jiija was going through emotional tidal waves brought on by unknown qualms. She had grown up *mukhabiyad* (housebound) but now was being told that she would be in front of hundreds of people watching her every move. And then she would soon be left alone behind a closed door with her new husband. She could hear the voices, *"You two, take care!"* and her mind responded, *aha, this is exciting and scary at the same time! This is good. No, I am in trouble!*

Iikar Aw-Mukhtaar was not that much into the wedding. In fact, he was ambivalent about the whole marriage matter. On the one hand, he would not mind managing his own family and having a woman exclusively to himself. That thought appealed to him. On the other hand, however, the possibility of losing his freedom to party at will worried him! *Why don't they leave me out of this wedding thing?* he whispered to himself. He thought about the groom's etiquette that he would have to adhere to during the wedding. He was not sure what he was going to say, how he was going to say it, when he was going to say it, and how he was going to look after those long hours in a suit, standing between two bridesmaids and a bride, shaking hands with people pretending to congratulate him but who were there to scrutinize and inspect every inch of him. He thought about the time involved and likened it to an imprisonment ordered by the highest court!

If he had a choice, he would have preferred to skip the wedding altogether and just take the bride home. Why go through all this trouble? He began to worry about the woman who had been pushed on him. If and when they were left alone, what was expected of him? Was he going to talk, or was he going to be all action? Action, what was that action going to be like? Iikar was bothered by these thoughts. What happened to his expertise of managing multiple women at one time? Where was all the *bravado* he used to throw around on women he did not know? Where was the alleged eloquence that could win over the ladies? Was it all imagined? Why was he so concerned about what words to use to open the door of love for his wife to be, his own cousin, Maana-faay? She was his own uncle's daughter whom he had known since childhood, the same Maana he had seen laugh and cry, the same one he had played with, had watched sleep, had walked with, and even had seen naked!

But it should be noted that since Maana had been betrothed to him, a great deal had changed between them. Now, whenever he ran into her, she looked like a stranger, not the Maana he knew. Iikar was baffled by the whole affair, but his family was brimming with excitement.

Aay-Soonto was happy, too. And why would she not be? Her first-born son Iikar was going to be married to a young lady tonight, and tomorrow he was going to have his own family and his own house. She was also elated that her daughter Jiija was going to be a wife. *I am not worried about Jiija anymore. She is getting married and will be safe with her virginity. I don't have to supervise her or watch over her anymore. All I have to do is to wait and see her with her own children,* she told herself.

Aw-Mukhtaar, her husband, was as happy as his wife but with a lot more responsibility. So, he was a bit more restrained.

Aay Caddeey, though, was less enthusiastic than Aay-Soonto but feeling a bit better than in the past days. She was upbeat about her son's impending marriage but less confident about her daughter's plans. She was very much worried about Maana. The fact that her daughter was in distress pained her. And the fact that she herself did not like Iikar Aw-Mukhtaar and would have preferred her nephew weighed heavily on her mind. She knew that Maana was not going to be able to withstand the pressure put on her by her father. The only thing she could do was yield to his decision. She was trying to let the excitement of her son's wedding substitute for her worries about her daughter Maana.

II

Here was Aay Caddeey actively preparing for the day's weddings. From early morning on, she had been engaged and was not able to avail herself of even the slightest window of time to have her breakfast. Tired, she took a seat to rest on a mat on the floor. But rest was not to be had, as the guests had begun to arrive.

A delegation of maternal and paternal aunts arrived carrying wedding gifts. Highly dignified, the army of aunts sat down on a mat and placed a large basket full of gifts between them. They picked out one item at a time and handed it over to Aay Caddeey, waiting for her approval. First was a bundle of seven *guntiinos*, and then a variety of *diricyo* followed, seven as well. All were put on the mat for a display; then the basket with some remaining gifts was given to Aay Caddeey. There was another bundle of long skirts. The items on top were examined. She let it be known that she liked their choices but more so the quality of the chosen gifts. And there was more: one, two . . . seven shawls or so (she could not count), bundles of *masaro* (scarves) too. There was still more in the basket: two kinds of shoes, *sookals* and *jabbaatiyo*.

"Where are the flip-flops?" someone asked. They were in there. Aay Caddeey picked a *sookal*, admired it, then said, "This one is too long." It looked as though she were not as excited about this item as she was about the others.

Even more gifts remained in the basket. She turned it on its side to reach the bottom. Nicely packaged bottles of perfumes and packages of soap fell out. One by one the aunts picked them up, massaged each with their palms, and handed them over to Aay Caddeey. Lastly, the most valuable gift revealed itself: a gold necklace with matching earrings, bracelets, and a ring.

Aay Caddeey lovingly accepted the wedding gifts for her daughter. She wanted to show off her daughter's prized gifts. She remembered the glamour of past weddings in the neighborhood and how she had wished to top them all one day. Aay Caddeey took this opportunity to remind the distinguished guests that they had an open invitation to *Sandalshiid* and to the bringing out celebration of *Kaay*. She was keen to offer the *Kaay* ceremony to as many people as possible, for she had been preparing gifts to pass on to her daughter on her wedding night since the day she was born. Despite her earlier disapproval, Aay Caddeey accepted the fact that the night she had been waiting for the past nineteen years had arrived.

III

Everything was in place for the double weddings to take their course. The families of the newlyweds opened the best parts of their houses to the public and adorned them with the latest, most expensive furnishings. As planned, Iikar and Maana were going to move into the third floor of Aw-Mukhtaar's house where even doors had been repurposed. The best weddings in neighborhood history were underway. All the neighbors and adjacent others were invited.

Two separate houses, where the brides were to be kept for their grooming, were made ready first. Jiija was going to be at her maternal aunt's house, where the young ladies assigned to serve her were stationed.

Maana was to be in her paternal aunt Ay Khayrto's house that morning where ten young ladies were ready for her for *Fadhiisin* (prettifying the bride). The selected young ladies knew the job well. They were ready to beautifully prepare and adorn the bride. They were going to prop her up with necessary tips on how to please a husband. But first they had to find her.

Four of these young ladies were Maana's relatives. Preparing to adorn and dress Maana, their celebratory mood was so loud they could be heard for miles, from Xamar-weyne to Boondheere. The preparation excitement started there. The four young ladies were given the assignment to fetch Maana and escort her to the *fadhiisin* house. Drunk from singing and drumbeating, the young ladies arrived at a house with an aged door with peeling paint. They knocked, ready to pick up Maana and go to work on her. A young girl wearing a *guntiino* but with no shoulder shawl opened the door. She let them in.

"Hello, Aamina, how are you? Are you at peace? Are you alright? Is Maana here?" they all asked at once.

"No, Maana isn't here," she responded.

"Where is she?" they asked loudly.

"I have no idea, maybe in school. I have not seen her since this morning," said the little girl.

Quieted down, worried, and losing the luster of their excitement, they looked at each other.

"Well, we have to wait for her, right?" one of them asked.

"Yes," another responded. Some of them made a noncommittal response by simply shrugging their shoulders; others just peered around Aamina trying to spot Maana in the house, and still, some of them just repeated yeses.

"Is Leyla at work?" one asked.

"Yes," said the little girl.

"When is she coming home?" another asked.

"Eight," said the little girl.

IV

Although Aamina had told the ladies that she thought Maana was at school, she knew that she was at Axmed Jaamac's. The night before, Leyla, knowing there was no time to waste, had told Maana to go to Axmed, knock on his door, and drop the whole problem in his lap. Leyla knew that the cousins would be coming for her in the morning for the *Fadhiisin* ceremony.

Maana had then called a taxi and deposited herself in front of Axmed's apartment. Feeling a chill, she walked to the door and knocked. An elderly neighbor woman saw her and asked, "My child, are you looking for Axmed?"

"Yes, Mother."

"He isn't there."

"Did he already leave for work?"

"He left yesterday. I am thinking that he is out of town."

"Are you sure? Where out of town?" asked Maana anxiously.

"My child, I am not sure where he went, but I overheard him say that he was given an assignment in another region. He said where he was going, but my memory is failing me. Was it Jammaame or Jarriban? I don't know! It was one of those places. Maybe …"

Maana was speechless. Her mouth was shut dry, and her tongue was suddenly heavy. She was on a roller coaster ride, feeling dizzy. Her heart was beating fast. She did not know where she was anymore. She turned and walked away while the elderly woman was still talking. She could not bear the news she had heard. She hated the elderly woman, blaming her for her alarming message. Tears welled up in her eyes. She began to cry but did not want the woman to see. She turned and walked off, destination unknown.

As she began to walk, her legs soon lost strength. She tried to stop herself from crying but could not. *Woe is me. This is a problem-ridden world,* she thought. *Why was I born? Poor me! Every door has been closed,* she lamented.

After crying both inwardly and outwardly for hours, she thought, *why don't I make sure that Axmed is away?* She headed to the Glass Factory where he worked. Wishing that she would find him there and that the neighbor woman was mistaken, she pleaded for mercy but to no one in particular. *Aw, bad news, please fade away and evaporate!* Arriving at her destination, the cruel fact met her head-on. The neighbor woman's news did not evaporate, and Maana's wishful thinking did not materialize. Engineer Axmed had left for an emergency trip to Jilib a day ago, she was informed. "He is going to be away for four to five days," someone said to her. *Who died, who is alive, and who cares when he is back? Forget about four or five days. I will not survive even a day without him!* she painfully thought, feeling lost!

There were no more doors to knock on. She had to return to Leyla's. As though she were pulling a sack of sand with her, dragging her whole self, she arrived back at the house an hour later. The torturous words of "Axmed isn't here. He left yesterday for another region on an emergency trip to Jilib" refused to allow her mind any respite. *Jilib should not exist! Why did they not send another engineer in place of my Axmed? What was the rush?* she thought.

V

As though afflicted with malaria, she was weak and could barely stand. Entering the veranda and confronted by the young ladies ready to groom her for the wedding, she hid her face in her shawl.

Unaware of Maana's mental state, the young ladies let out a thunderous ululation with a chorus of clapping. Urgent excitement began to stir. Trying to get her to join them in celebration they began singing, "Hey, you are the bride we have been waiting for." Her cousin Shariifo, who normally was not the talkative type, took the lead and said, "Where have you been, girl? You have exhausted us."

Maana just walked by her without a word. Their commotion added to her ache and pain. The wedding they were waiting for was making her ill. The stirred-up excitement was waging war in her. She was laboring under the weight of their witless cheer.

"Hey, why is her face so flat?" one snapped.

"She does not look happy," added another.

"Has anybody seen a bride with such a gloomy face on her wedding day?" another followed.

"Do you think she is serious?" asked a third.

"She must be happy inside," one answered. Putting her hand on another's shoulder, she went on to say to Maana, "Let's go, Maana; people have been waiting for you long enough."

Shariifo, who had become suspicious and serious, walked over to Maana and said, "Maana, what happened? Are you sick?"

"Yes, I am so sick. So please leave me alone!" were the first words they heard from her. She was not actually ill but psychologically defeated.

"Young lady, you are making us late. Let's go, I said," barked an airhead.

Shariifo did not appreciate the insolent attitude of some of her team. She concluded that the issue at hand was more perilous than all had imagined. She somehow understood that Maana's case needed a delicate hand if they were to succeed with their assignment.

Shariifo, trying to appeal to Maana, said in a low voice, "Maana, would you please; the wedding ceremony is upon us, everything is ready, and your seat at the ceremony has been set. So please, people are waiting for you. We have to take you there."

"My sister, I don't care one bit about that wedding," said Maana with stern enunciation.

At this announcement, the young ladies turned to each other in shock. Each one was trying to shut the others off when one walked over to Maana and asked, "What's going on?" And then continued with, "Iikar is a good guy, he is your cousin, he is handsome, and he isn't missing an eye or a limb. Nothing is wrong with him. Why are you saying no to him?"

"That is true. He is a great guy," another followed.

"He is good, and he may be great to you," Maana responded. "But I don't care. I am not going to marry him. He isn't going to come anywhere near me. If you want him, why don't you marry him yourself? If you believe in Islam, if you fast and pray for the fear of Allah, please don't ask me to marry this man. You have to leave me alone!"

Shocked, the young ladies looked at each other with disbelief.

"Let us leave her alone; there must be something that we don't know. God knows what is in her mind. We need to inform the people who sent us," said one of them. The rest agreed. In the same way that Maana had arrived, they left dragging their feet, dejected. The excitement that had brought them to Boondheere did not take them back. The celebratory cheers that had started in the morning were now substituted with disappointment and sadness. Arguing all along the way, they headed to Xaaji Muumin's house with their news.

As they turned the corner, Aweys, who had been waiting impatiently, came excitedly out to greet them.

"Hello, you took her there, right?" he asked.

Nothing but silence met him. Without a sound, the young ladies looked at each other, as though each one was waiting for the other to speak first. No one wanted to be the spoiler of Aweys's happiness.

"Why are you so quiet? Why are you not talking?" he asked.

They all looked at Shariifo. And then Shariifo began to speak, "Hey, friend, open your ears! We brought nobody home with us. Nobody is coming! The young lady refused to come with us. 'I am not going to marry anyone, particularly that man' she said to us."

"What? What are you talking about?" Aweys wailed, seemingly unaware of himself and his wounded pride. This negative news hit him hard and caught hold of his judgment. He was upset with the messengers. But upset or not, nothing was going to change the fact that Maana had refused to come. He started to repeat the same questions over and over. And the ladies repeated their story over and over. Word by word they rehashed the exchanges they had with Maana.

Suddenly, he ordered everyone to stay where they were and to keep their lips shut until he came back. He knew that if the news got out it would reach Aw-Mukhtaar's family, and the flames of anger would fuel the already burning fire. Dashed would be his dream to wed his beloved Jiija.

Aweys was shocked that Maana had refused to return with the young ladies for the *Fadhiisin*. He stumbled under the weight of what he had heard. He was no longer able to walk with his normal gait. A thousand ideas came to his mind. He would abandon one thought as soon as he conceived another. He would see something one way for a second, and then would change his mind the next. At times he was thinking of running to Maana to bring her in regardless, then he thought it was better to let his father handle it, then he thought to inform the rest of the family, then he thought he should take advantage of her being stationed at Leyla's house in hopes she would change her mind.

He picked up and then dropped one choice after the other. Finally, he grasped hold of one and ran with it. He got into a taxi and headed to Boondheere. Furious, he reached the house and stood over his sister, who was lying in the same bed in which the others had left her. In an angry voice he began: "You, Maana, what are you doing? Why the hell are you still here? Let's go, people have been waiting for you!"

Maana did not respond, nor did she move a finger. Recognizing that it was her brother talking to her, she became sicker. Blaming him for the trap in which she was caught, she thought of herself as the sacrificial lamb to be served during his marriage to Jiija. To her, Aweys and her cousin Iikar were both her kin. At this moment, though, Aweys was the one she could not stand looking at. Every word that passed from his lips licked her like flames of fire. He, on the other hand, expected her to bend to his will, in compliance with tradition. As far as he knew, his sister had loved and listened to him. He did not think Maana would send him away in defeat. But it was now clear that he had miscalculated the power of her determination.

He spoke to her in loud, low, harsh, and healing tones. He threatened her and then treated her like royalty by opening his heart wide. He reminded her of their past treasured sibling relationship. He told her that he was in love with Jiija. If she were to reject Iikar, Jiija's parents would deny his marriage to Jiija. He told her that she should not dishonor herself nor her family. He begged and pleaded with her, but to little avail. "You are only thinking about yourself," She confronted him. "You don't care about me. If you want that young lady, why don't you go for her? What do you want from me? If she rejects you because of me, she did not want you in the first place," she went on to say.

When he realized that he was not getting anywhere with her, he began to threaten her. He was going to make her marry the man who had been chosen for her. He thought of ways to force her into a taxi to take her with him. At that moment, however, his brother-in-law Ciise walked in, making him nervously hopeful. He was nervous because he realized that he was not going to be able to force Maana into the taxi in the presence of his brother-in-law, but was hopeful that Ciise might be able to persuade her to submit to his summons and to the arranged marriage. He thought she would be too modest to say no to her brother-in-law.

When Aweys told Ciise what had happened, Ciise too began to pressure her to obey her parents' wishes and urged her to go with her brother.

Like all the others, his plea fell on deaf ears. It did not sway Maana an inch. Aweys had to go back defeated. Dejected and hurt, he rushed to inform his father about the "calamity" that could descend if Maana's refusal were not reversed. Fuming with anger, his father jumped to his feet. He could not take it that his daughter was such an apostate. In a rage, he stormed over to Leyla's house.

Maana knew the next person to expect would be her father. The waiting frightened her, for she had no idea what he would do to her. *I have been able to get myself into trouble, but I am not able to escape it*, she thought. She regretted that she had refused to go with the young ladies that morning, and she regretted that she had refused to go with Aweys or Ciise. She simply had not been able to calculate the outcome of her actions. Her mind was frozen in a fog of confusion and fear. The last decision she acted on was to look for Axmed, to ask him to take responsibility for her. Since she failed with that, she had been unable to think straight.

Her situation was at a perilous stage. Her father was on the way, in a fury. *What should I do? Should I surrender? Should I hide myself? But where? Should I stick to my decision, so he has to physically remove me? Should I kill myself before his arrival, but how?* were thoughts which ran through her mind.

Sadness isn't going to save me. Use your mind. What should I do? she repeatedly asked herself. And since Leyla was not there to help her, she was completely alone at this dangerous impasse in her life. She missed her sister, thinking, *why don't I go find her? Leave the house, find Leyla at the hospital, and consult with her.*

She checked whether her brother-in-law was still in the house. When she did not see him, she slipped outside into the alley. In case another emissary group would intercept her, she avoided the main roads. She remembered Leyla's words, "If Axmed can't rescue you today, you have to submit to the wishes and wisdom of your parents." She repeated them to herself, *If Axmed can't rescue you today, you have to submit to the wishes and wisdom of your parents.* More worried now, she stopped in the middle of the road. *Wait a minute, where is my friend Sahra? Why didn't I remember her all that time? Why can't I ask her to help me?* She was somewhat relieved by recalling that she had a friend in town to whom she might be able to turn.

Stopping at a strange house, she knocked on the door and asked to use their telephone. Dialing the number, she put the receiver to her ear.

"Hello," at the other end.

"Is this Dhaxagtuur High School?" she asked.

"Yes, it is," responded someone.

"My brother, can I talk to teacher Sahra Yuusuf?"

"Please hold. I am going to call her."

A while later she heard the voice of her friend, "Hello."

"Sahra?"

"Hey, is this Maana? I shouldn't talk to you. Why did you not come to see me? Where have you been? What happened, Maana? Are you crying? What is this sobbing all about? My sister, what happened to you? Woe is me, woe is me! What happened to my girl? Maana, please talk to me! What happened to you?"

"Eee, Sahra, eeeee, sister, tonight..."

"Please tell me, in the name of Allah, what is going to happen tonight?" asked Sahra quite anxiously.

"I am going to be married off."

"Married off, what is this marrying off about? Are you crazy?"

Maana responded with an accelerated wave of tears.

"Maana, please talk to me. What is the issue?"

"Eee..., my sister...!"

"Woe is me, my girl has been afflicted by God's wrath. Maana! Where are you now? Just tell me where you are, and I am going to get you!"

Once Maana told her where she was, Sahra rushed out the door. She made a mad dash to a nearby taxi and got on the road.

"Would you please drop me off in Boondheere?" she requested hurriedly.

She could not have heard worse news than that Axmed Jaamac was not the one who was going to marry Maana. On her way, many questions came to mind: *Who was the damn man that Maana was going to be married off to today? Where in hell did they get him from? When was this hasty decision made, for they (she and Maana) had not been away from each other that long?! Had Maana kept the news to herself because she thought Sahra might tell Axmed and that could have made it worse?* In five minutes she was with a sobbing Maana.

Once Maana saw Sahra, she let loose whatever she was holding on to and wept even more. Immediately Sahra took her by the hand and said, "Let's go."

"Where are we going?" Maana asked.

"Just let's go. I will let you know later, but now we need to not talk." Sahra ushered Maana into the waiting taxi, knowing that Maana was now her responsibility since Axmed was out of town.

She went to her place. And after putting Maana inside, she padlocked the doors. She picked up the phone and called Leyla at work. Although Maana had told her that her sister was on her side, Sahra was not fully confident to trust Leyla with this sensitive issue. However, she was fully aware of how much they both needed her assistance. She began a phone conversation with the perfunctory "hellos" and "how are you?"

Leyla was glad that Sahra had called her. She had felt isolated in her knowledge, and this isolation saddened her. She was worried about what step Axmed might be forced to take. She knew that he was in love with Maana, but she had no idea of where he stood when it came to marriage. Until Sahra called, she had not known that Axmed was out of town and that Maana could not find him.

Leyla told Sahra all she knew, hoping that she could shed a light on what her cousin had planned for her sister.

Sahra allayed Leyla's concerns by telling her how Axmed had been preoccupied with how to make Maana his wife and that he would sacrifice his life for her.

Leyla's candidness on the phone gave Sahra the courage to open up and share the news that she was hiding Maana in her place. She made it clear to Leyla that she could speak for her cousin, Axmed, and made it absolutely clear that he would do right by Maana. In return, Leyla promised that she was going to guard the secret close to her heart and would support anything and everything that was going to make it possible for Maana and Axmed to unite.

Leyla decided to run to her family under the pretense that she had no knowledge that Maana had left home. She wanted to go to them before they came to her. She did not want to be blamed for planting the idea with Maana to reject the arranged marriage proposal.

She rushed through her lunch and was about to leave when her father arrived. Like a thief caught in the act, she was rattled, nervous, and filled with regret. She was regretful because she had not reached a satisfactory decision. She was rattled because she had not prepared what she would say to her father. Nervous due to her father's unexpected arrival, she blurted out, "Maana left before I got home from work."

Her father let loose his anger that had brought him all the way from Xamar-weyne.

"I am blaming all of this on you. I know that you have become disruptively disloyal. You and Maana are in this together to undermine your parents. You will see where this will get you. You tell that monkey sister of yours that if she isn't home by this evening, she may never show her face at my house again. She should walk off onto the streets. And you know what? No, no one is going to believe that the bride is simply missing!" he added furiously.

VII

The anger that had brought Xaaji Muumin to Boondheere was worse in Xamar-weyne. The whole neighborhood was now at war. While he was on his way, the young ladies who would have groomed and molded Maana into a ready-made bride added fuel to the already smoldering heat. They told Maana's story for all to hear. They let everyone know what she had said and what she had done. Each person who heard it told someone, and that someone told another and another.

An hour later, the news arrived at Aw-Mukhtaar's doorsteps where Iikar received the inflated and selectively sorted-out gossip.

"Who the hell does she think she is? Despite my reservations, I have been preparing myself for her, and she is scoffing at me, ready to humiliate me. My goodness! You people, begging a woman for me, and all the while she is destroying my integrity? This is all my father's fault! That is it; I am going to bury myself," responded an enraged Iikar.

In comparison to his mother Aay-Soonto, Iikar's anger was not too severe. Aay-Soonto, whose fury rose up to high heaven, held the hem of her gown above the ankle (which, for a Somali woman of her age, particularly her subgroup of Reer Xamar, meant she was revealing more than allowed), opened her mouth wide, and let the words spew out. She let the verbal assault flow and supported it with a pantomime, beating on a table as if it were Maana herself.

"Hah, the nasty one did this and that! Who does she think she is? The monkey-look-alike, the one with no hope of ever attracting a suitor! And the same one we have been pleading with my son to have mercy on and marry her, even though she is too old for him. She is insulting us with a refusal! Why have we done this favor for a spinster who had no one else offering to marry her? Well, if she should come through the door right this moment, there is no way I would allow my son to have anything to do with her. There are countless others out there, swooning over my son. He is able to have any woman in Mogadishu his heart desires," she fumed.

Wearing neither shoes nor shawl (yet another social aberration), she ran out of the house and into the street. She continued to curse Maana while swearing her allegiance to her daughter, Jiija. She ran to her sister's house where the young ladies were grooming and preparing Jiija, the other bride involved in the marriage swap. She walked in on them, busy singing but hard at work. Jiija, sitting in the middle of a bunch of humming young ladies, was very excited. She was being attended to like a queen with her army of servants gathered around her.

Like a mad spirit, Aay-Soonto crashed the *Fadhiisin* celebration. She ran through the happy troop and brought all to a halt. Their eyes just followed her, their ears heard her words, and their minds bore the unfiltered filth her lips unleashed. Everything stopped. Pushing her way through, she shoved some attendees out of the way, stomped on any feet in her path, and kicked over a bowl of henna which they were using to paint Jiija's hands. She grabbed hold of Jiija by her hand, ordered her to stand up, and marched out the door with her. The prospective young bridesmaids were left baffled and without the bride. Like a camel herder who has lost his she-camel to a lion and too fearful to chase after the lion, they just sat there quietly, staring at each other.

All of what had just taken place soon fed the neighborhood gossip mill. The news multiplied and, like a wildfire, it intensified as it spread. Marching across the miles, it arrived at Aay Caddeey's door, who despite her earlier protest, was now minding her own business by dutifully dealing with her daughter's impending wedding. Several women, each clamoring to be the first, brought the bad news to her.

Standing outside for all to hear, the women gave the incendiary rallying cry to Aay Caddeey, "What are you waiting for, Aay Caddeey? A woman of your peers has insulted your daughter in public!" Before she knew it, she was on her feet and running downstairs. She took to the road and quickly found herself at Aay-Soonto's house. Yelling as if there was a fire, Aay Caddeey tore into the kitchen. Aay-Soonto, who had brought her own daughter back home, had settled down somewhat and was now busying herself with household matters.

Aay Caddeey fumed with rage. "You, when did you decide to trash my child? To begin with, Maana did not want your son. We begged and pleaded with her to marry that loser. Isn't that the case? She was really waiting for her maternal uncle's son. Listen, you will never again badmouth my child! For starters, your son is a useless loser, the one who comes home every night at 3:00 a.m. Does my daughter deserve this type of man?"

Insulted and besieged, Aay-Soonto was beyond furious. She let her lips loose, and, attempting to employ all her flailing limbs on Aay Caddeey, was held off by the others around her.

Although by now both women were being held apart, Aay Caddeey continued to battle, spewing anger on other family members, specifically on her brother-in-law's family. With that accusation thrown about, Aay Caddeey sobered up enough to sense that she might have gone too far. Suddenly, she realized that here in Aay-Soonto's house she was on the wrong side of things. She stopped her tirade and gathered enough wit to pull away from the throng of women and head home, leaving Aay-Soonto there still being held by several women.

Back in her house, Aay Caddeey was once again furious. Taking out the accrued frustration on her possessions and her family, she began breaking tea glasses, and even cursed at and slapped her youngest child

Cumareey. The innocent child stopped playing and started crying. Gluing himself to his mother's legs, he pleaded "Mom, Mom," begging her to bring back her better mood. Furiously blaming her husband, she burst out, "Be quiet. I've had it with you. Be quiet. I let my mouth run on to 'She-who-has-a-foul-mouth.' I would not have been in trouble had it not been for you. It was yesterday when I said to you 'Don't make me say bad things to that woman.' I was afraid this was going to happen," she ruefully moaned.

All that, however, was a warm-up for the fight she was waiting to wage against her husband, who was on his way from Leyla's home. As soon as he walked through the door, she greeted him with a salvo of indignation. Any thoughts of Maana or Leyla instantly left his mind due to the fire from his wife's mouth.

It took some trying, but he managed to reason with her and calmed her down. Only then did she begin to bring him up to speed on all that had happened between her and Aay-Soonto. Soon he gleaned enough from her debriefing to realize the gravity of the situation. To put out the blazing fire and salvage whatever was left of their family dignity, he ran out of his house to his brother Aw-Mukhtaar.

Aw-Mukhtaar, who was not there when the wives fought but had heard the news while out in the community, was back in his house. There he found his daughter. She should have not been in the house but at the *Fadhiisin*, the grooming ceremony, preparing herself for the wedding reception. Sitting angrily beside her was her mother. She did not say a word, but the children and others began to tell him about the fight and the chaos that had preceded him.

With that, Aw-Mukhtaar's blood began to boil, and the world around him started to spin. He was not sure of what was happening to him. Was he mad as hell? Was he sad? Was he shocked? He knew one thing, though, and that was that it had been his wife who had initiated the fight. At the same time, he also confirmed that his wife, like Aay Caddeey, had been blaming the whole mishap on the secret, deliberate, dictatorially-arranged marriage decision that he and his brother had made. And now, contrary to the views of Aay Caddeey, his wife was mad because she thought her son, Iikar, had been grievously wronged as well as smeared.

Aw-Mukhtaar was furious. He paced in circles through the house. He did not know what to do next when Xaaji Muumin walked in on him. Aw-Mukhtaar's stomach churned, and his mind filled with the sounds of his wife's unfiltered version of the event.

He turned on Xaaji Muumin, but as though talking to himself, he said, "It's life that has forced us to deal with this kind of disgrace today." He paused, and then continued, "Your wife invaded us in our home. You know that? I knew you were under your wife's thumb." Raising his voice, he went on to say, "If you were not that type of man, your daughter would not have dared to disobey and dishonor you by refusing your deliberate decision to arrange for her marriage to my son. And your wife would not have attacked us in broad daylight in our house. What is clear to me is that you are in support of this behavior."

The harsh words from his brother's mouth added salt to Xaaji Muumin's already wounded soul. The anger he had at Maana, the aggravation caused by his wife's fight, all this brought humiliation upon him. And that his brother was now berating him, laying the blame squarely on him, greatly pained him. It also forced him to ask why his own brother was demeaning him. *Did he not know how devastating it was to him to hear that his own daughter, Maana, had disobeyed him and that his wife had come over to fight with his own brother's family?*

The troubled thoughts continued to run through his mind,

How could I be indicted and insulted with being under my wife's "thumb"? All my hard work has gone up in flames and not a note of appreciation has been addressed to me. What on earth was Aw-Mukhtaar talking about? When he sided with his wife, how could he forget that she was the one who had hurled insults at my wife, and then, holding their daughter by the hand, walked out of Fadhiisin with her? he asked himself.

In seconds, all these questions filled Xaaji Muumin's mind. He was close to exploding and was fearful of lobbing grenade-like words that could return to haunt him. But he firmly held on to his self-control, hoping for reconciliation and their children's marriage. He had high regard for his brother and respected him as the elder of the two. Thus, he licked his wounds, took the undeserved pill, and swallowed it whole. He tried his best to hide how mad he was and selected the path that he thought would calm his brother down. He started with soft words and went on without deflecting the blame or blows. He promised to redress whatever had been amiss and requested that his brother help mitigate the mindless mound of mistakes.

It did not work. Insanely irate, Aw-Mukhtaar did not listen but rather went on with his list of malfeasant allegations.

Just then, Xaaji Muumin reached the point at which he was no longer able to withstand the waves of blame coming out of his brother's mouth. He had had enough.

"Let us cut the cord of the partnership that has kept us tied to each other," he exploded. "We should separate and sort out our shared business and properties. Let each of us go his own way! We are done," he concluded. It looked as though the knives were out of their sheaths, and the fire fueled by gasoline was about to flare.

That date, the 13th of Mowliid, which was planned to be the happiest day in the history of the family, had turned out to be the most troublesome. The families of the two brothers were torn apart and at war. The neighborhood that had been planning to celebrate the double wedding had turned into a gloomy town. The happy faces that were all smiles in the morning were all lifeless now.

Jiija was the most disappointed and gravely sad. She thought nothing worse could have happened to her. But despite the distress and pain, she bit her tongue and tried to force a fake smile, to escape the societal disdain of "she is so sad because she wants a man so badly." But she was in a pit of anguish. In fact, she was bothered more by her inability to express her sadness than by the loss she was forced to endure. She had neither the stamina nor the idea of what to do next. She felt imprisoned by an old-fashioned custom in an ancient, rigid culture. She wished she could openly express her suppressed grief, but was obliged not to share her emotions, as Maana had done, by simply crying. Instead, she was weeping inside while forcing an outward smile.

Aweys, the man she wanted, was no less anguished, but he did not feel as completely helpless as Jiija. He was also willing to limp along with his emotional injuries. Sure, others insisted that it was all a *fait accompli,* but it did not matter much to him whatever it was called. The speed at which the misfortune unfolded chased off all orderly thoughts.

Leaving the house, he walked southwards. Reaching the ocean beachfront, he sat on a rock that was hugging the shore and bit his middle finger to withstand the emotional pain. As though he was trying to gather from the sea all that he had lost, he looked out. At times it seemed that a solution was so close yet remained far from his grasp. He was, however, leaning toward eloping with Jiija, and leaving the rest to chance, despite the enormity of the challenges ahead.

CHAPTER NINE

I

A long white sedan pulled up in front of a red building with an aluminum roof. The corpulent man in the driver's seat revved the engine three times, a signal to the madam inside the building. He knew the sound signal would reach its intended target.

Beyddan Shabeel, in the middle of all the entertainment her guests could desire, received the signal inside. In the main room of the house, two men were propped against pillows in separate corners. Two young ladies not much older than eighteen attended to each. Wedged between the legs of those men, the girls sated each one's need while intermittently feeding him *khat* leaves, like a mother feeding her baby.

The din of the music and excited chatter made it hard to hear anything outside. But Beyddan Shabeel had trained herself to multitask, and so, even while focusing her attention on her guests, she kept an eye out for the arrival of any new guests. With years of finely-honed skills, she was able to keep the inside Johns happy while making those awaiting her outside feel important. Suddenly, she ordered the girl working for her, "You, the-little-one, see the car outside!"

The haggard little girl, wearing a tattered and torn *guntiino* from all the hard work and abuse inflicted on her by her employer and the demanding guests, ran out. The little girl shouldered a heavy burden so that Beyddan could reap the reward when the guests let their hands travel deep into their pockets. The poor girl had gotten used to the endless orders barked out by her employer.

"You, the-little-one, clean up this room for the guests. Go upstairs and clean it too. Make some more tea. Light some incense. Get water from the well. Put some more water in the bathroom. Wash all the *Macawis* and bed sheets for tomorrow's guests," were Beyddan's barking orders.

Toiling from dawn to dusk, it was quite apparent that 13-year-old Faadumo did not have the luxury of time to process the dirty profession that the madam was in. Faadumo's father, a small farmer in Afgooye, had died when she was just nine years old, just a year after the death of his wife, Faadumo's mother. Assuming responsibility for her younger siblings, she had packed them up and moved to Mogadishu. Since then, she had put up with assault, injury, and servitude just to be able to keep her young family clothed and fed. Often she would save scraps of food for them that had been slated for the dump.

Faadumo returned quickly with the news. With her meek disposition, she stood in the doorway and timidly reported, "It's the heavy man with the big white car."

In her line of business, Beyydan was not able to tell which heavy man had arrived. She knew a number of male customers meeting that same description. Sternly staring at the little girl, she asked, "Which heavy man?"

"The one you paired up with Saynab last time," Faadumo hinted further.

Saynab, who was one of the two girls attending to the two men inside, immediately knew who it was.

"She is talking about the old man, Jaamac-dhegey," she volunteered.

Beyddan hurriedly jumped up and ran out. *If I want to remain in business, Jaamac-dhegey should not be neglected,* she thought. He was one of her most valued customers. She was a little disappointed that she would not be able to accommodate him tonight. She already had a full house but did not want him to feel ignored. She was worried that he might feel slighted and hold this night against her. Leaning on the window of his car, she lifted a foot, rested it on the base of the door frame, and said, "Hello, Jaamac. So, it's you. Long time no see. How have you been? You caught me at a bad time tonight. I am dealing with a stubborn group." With eyes quickly scanning the inside of his car, she continued, "Could you pass me a cigarette?"

Before he responded, he reached for an open pack of cigarettes and a box of matches from the dashboard, pulled out a cigarette, and offered it to her. As she placed it between her fingers and raised it to her lips, he pulled out a matchstick, struck it on the side of its box, and motioned to light it when his eye caught a young, dashing beauty crossing the road. The young lady, Maana-faay, was coming back from Sahra's house where she had been hiding since yesterday. Now she was heading to her sister Leyla's home. Distracted, he forgot about the lit matchstick in his hand until the flame licked his fingertips. He threw it down fast.

"I see that she has hypnotized you," said Beyddan looking at him.

"She has not only hypnotized me, she has sedated me," he said. "I dare you to bring that type of woman into your realm which until now has only been occupied by low-class escorts."

"You are insulting me. As you are well aware, I don't offer inferior services nor low-class ladies. Even that one you are looking at isn't out of reach if you so desire her! I can bring her in tonight. But the way you are talking to me, you hardly deserve it," Beyddan said.

He swiveled and pushed himself out of the car and turned toward her.

"Do you swear you are going to do that? Do you know her?" he asked with obvious enthusiasm and lit the cigarette for her.

Taking the cigarette away from her lips with a self-inflated stroke, she puffed a circle of smoke into the air and said, "You have yet to know Beyddan well. Do I know her? Do I know her? Not only do I know her, but how many others with her angelic beauty have I scored? What will you do for me if I snare this one for you?"

"You keep all the others for yourself, but this one, I dare you to bring her before me just once and in return just ask me whatever you want!" he taunted.

"I know Maana is not that hard to get. She is in Beyddan's hands. What I have been saying to you is," she began to say, but with a smirk to show her confidence in her impending task, she interrupted herself to change the subject and said, "I am starving. Let's have dinner." She turned back and barked out a command to Faadumo. "Hey, you the-little-one, come here. Go and get a take-away dinner from that restaurant." And turning to Jaamac, she added, "Give her the money for the order."

Beyddan knew that Maana was not going to be that easy to trap. She certainly did not care much about dinner, but she needed to distract Jaamac. He knew it and she knew it too, but neither one said it aloud. Through experience, she had learned to use men's temptations against them to the full.

Jaamac-dhegey, putting his right hand into his back pocket, asked,

"What did you say her name was, Muuna? Can you repeat it for me?"

"Maana-faay: One-no-one-can-compete-with."

"Tell me about her. Is she with her family, or does she belong to the streets?" he asked, withdrawing a bundle of green notes from his pocket as an incentive for Beyddan to move quickly on her promise to snare the girl.

Softening her voice, Beyddan said "She is safe in her home. She is as pure as the vitamin from sweet nectar. She does not deserve the thoughts you have of her in your mind. You aren't the only one who has expressed interest in her. I have denied many others who have demanded her. But I can't say no to you because you are Jaamac, although I am well aware that you are only friendly towards me when you are in need. Today you are in need, so I, Beyddan Shabeel, will have mercy on you, but will deliver."

"You will find me forever appreciative," he tried to assuage her. "Now, when are you going to tie her to me?" he asked with an authoritative voice.

"Add it to your agenda this Friday."

"Sure, though Friday is too far away for me."

"Friday is just four days away and Maana will be on your menu. Don't make other plans."

"Do I have your word? For sure that Muuna is going to be in your hands by Friday?

"Maana, not Muuna, is for sure going to be in my hands, thus for you."

"Can you reveal a bit about the snare you are going to lay?"

"That is a secret which will remain with me. I know how to get there and what road to take. I promise you a ready girl. Don't push it."

"Your word is the deed. Just tell me the time to arrive."

"I will come to see you on Thursday to inform you and tell you what is needed of you and the time."

"OK, deal. Bye now," he said and drove off.

"See you later," Beyddan said, but to no one.

II

The past week had been the worst of Maana's life, or so she thought. She had imprisoned herself in her sister Leyla's house, the same house where she used to refresh herself when she needed relief. Now this same house had become the object of her despair. The same Leyla who used to comfort her was mad at her, blaming her for the strained relationship between her and their parents. Their parents believed that Leyla and her husband had encouraged Maana to marry their son-in-law's friend rather than obeying their wishes for matrimony with Iikar.

Whenever Ciise was home with Maana, he would engage and entertain her. But now he too was only worried about what was taking Axmed so long.

These days the only thing that could keep Maana's spirits upbeat was the hope that Axmed would soon be back to rescue her. Ciise and Sahra both kept telling her the same thing—that he would be back for her soon. Maana called again and again at both Axmed's house and his workplace but kept receiving the same heartbreaking answer: "He isn't back yet." The five days he was away were longer than five years to her. Countless were the times she went to his apartment, even knowing that he was not going to be there.

When Ciise was not at home, she would usually go to Sahra's place, though Sahra herself was in great distress.

Sahra was feeling the burden of being related to the much-desired but missed Axmed. She had been calling and telegramming her cousin, but to no avail. At one point, she thought about sending Maana to Jilib to join Axmed there so that they could have their engagement, but she could not bear to make that decision alone. Then she thought about involving her uncle, Axmed's father, but thought better of that too. *Who knows what he would say?* she asked herself, knowing that the elders had their own lenses to view matters related to the younger generation. She was fearful that she might exacerbate the matter more.

It is better that we should wait for him. He is going to be away just for a few days. So, I should try to keep Maana occupied, she thought.

Maana had been meeting Sahra every day since Axmed's departure. This particular afternoon, however, Sahra went to Leyla's house looking for her. But while she was on her way, Maana had gone to Sahra's home looking for her. Arriving at Sahra's and discovering that no one was there, she left disappointed and soon found herself standing in front of Axmed's apartment. When she noticed that the door was open, she began to tremble. Was she scared? Was she overjoyed? Was it a combination of both? She could not tell. But she could hear her mind saying: *hurrah, my sweetheart is here at last! What a blessing!*

With urgent haste, she did not knock on the door but burst in and laid eyes on a figure on the bed. The figure lifted the sheet off himself and raised his head. Maana jumped back and her heart dropped.

"Hello, Maana. What happened to you? Did I scare you?" he asked.

Maana collected herself and said, "Nothing."

The man, Kulmiye, sat upright and got off the bed. He walked over to Maana standing at the doorway, gently took hold of her hand, and pointed to a chair. "Please take a seat. Welcome, feel at home. How are you doing?"

Unbeknownst to Maana, Kulmiye had asked Axmed to loan him the key to the apartment. "I am going to house-sit for you while you are away, but I might also use it in case a need arises," he told him. But all along he had his own plan: to stalk and seduce Maana in Axmed's own apartment. He knew she was going to come checking on whether Axmed was back. He was hoping to get a chance to make a move on her. He too was hypnotized by her beauty and hoped to win her over. *I have to take advantage of this opportunity, now that the beautiful one is here,* he thought.

For the first two days Axmed was away, Maana had not bothered to come to his apartment, but Kulmiye himself was preoccupied with his own affairs. He did not visit the apartment.

Recently, Kulmiye's luck had been on a downward spiral. He had been drinking and was frequently inebriated. He had neither time to go to work nor time to attend to other necessities. And because of his poor attendance at work, he had received numerous warnings and write-ups for low productivity. His employment was in jeopardy, and he was in trouble with his family. It had become a daily routine that either his job or his family was looking for him. He would later surface somewhere on the streets staggering drunk, or he would sleep it off in some God-forsaken alley. His last day of work was imminently approaching, but he did not care. His relationship with his well-to-do family was fast deteriorating. His father had had enough of Kulmiye's wasteful ways, it seemed.

"Son, stay off of my property, so that the other children don't follow in your footsteps," his father told him.

Kulmiye was having a hard time financing his predatory behavior and drinking habit. Many of his socialite friends had abandoned him when he no longer was able to shoulder his share of excessive party expenses. He was desperate and in despair. He was fighting against all and with himself. Many a time he tried to change but failed. He loved his family and wanted to do what they asked of him but was unable to follow the prescribed path.

Kulmiye was not a bad guy. In fact, he was not even able to smoke in front of his father, let alone disobey him. He listened to all his father's sage advice, promising to use it against all highlighted youthful mistakes. But whenever it was time to act against temptation, he was unable to awaken a whiff of courage within. Like a man on fire dousing himself with gasoline in place of water, he used alcohol and women to mask his failure.

This afternoon, he decided to try to compensate for his failures with Maana. He was excited that she had come into the apartment. Welcoming her with an ostentatious air, he began trying to tell her stories, full of jokes, attempting to ease her initial alarm.

This friend of my sweetheart is nice, she thought, laughing lightly at his stories. Unbeknownst to her, however, he was honing his knives for an attack. Step by step he maneuvered each story and joke into position.

Suddenly, the delicate dance missed a step when Maana asked, "Have you heard from Axmed? Do you know when he is coming back?"

He knew when Axmed had left the city, and must have known when he was coming back, but did not utter a word about Axmed.

"He told you that he was leaving and when he will be back, right?" he asked.

"No," she said candidly.

"How could that happen?" he asked feigning surprise.

"It was unplanned, sort of an emergency, I was told," she tried to deflect.

"What? He had told me a week prior to leaving that he was going to Jilib," said Kulmiye.

"Really? You swear?" asked Maana irritably.

"That was not nice of him, and I will take it up with him when he comes back," he continued his deceitful tale.

"Are you telling me that he told you a week before he left for Jilib?" Maana asked again in disbelief.

"Yes. As a matter of fact, I had overheard him telling Mulki before he told me."

"What? What?" Maana, who could not believe that she was hearing the name of another female, repeated "What? What? Who is Mulki?"

"His girlfriend, don't you know Mulki? The one who passed you at the door when you were coming in!" he replied with a malicious lie.

"I didn't see anybody leaving here," Maana responded in an agitated voice.

He turned to his side, opened a drawer, and withdrew a photo of his own girlfriend that he himself had earlier placed there.

"You don't know about Mulki. Here is her picture."

She snatched the picture from his hand, looked at it for a second, and threw it down, buried her face in her lap and began to cry.

Secretly joyous, Kulimiye picked up the picture from the floor and put it back in the drawer. *Yes! That is what is needed,* he told himself with a sense of victory.

"You do know each other, right?" He asked, feigning disbelief.

When she did not respond, he moved closer to her as though he were consoling her and said, "What happened, Maana? What is this? I am sorry; I don't want to create a problem between you two. I shouldn't have told you about Mulki. If I knew that you didn't know about her, I wouldn't have said anything. He had told me that you two knew about each other and that you, Maana, were content that Mulki was his first choice and that you didn't mind settling for second. I am so sorry about the secret I exposed. But this is not a major problem, is it? Please forget about everything that I have told you. People in our generation are not interested in monogamous relationships. You know that. You yourself, I am assuming, are involved in more than one relationship! What I mean is, if you're not, it would be your loss, and you need to learn fast!"

Kulmiye kept on talking, trying to ease his way toward asking her for a date. He told her that he had been attracted to her for a long time but did not want to violate his relationship with his friend. "Nevertheless," he said, "my attraction to you and affection for you have reached a stage where I can no longer put anyone else's interest before mine. Love has a way of prioritizing itself."

Initially, Maana was not able to process the whole story. She was no longer aware of herself. Hearing "his first choice was Mulki" was like hearing of Axmed's death.

The way Kulmiye was talking and looking at her, how he was moving in closer and closer, with his hands slowly moving onto her body, startled her, and brought her back to reality. As though awakened from sleep, she raised her head. She stared at him from head to toe. *Who is this guy anyway?* Maana asked herself. *Is he not my sweetheart's friend?* Suddenly, he looked much uglier than she had ever thought. He was no longer the same person with whom she had been laughing with. In seconds, she sifted through all he had said and more. With disgust, she stood up and walked off. "Excuse me, my friend. I am not the kind of woman you have in mind. I was mistaken about you. If I had known who you were, I would not have sat here with you. Goodbye!" was her last word with him.

Kulmiye did not want to accept the loss and tried his best to dissuade her from leaving, but could not. Afraid to attract the attention of the neighbors sitting just steps away outside in front of his place, he was forced to let her leave.

III

Embarrassed and sitting in the same room ten minutes later, he heard a man's footsteps approaching. Before he had a chance to grab his backpack to escape, the man arrived at the door.

"Hello, Axmed. Welcome back," said Kulmiye, trying to hide his disgrace-ridden anxiety.

Eager to address his urgent concern, Axmed asked, "What news do you have of her?"

Kulmiye was startled. The question sounded to him like *what possessed you to do what you did to my girlfriend?*

"Who is the 'her' you are referring to?" asked Kulmiye, pretending that he didn't understand.

"Who else am I talking about but Maana?"

"Oh, your girlfriend. Yes, I saw her."

"Well, I guess you did your job then," Axmed said. "So, tell me, how has she been?"

"You should not ask that question," Kulmiye said.

"What happened?" followed Axmed, suspicious.

"I would rather you don't ask. It's better for you not to know."

Alarmed and with fear on his face, Axmed moved in close to Kulmiye and firmly said, "Don't play an evasive game with me. Just tell me what has happened."

"There is nothing much to say, my friend," said Kulmiye, trying to deflect the blow. He knew that the news was going to upset Axmed and was not sure how to break it to him. He would have to finagle him into a position that would make it look that he was being forced to reveal what had happened. At the same time, he was trying to put together the parts of his plot. He had to make it appear to have been Maana's fault before she would have an opportunity to tell Axmed her side of the story.

"It isn't good to tell on people. But you are my friend, and I can't hide anything from you, OK? I'll tell you." He started, "Last night I saw Maana where she shouldn't have been. I was so surprised. It wasn't a place for an educated, decent young lady to be, hanging out with disreputable characters. We surprised each other. I forced myself to approach her. I took her by the hand and pulled her aside to talk with her. She began to curse me. Her date, who looked a little frightened, jumped in and wanted to fight me. But his friends stepped in and separated us. They all went on, accusing me of instigating a conflict between the man and his girlfriend. I told them that she was not his girlfriend but my dear friend's and that I was admonishing her for her bad behavior."

Kulimye began to assess the effect of his words. He looked at Axmed rising from his seat and falling back with anger. Kulmiye went on, relieved and satisfied with his mischief.

"I can go on and on, but let me say Maana and I parted ways that night. You remember that I had warned you about women of today and how you can't trust them. They show you their angelic side but behind your back prepare a poison by courting hundreds of other men!"

Axmed was shocked, his head was heavy, and blood pulsed hot through his veins. He thought he knew this man who was feeding him such vile news. He wanted to believe that what he heard was not true, yet he was worried sick. *Had I severed the relationship long ago with this man, I would not have to deal with this pain*, he thought.

Axmed threw himself on his bed and asked Kulmiye to leave. He tried his best to rest but could not fall asleep. He had to find Maana, but first he had to clean up. *Whatever I do, I have to find her tonight*, he thought. Thinking that Sahra was the only one who would know where he could find Maana, he quickly showered and took off for her place. He reached her home, but no one was there. *Where in the world can she be?* Searching his mind for where to find her, he walked for three hours before he realized that even if he did find her it would be too late to go to Xamar-weyne to see Maana. He resigned himself to defeat and headed back to his apartment, cursing Sahra Yuusuf under his breath.

Look how this woman has ruined my evening. I declined my friend's suggestion to spend the night in the town of Jannaale to rest, for I was rushing to see her this evening. Now I am going to go to bed without laying an eye on her. The darkness of night will soon descend, but it will bring me neither sleep nor comfort, he moaned.

Axmed did not know that Maana was not locked in her house in Xamar-weyne. Had he knocked on Ciise's door during his search, he would have found her there, and he would have saved himself a ton of grief and time. He would also have bumped into Madam Beyddan Shabeel, who was in the house setting the snare for his girlfriend. They were both there, sitting in Leyla Xaaji Muunin's kitchen. Beyddan was showing Maana her basket filled with 'clothes for sale.' He certainly would have startled Beyddan and sent her packing. He would have saved Maana a load of trouble ahead.

Beyddan was a very social, gregarious, and clever woman. She would appear friendly and generous to put those around her at ease. She had come to Leyla's house in a commercial disguise.

Beyddan and Leyla were acquaintances but did not know each other well. Leyla thought of her as a mature woman who deserved due cultural deference. However, a faint wind had brought a scent of suspicion. Through the grapevine, Leyla had heard a vague warning that Beyddan Shabeel had schemed to use neighborhood households for nefarious purposes. Yet that alarm of concern did not sound for Leyla that day.

Leyla was unprepared when Beyddan, who had not asked permission to enter, walked into the house with her inflated ego, sat down next to Leyla, and began to chat. She disentangled a bundle of clothes from a basket.

"You, daughter of Xaaji Muumin, should take a look at some of the items I have for sale today. Once you see them, you will feel like you are in high heaven," she declared.

Tempted, Leyla asked, "And what exactly is it that you are selling?"

"Twenty or so varieties of new clothes arrived today," she claimed. Beyddan pulled out two *guntiino* and offered them to Leyla, thinking, *I am really not into all of this. Where is Maana?* She had thought that once she entered the house, she would find Maana there. She felt a bit disappointed. To avoid suspicion, she was careful to not ask Leyla if Maana was around.

Now she feared that Maana might have returned to her parents' home, and if she did not find her tonight, the commitment she had made to Jaamac was in jeopardy.

Leyla continued looking at the clothes as Beyddan considered a line of questions she could use that would not raise suspicion.

Suddenly Maana entered the room. "Leyla, your child is awake."

Hurrah! It's her! Don't let her go, Beyddan's inner voice ordered her.

"Is this our Maana-faay? My daughter, how are you? How come she is so thin? Leyla, have you not been feeding this poor young lady? You yourself are too young, and you are trying to help raise another child! Look at this young lady and how weak she is! Her eyes are hidden deep in their sockets. There are food supplements that are full of vitamins, you know. I have some in my house. I'll bring them with me when I come back tomorrow. 'My niece,' can you come here?" she asked.

Maana approached, thinking that the woman was concerned for her well-being. Leyla nodded in agreement, for she herself had been worried about Maana's recent weight loss.

Beyddan went on to say "My daughter, it is not good to worry and think too much. You should know that life is short, and you should not waste a minute of it…"

At that moment, Leyla stood up and said, "I'm going to the corner store and will be back in a minute."

Beyddan, sensing the opening, decided to take advantage of Leyla's absence. "While you are still young, you should live life to the fullest."

She continued, "I saw you crying the other night, and it frightened and as much saddened me. You don't have to give your life to a man. If you do that, he will lose interest in you. Maybe he is already dating another woman. You are too young. But you must restrain yourself. Don't cheapen yourself."

Maana, who had lost interest in this meddling woman, stood up to walk away. What she most hated was when people would say "Be careful" or "Don't be in love with Axmed." Anybody who said something negative about Axmed also made her feel like cutting his/her lips off. And, fueled by anger, she would get close enough to lash out at them.

After all that preaching, Beyddan understood that Maana was truly committed, and that there was no hope of changing the mind of someone genuinely in love. She instantly decided to change her approach. Holding Maana by the hand, she said, "Come here, my daughter. I was just talking about men with bad manners, but yours is a nice guy. Look at yourself though. While you are thinking about him, you have forgotten to care for your attire. Can you look at these clothes that I brought in? They are the latest fashion, the best in town. You must at least try them."

Maana had no interest in new clothing, but Leyla, who had just joined them again and wanted to distract Maana from her worries, pressed her, saying,

"Can you take a look at least, sister? If there is anything you like, I am going to make sure you get it."

Beyddan, trying to seize the opportunity, added, "I know the item Maana would have liked, that she would not have been able to turn away from. Everybody likes the brand I am talking about. But on my way here I sold out of it. "

Intrigued, Maana asked, "So you have no more?"

"Yes, I do. I have a variety of it in stock, but they are at my home, not with me now. It is better we go there, so you can choose. You are like my child, so I will give you a discount too. I will give you some medication for your depression as well. It will help put some meat on your bones too!" said Beyddan.

"Where do you live?" asked Maana.

"Here, in the Boondheere neighborhood, just down the hill, the house painted red with a green door, next to the old two-story building that is under reconstruction. I am going somewhere tonight and don't want to be late, but tomorrow night at seven I will be waiting for you. Come by then and make your choice. Leyla and I will work out the price. Isn't that so, Leyla? You don't have to pay now; you can pay for it any time in the future, even in installments."

"Sure, auntie," said Leyla, with a bit of suspicion, but hoping for anything that might distract Maana from her gloom.

Giddy, Beyddan left Leyla's home, thinking that she had earned her stripes. Now she might be able to deliver the promise she had made to Jaamac-dhegey. She knew, though, that the issue was not settled. The hard part was how she was going to get a young lady who was in love with a young man into the hands of an older man. Using her experience, she knew what road to take. She would first have to try to dissolve an intimate, thoroughly-matured relationship. She had been there before and had failed. But that would not deter her now. *Where do I start?* she thought.

She had tried to snare Maana earlier with little success. And she knew it would be a difficult task to turn a young woman away from a current lover. So, she decided to look to Axmed. Aware of how little time remained, she had to act quickly before Maana and Axmed saw each other again. She decided to see him that next day early in the morning to plant the seed of conflict. During that same trip, she would try to fleece the dirty old man and charge him more! While she had his lust in her hands, she should milk it for as much as she could.

IV

Jaamac was resting his head on a fancy chair in his office. He pushed the buzzer and left his thumb on it to let it whine annoyingly. A young lady, his secretary, came running with a notepad and a pen in hand. As she looked at him, he said, "Listen, no one should come to see me this morning. I have a lot to do, do you understand?"

"OK, Sir," she said and abruptly turned back.

Rifling through his financial ledger, he remembered something, lifted his head up, and called after her. "Hey, listen, are there people waiting for me now?"

"Yes. There is a crowd out here," she replied. She stopped and walked back toward him as though in sympathy with the people who had been waiting for him.

"Who are they?"

"Some are your branch managers, and..."

"Tell them to carry on with their assignments and not to bother me," he interrupted her.

"And some are regional managers..."

"Tell them I will meet with them tomorrow."

"There are also employees of yours out here who have not been paid in several months, and they are complaining."

"Why are they here? I told them to go to the human resources office. Do I have to do everything myself? Tell them to go back to work and get all this traffic out of my office. They are so selfish!"

She wanted to say. *They aren't selfish. They just have no faith in you. They want their rightfully earned wages. What should they do when their children have nothing to eat? Where should they go?* But she dared not say that aloud to her boss.

"Are there others out there? Anyone from the general public?"

"Yes, there are a number of them."

"Who?"

"For one, there is an older woman who almost knocked us over. She said she has 'to see you urgently by any means.'"

"What does she look like? Did she tell you her name?"

"She is a bit on the heavy side. She also came to see you the other day. Her name is either Barni or was it Beyddan? I am not so sure!"

"Is it Beyddan Shabeel?"

"Yes, I think that is what she said."

"Let her in. I have to give her an assignment. And tell the others to leave."

"OK."

When Beyddan came in, he stood up from his chair and ostentatiously walked over to the middle of his office.

"Welcome, welcome, Madam! How are you?" He indicated to her that she should take a seat, and he sat down next to her.

"You can't believe how anxious I have been all morning waiting for your call. Your visit proves that you are a person of your word."

"What word? You got me troubled," began Beyddan. "I haven't been able to do anything for myself for the last two days, mind you. All I have done was to run after this young lady for you."

"But you finally prevailed, did you not?" he asked, thinking, *And I know you want to be paid.*

"That's for sure," she said. "When Beyddan makes a commitment, she delivers. But the major problem is that the woman is in love with a young man. And you know about the younger generation and their love issues. I am telling you; she is blinded by love. So, unless we pry her away from him, we cannot finalize a deal with her," she warned.

"What kind of a young man is she with?" he asked with a voice tinged with jealousy.

"He is one of those losers that hang around."

"There is no such thing called love. What is she going to do with a street boy with no means to support her? When she sees wealth and prestige, she will leave dry," he continued.

"I don't think she is going to let him loose unless she is made to do so."

"How are we going to achieve that goal?" he asked. "How much money is needed?" he added, putting his hand into his pocket.

"Give me three thousand shillings for my hard work, and I will add the rest."

Surprised about the amount, he pulled out his hand, thinking, *Oh, greedy woman! What is she going to do with three thousand shillings?*

"Three thousand shillings! That is almost what I paid for my new car."

"Oh, you are so stingy," said Beyddan. "Three thousand shillings means nothing to you. I'm going to need it for the party I'm planning for you. I'm inviting several people. I need to buy *khat* and alcohol, food and other party supplies. Three thousand alone will not cover it all. I am going to add another three of my own," she chided him.

She was right that Jaamac was normally very tight with his money but lavishly wasteful when he was spending on young ladies. In his pocket were several hundred shillings; not enough to cover what Beyddan was asking for. He called the agency's treasurer and demanded,

"Get me three thousand shillings out of the Hospitality and Executive Fund. And call one of the drivers to my office."

After the money had been handed to him, he passed it all on to Beyddan. And when the driver walked in, he barked, "Work with this lady today and tonight. Make sure you have enough fuel in your car." By "enough fuel" he meant gas paid for from the public funds.

"Yes, boss. But the employees will be waiting for me to take them back home after work, and my department has a lot of chores for me too," said the driver.

"Stop talking back. And don't try to change the subject to things you have no business going into. Carry on with this responsibility. You don't take orders from anyone else but this lady today. If anyone talks to you, tell him or her that you have received an order from me. Go!"

Beyddan walked out with the three thousand shillings and a driver with an Executive Order. "Take me to the Glass Factory, and make it quick," she barked.

V

As usual, Engineer Axmed Jaamac had come to work early. But this morning he was not productive. He sat staring at a pile of paperwork that had accumulated on his desk while he was away. He wished to start on it but did not know where to begin. He was physically present but absent in mind. He was thinking about Maana, wondering whether or not he was going to see her tonight and worried sick because he had not found her last night. He was burdened by the weight of the news that Kulmiye had delivered to him.

Just then he heard heavy footsteps heading his way. He lifted his head up from the table and behold! There in front of him was a lady, heading straight for him. As she slowly swaggered into his office, she let out a loud greeting, "Hey, Professor, how are you? Ah, I am so tired from my trip to get here. You are so far away. Wow, you have grown fast! Last time I saw you, you were a baby." Putting her purse on his table, she took a seat on a chair before him and continued, "I am really tired. Axmed, I need your help today. I am carrying a letter with me that I would like you to present to your boss." Having noticed the disturbed feeling on his face, she changed the subject, "You seem like you might not know me, and it isn't your fault because I was away in Kismaayo while you became a man. I am your aunt. I know everyone else in your family. I know about you too, and I was happy to hear recently that you are getting married to a very good young lady. Congratulations!" She paused for a moment to check the effect of her last words on his face, and then continued, "Today's youth is more modern than we were. In the olden days, ladies who openly dated, like your fiancée, would have had no prospect of marrying anyone. But your generation has no issue with that. You don't care if your partner had a good time with others in the past. That's fine with you." She let her words slip into him without taking a breath, not allowing him a chance to get a word in.

Axmed patiently listened to her babble on until she stepped on his injury that hurt the most, "You don't care if your partner had a good time with others in the past."

"Listen, Ma'am, do you know my fiancée?" he asked.

"Mercy on the uninformed! Are you asking me, the daughter of Shabeel, whether I know Maana-faay Xaaji Muumin? The same Maana I helped deliver as a midwife? I have been following her ever since."

"If you know her, do you know her as an escort?"

"Well, frankly, with her beauty and all, she is good enough for a wife. But she is a bit outgoing, and there are other things that can be overlooked. That is if you don't mind her going out at night and chewing *khat*. You just need to counsel her about alcohol and such. A few nights ago, she was with an unruly group of men, I am told. Their influence could lead her onto the wrong path."

Losing sense of where he was and with the world spinning around him, he hit the table in front of him with the palm of his hand and in a loud, angry voice asked, "Where did you see her?"

She pretended that the words had slipped out of her mouth and said, "Pardon me, sir. I saw nothing, heard nothing, and I told you nothing. I made a mistake. Forget about what I said. It was my imagination," while secretly thinking, *I got him exactly where I wanted him.*

Elbows on the table, Axmed opened his eyes wide and said,

"Listen, lady, you said it and I heard it. So, you can't take it back now. I want you to prove it so that so that I can know it's true. Or I am going to sue you for libel. You are peddling lies."

"If you want to touch the truth, then come to Boondheere at 8:00 p.m. Tonight. As you descend into hell, you will see an old two-story building under reconstruction. To its right is a red house with a green door. Be there with your eyes open," she said with a self-assured manner, while standing up and grabbing her purse to leave.

Axmed who had no patience left in him, feared that he was going to lose his self-control on this old woman, and would disgrace himself in front of the male employee entering his office with paperwork.

Beyddan walked out saying in a low voice but meant to be heard, "As the proverb goes, 'Do favors for no one, and you will see no evil.' I should have kept quiet," while saying to herself, *Mission accomplished! The next and final goal should be scored tonight.*

VI

As she made her way out of his office and out of his sight, Axmed began to mull over what she had said. He went through it all as though it were a film. *Who the hell was that person? Who sent her? She said, 'You don't mind her going out at night and chewing khat.' The hell with your evil khat chewing. Is it possible that she is not lying? No. When did Maana learn to chew khat? No, no, that can't have happened. She can say whatever she wants but that, no. Well...*

Trying to ignore the ringing phone, he lifelessly picked it up, put it to his ear, and in a weak voice said, "Hello."

An energized tone of "Good morning, Axmed!" came through the other end.

"Good morning, Ciise!" Axmed responded, trying to inject a bit of life into his own voice.

"Welcome back. Your father told me yesterday that you were back."

"Thanks, brother. How is the family?"

"All is well. Thanks," he answered, and then cut to the chase.

"We missed you, but Maana is fine. She has been with us for the last few days and..."

"Who? Maana?" interrupted Axmed.

With ease in his voice, Ciise continued, "Well, while you were away, some minor family issues arose. So, we decided to have her stay with us until you got back. It's good that you are here now. We will wait to see you to tell you all about it."

When Axmed asked what the issues were, Ciise repeated that they were minor and that they should talk about it when he got to their house.

Again, Axmed's world spun. This was worse than the previous update. He was worried. His mind was working harder now. He hung up the phone but needed clarification of what Ciise was referring to.

It was hard. Axmed was bothered by the unsavory update that he had received that morning and was now going over all that he had heard,

yet he did not want to believe any of it. He remembered what Kulmiye
told him a day ago. He remembered the rotund woman and what she
said. He could see the picture of the red house with the green door that
she had told him about, and he tried not to imagine what was happening
inside there. He sighed and turned away, but the bothersome images
remained. *There is Maana leaving the party late at night. She knocks on the door of
her family's house about midnight. She is turned away by her family, who have
disowned her. She goes to see Kulmiye. She goes out with him and other alcoholics who
welcome her into their circle. She swims in the ocean of debauchery with them, and
there the madam finds her. That's how Ciise becomes involved. He agrees to bring her
home until I get back and take responsibility for her.*

*Yes, I understand Ciise and Leyla now. Who are trying to trap? I am at a loss.
I can't believe what and who Maana turned out to be! What in the world happened?
This is not the same Maana that I met. The results of whatever tests I tried on her
are inaccurate! What in the world have they done to her? Has she been bewitched?
There is no such thing as being bewitched…All the signs must have been there, but
am I that dumb? The woman bamboozled me. She will not fool me anymore, though,*
he said to himself. He paused briefly and then continued to think:

*Are all those people pulling my leg? Isn't Maana the same meek, decent woman I
have come to know? How did she get the time to do the things that she has allegedly
been doing behind my back? How was she able to do this during the one week that I
was away? Connecting with countless people! This can't be possible! I shouldn't
listen to anybody! But what Ciise told me could be true. He is the one who said, 'It
was a minor issue, nothing else.'*
*Why would I trust Kulmiye? I should forget about that rotund woman, too. She who
strutted in and let her mouth run free like sea water. You are all liars. Leave me
alone. Don't dismantle the family I have been planning to build. If I can't have
Maana, I will never marry in my life. I recant the statement I had made when I
came from abroad that I want to find a good Somali wife to settle down with and
raise a family.*
*Forget it, forget it. There is nothing to worry about. I am sick with unwarranted
suspicion. Foreshadowing bad luck isn't good for the soul. Dithering is not good for
anything. I must yield to my parents' wishes. I need to be married in a week. And I
need to let Maana know about it in the hope that she will accept my marriage
proposal.*
*No, when you first see her, get to the bottom of what this was all about. Well, she
will be shocked if I dump all those lies about her on her lap. No, no, she knows
something. Don't let her hoodwink you. If she weren't guilty of something, why did
her family put her out?* he argued with himself, confused.

He talked to himself hour after hour, repeating the same thing over and over, contradicting himself again and again. Nothing he tried to eat had any taste and he found no rest. He kept thinking: *will the sun never set?*

The minute the sun dipped behind the horizon, he left his apartment heading for Boondheere. Shortly before 7:00 p.m., he knocked on Leyla's door. A skinny little girl opened it.

"Is Maana here?" he asked. Before the words had left his lips, he realized he had made a mistake. It would have been more culturally appropriate to pretend that he had come to visit the family, not Maana. He heard the girl say, "No, Maana isn't here."

The answer was hard for his ears to take, but it was more painful for his heart. Somewhere in his inner soul there was a tear of pain. Through clenched teeth he asked the little girl, "Is there anybody else in the house besides you?" This was how he would have liked to start.

"Yes, there are others. Please come in," the little girl said.

As he walked in, he realized that the others she was referring to were a little boy, Burhan, and a younger aunt who was babysitting him. The girl told him all she knew about where the rest of the household was: Ciise had eaten his lunch in a hurry and gone back to work; Leyla had made a house call to a sick neighbor; and Maana was trying to purchase items of clothing from a nearby house. The last part of her statement gave him a bit of renewed hope about his love Maana.

With that glimmer of hope, he calmed down enough to take a seat and wait for Maana to return. As time went on, he began to feel restless and bored with both the waiting and the children. The hour ticked on to 7:10 p.m., then 7:15, then 7:20 p.m. and then 7:30 p.m. Still no Maana. His suspicion set in again. Talking to himself, he was beset by the same worrisome argument that had previously attacked him. At about ten minutes to 8:00 p.m., his patience ran out. Hitting the table in front of him with his fist, he stood up, and without a word of farewell, walked out of the house. His recollection of what the fat woman had told him gnawed angrily within him.

She is not coming back here. What that fat woman told me was true. I am a fool. I should have welcomed that old woman's news and asked for more. Who owns that house she was talking about? Well, it could be a bachelor's dwelling. It would have been nice had I asked the woman her name and where I could find her later. Where in the world was the place she was directing me to? Let me see! Here, I am in Boondheere. Hey, where could that hell house she was talking to me about be? It must not be far, he told himself.

He descended from the hilltop on which he had been standing. At the bottom he looked around at the nearby buildings. *Where is that two-story building she referred to? All I see are ugly huts and shanty look-alikes. She has doused me with lies!*

He recalled that the building he was looking for was painted red with a green door opposite a two-story building. But he had turned in the wrong direction. Had he turned left as he entered the neighborhood, the building would have been within fifty feet, and he would not have missed the unmistakable house of Beyddan Shabeel.

VII

Beyddan's living room was full of guests, but she had one important task to attend to: someone had to be stationed at the door that Engineer Axmed was expected to come through.

Three out of four corners in one of the rooms of her party house were occupied by three men, each paired with a young lady. Bundles of *khat* leaves covered the mattresses on the floor. On a small coffee table were cups, cigarettes, a thermos full of sweet tea, and a pitcher of water. Bottles of perfume sat in front of each entangled pair. In the middle of the room was a *burjiko* in which burning incense blended with the smoke from cigarettes, conspiring against any fresh air that could have entered the room. In the fourth corner of the room next to the door a man sat alone, quietly munching on *khat* twigs. Seated on a nearby mattress was Maana-faay. Next to her lay a small bundle of women's clothing for her to look through.

Earlier on Maana had arrived at the appointed time of 7:00 p.m. to buy clothing from "Aunt" Beyddan, who had welcomed her warmly and maneuvered her onto the mattress. She poured praises on her, to encourage her shopping and to distract her from the party activities.

Now, looking at Maana, Beyddan spoke softly to herself, but loud enough to deliberately let Maana hear her: "What in the world is holding her back?"

"Who are you talking about?" Maana asked Beyddan.

"It's a young lady who has the key to a locked drawer where I keep the best *guntiinooyin* I had selected specially for you."

"So, is this all?" Maana asked as an excuse to leave.

"No, no, my 'niece,' she will be here soon. I just told her to run an errand for a neighbor, but she is taking longer than I had hoped." She handed Maana a photo album. "Take a look at these pictures. You may find some people you know in there."

The young woman on errand did not exist, but Beyddan needed an excuse to keep Maana occupied until 8:00 p.m., Axmed's impending arrival time.

Beyddan stood up and walked into an adjacent room. She returned with another small pile of clothes. "My child, that young lady is so late with the key. I don't want to keep you much longer. Take a look at these and see if there is anything you like."

Maana rifled through the pile.

"No, I don't think I see anything I like."

"What is it with you, my child? There are good ones in there! Don't you see? Your friends would love any of these," she said, pointing to some of the *guntiino*. Suddenly, she took Maana by the hand. "Let me take you to others who can help you choose." Pulling Maana up with one hand, she scooped up the pile with the other and led her into the smoke-filled room. A bewildered Maana followed.

Beyddan put the pile of clothes in front of the man sitting alone in the far corner of the room and said, "Muuse, you have great taste in women's attire. Can you recommend a good *guntiino* for this beautiful young lady?" She looked at Maana, adding, "My daughter, take a seat here for a minute," pointing to the mattress the man was on.

Puzzled but cornered, Maana felt that she had no choice. She tentatively stepped to the mattress and sat down.

"Muuse, please hurry up. My child has already wasted enough of her time here. We don't want to keep her much longer," Beyddan barked but winked at Muuse, who was well aware of the plot beforehand. He knew that she meant, *you know what to do with her. We are breaking her down.*

Muuse, along with the other room occupants, abandoned their interest and began attending to the task of enticing the new young lady into their circle. They took turns to entertain and humor her. Using the clothes before Maana as a pretext, they turned the whole charade into a competition among them. "I recommend this one," a man would say. "No, I recommend that one," another would counter. "No, I know what angels prefer," yet another would chime in.

Once they were all engaged in the game of pretending to select the best items for Maana, Beyddan slipped out of the room with an excuse that she heard a voice that sounded like the young lady returning with the key. But she left when she realized that Axmed's arrival time is approaching.

When she came out to the veranda, she told the little girl Faadumo, "If a woman comes in and asks you about Maana, tell her that she has left. But if it's a young man, tell him to go into that room. If anyone else is looking for me, tell him or her that I am going to be back in thirty minutes."

Beyddan left to hide in a neighbor's house while her team in the smoke-filled room executed her mission. As the chicanery of teasing Maana went on, they proceeded to make a case for the narcotics, the *khat* they were all chewing, too.

"What do you think about these grownups grazing on this green vegetation, like animals?" Muuse asked Maana deceptively. "Have you ever seen this before?" he added, giving her a twig. She had heard of *khat* but had neither seen nor ever been anywhere where it was being consumed. She did not know what it looked like and did not know that it was this dull vegetation. She had a different image in mind. "Is this the famous stuff, *khat*, that is being talked about?" asked Maana. She gave the twig a thorough exam.

Having noticed that it was time for Axmed to arrive, Muuse, began to give Maana a long lecture about *khat*, while the other pairs deliberately turned their attention to each other, with renewed kissing and groping.

Suddenly, someone burst in. His eyes registered the amorously engaged couples. Before he could process the scene, he heard a distinctive voice of, "Hey, Axmed, sweetheart!"

The words shot through his body like a bolt of electricity. His heart raced a thousand-fold, and his eyes followed the voice, landing on Maana. She threw down the *khat* twig and leapt at him like a body possessed. She completely lost her sensibility in an attempt to envelop him in an exuberant hug.

Axmed had lost his sanity at the first sight of Maana throwing down a *khat* twig and a bare-legged man on the mattress next to her. Strand by strand, his hair stood up with rage. He wished he were an exploding grenade taking all inside that room with him. He jumped back and away from his love's attempted embrace and landed an open-handed slap on her face. The force of the blow dropped Maana to the floor like a rock thrown from a rooftop. The shock that had greeted her, the disappointment and the pain of his assault, converged on her all at once.

Her vulnerable mind could not grasp the magnitude of such hurt. Unconscious, she remained where she fell.

Axmed did not fare much better. Unlike her, however, he did not pass out but lost all rational thought. He did not know that he had slapped her, he did not know when he left there, and he did not know where he was heading, but eventually he found himself wandering on the beach. He was not sure whether he was sleepwalking or dreaming when he stopped to collect himself.

CHAPTER TEN

I

Leyla was worried. Maana had not returned home, and it was getting late. Since 8:00 p.m., she had been repeating the question to herself, *what happened to Maana?* She knew that Axmed had stopped by at her house while she was out. For just a second, she felt some relief at the thought that perhaps Axmed and Maana had run into each other on Maana's way home. Yet her instincts were telling her that something was not right. *Had she been hustled by street boys? Was she lost? Why did I send her alone?* she asked, blaming herself.

Around 10:00 p.m., she put on a *guntiino and* shawl. Trying to remember the directions Beyddan had given them the day before, she headed out to find the house.

Unsure exactly where she was headed and feeling lost, Leyla was about to turn around when she heard a female voice calling out, "Nurse Leyla Xaaji Muumin? You have come a long way tonight."

When she turned to look, she realized it was Xaawo, a woman she knew from the neighborhood.

"How are you, Xaawo? My sister, do you know a woman by the name of Beyydan Shabeel in this neighborhood?"

"Beyddan Shabeel? For God's sake, how are you involved with Beyddan Shabeel?"

Startled by Xaawo's question and with her eyes wide open, Leyla put her palm over her mouth. When she found the words to ask Xaawo what business Beyddan was in, she confirmed Leyla's refusal to suspect that Beyddan Shabeel was a courtesan. Leyla felt ashamed and embarrassed. Xaawo went on to explain how Beyddan's house was not a place for decent women.

"It doesn't matter what brought you here," Xaawo continued, "What matters is if you are seen entering or leaving this house, the neighbors will think you are a prostitute or a call girl." Now worried not only about her sister but also about herself, Leyla lamented, "Oh, who is going to have mercy on me tonight? I can't go into this place. But if I don't go in, how will I be able to find my sister?"

Xaawo took on the responsibility, suggesting that the two should go in together. If she, a respected neighborhood elder, was with her, Leyla would be protected from libel and tongue-lashing.

Together they walked through dark alleys to Beyddan Shabeel's house. Picking up the pace, they saw a silhouette of a human figure walking ahead. The figure took a few steps, squatted, stood up, took a few more steps, and squatted again. As they came closer, they saw that it was a small, frail girl carrying an earthenware pot of water. The child was wearing a wet, threadbare *guntiino,* shredded at the loose ends. The weight of the earthenware pot was forcing her to frequently stop, sit down, and re-adjust the load. By now she was drenched in water overflowing from the pot as she waddled through the alley. The overflowing water from the pot on her, along with the drizzling winter showers of Mogadishu, had weakened her with cold.

Tired and hungry, the little girl put down the earthenware pot just as the two women caught up with her.

Realizing how increasingly difficult it was to lift the pot, she asked in a feeble voice, "My aunts, would you help me put the pot on my head, please?" From the way they were looking at her, she could tell that they were sympathetic to her plight. And though she wanted to rest a bit longer, she feared that she might not find anyone else to help her if she let them pass her by.

Recognizing the little girl, Xaawo sighed with sadness and said, "Ah, you poor little girl! Is it you, Faadumo? How many times have I seen you out late at night with so much weight on you? My child, is it that fat woman who has sent you out this far to get water? Let me help you, my child. That woman will pay for her crime in the hereafter. And why did you not get this water earlier in the day rather than endangering yourself this late at night with the cold, street boys and all?" She scolded her in a motherly way. Xaawo lifted up the earthenware pot and placed it on her own shoulder rather than on Faadumo's.

"I have been doing this since sunset," the little girl replied.

"And where have you been pouring all of this water? Were you watering a herd of camels?" Xaawo asked.

"She told me to fill a whole barrel. If the men at her *khat*-chewing party run out of water, I will be blamed."

"Why then did you not at least tell her that the earthenware pot was too heavy for you?"

"I did!"

"What did she say? Nevermind."

"She told me I could leave if I was not able to do the job."

"To hell with her and her whorehouse! She is so cruel."

Leyla was not aware of the whole story, but was pained by the plight of the poor little girl. She deduced that the "*khat*-chewing party" the girl was referring to was taking place in Beyddan's brothel. But to make sure, she asked Xaawo, "Is she talking about Beyddan Shabeel?"

"Yeah, she is putting this poor child through hell on earth."

"Why doesn't she have running water for her men? She is a woman of means, I assume?" asked Leyla.

"There was running water in the house, but she shut it off. She told the people in the neighborhood that her water pipes were rusted. So, she shut it off. She has also told others that all that human traffic in and out of her house was costing her a fortune. Thus, rather than paying money she thought that she could use indentured servitude. She got this poor child for that. It is only when this child is busy with her other errands that Beyddan buys water from a water-donkey merchant," answered Xaawo.

Leyla looked at the wet, frail, and shivering Faadumo and asked, "Why don't you quit working for this cruel woman?"

"My sister, I have nowhere else to go."

"Where are your parents? Are they still living?"

"No, they passed away."

"Do you have older siblings?"

"No. I am the oldest."

"And where are the others?"

"The two boys closest to me in age are in Mogadishu. One shines shoes, but I have no idea where the other is. I have been told that he is a street boy. He is either snatching food or money from others in order to survive, or eating out of dumpsters."

"Oh, poor child! What about the others?"

"The rest are still too young. They live with grandma, who herself is very poor."

"So, your father is deceased? Did he leave you anything, inheritance I mean?"

"A farm."

"And what happened to the farm?"

"In the beginning we were too young to farm, and then when we tried to start farming, we realized that a wealthy man had taken it away from us, annexing it to his neighboring farm."

"Did you try to take him to court?"

"Yes, we did."

"What happened?"

"They said that we were not farming the land, in which case the law is with the person who can use it."

As Faadumo continued to share her story, she realized they were very close to her destination. She quickly lowered her voice and began speaking fast, "Aunt Xaawo, hand me the earthenware pot. If I am not the person carrying it, Beyddan will yell at me and more."

While Xaawo was transferring the earthenware pot of water onto her, Leyla asked, "Listen Faadumo, is there a young lady by the name of Maana-faay in there?"

"Maana-faay, Maana-faay. . ." The name sounded familiar, but she could not match it with a face.

"I can't tell one girl from the other. There are many of them entering and leaving; some in cars and others by foot. It's hard for me to keep up with their names."

"Listen, it's a girl. . ."

"No, no," Xaawo interrupted her. "Leave her alone, Leyla. She can't, as she said, keep up with it all. We will deal with the woman ourselves." She looked at the little girl and asked,

"That old woman is there, isn't she?"

"Yes, she was there when I left."

"Tell her that we are waiting for her outside" she said, then whispering to herself she said, "We don't want to be in the middle of her mess."

"OK. Thanks," said the little girl and walked into the house. Inside she poured the water into a barrel, then turned around and went into the room where she had last seen Beyddan. She stood outside the door and said, "'Aunt' Beyddan, there are two ladies outside waiting for you."

Beyddan guessed that the two women waiting outside for her had probably come for Maana. She knew that if it were her usual crowd, they would not have hesitated to come in. As though the child had committed a crime, she looked at her with a stern stare and said, "You tell them she is not here." She looked around, lowered her voice, and added, "If they ask you about a young lady by the name of Maana-faay, tell them we didn't see her. Do you understand? Go, you-with-the-wet-and-dirty-body. Did you bring the water?"

"Yes," the little girl responded and walked away to avoid being yelled at again. Taking a few steps, she realized that the name Beyddan just uttered was the same name the two women had asked about. She now knew that she had heard that same name at least three times in the past. She recalled she had heard it first from Beyddan.

Maana-faay, Maana-faay. OK, now I know. It's the young woman she was talking about earlier this evening, 'If a woman asks you about Maana-faay, tell her that she has just left, but if it's a young man, tell him to go into that room.' So, what should I tell those who are asking about her now? she asked herself.

She dallied on the veranda for a while. It was hard for her to face the two women waiting outside. She debated whether to tell them the lie that Beyddan had ordered her to tell or to tell the truth as she knew it. If she told the truth, she was disobeying her boss. She was afraid of Beyddan, who could easily hasten the arrival of judgment day for her. But she knew that telling the truth was the right thing to do, and she did not want to lie to the two women who had been so kind to her. Faadumo also remembered that there had been other times in the past when Xaawo had stepped in to protect her from Beyddan.

She weighed how much she liked Xaawo against how much she hated Beyddan. Still, disobeying Beyddan was hard to bear. Conflicted, she went back outside to the women waiting for her.

"Faadumo, where is the madam?" Xaawo asked.

"She told me to tell you, 'She is not here.'" Once the words had passed her lips, she put her hands over her mouth as though the words had just slipped through, adding, "I don't know what to tell you. She isn't here."

Xaawo and Leyla looked at each other and said at the same time, "What did you just say?"

"She is not here," repeated Faadumo, avoiding eye contact lest she expose her internal war.

"She isn't here?" repeated Xaawo.

"My child, come here, please. Let us move to the side. This is just between the two of us," said Xaawo, taking Faadumo by the hand and moving into the alley away from the light. "Let me ask you, my child," she went on in a hushed voice, patting her on the head, "She told you to tell us that, right?"

Faadumo took her time, and in a soft, sniffling voice said, "Yes."

"It doesn't matter. But what I would like to ask you is, are there young ladies in the house?"

"Yes."

"What are they doing?"

"They are chewing *khat* with the men."

"All of them?"

"Yes."

"Listen, I know you are a good girl and you know that I have been much kinder than Beyddan. So can I ask you a favor?" Xaawo asked.

"Yes."

"Without attracting attention, I would like you to find out whether Maana, a very light-skinned young lady, is one of them. And I am going to tell you how you will go about that, OK?"

Silent for a moment, Faadumo blurted out "She is!"

"What? Who?" said Xaawo and Leyla who had sidled in to join them.

"There is a young woman in there by the name of Maana-faay," said Faadumo.

"Are you sure?" Xaawo asked.

"Yes," Faadumo responded.

"So, were you hiding it from us earlier when you said you didn't know if she was there?" asked Leyla.

"I wasn't sure then, but the madam reminded me."

"What did she say to you?"

"She told me that 'if they ask about a young lady by the name of Maana-faay, tell them she isn't here.' She said the same earlier."

The two women looked at each other.

"In the evening I saw Maana sitting on the veranda," Faadumo started to open up quickly. "The madam was showing her some clothes for sale. They both went into a room where men and women were partying, chewing-*khat*. When the madam came back out, she told me, 'If a young woman asks you about Maana-faay, tell her that she is not here. But if a young man is looking for her, let him into that room.' The young man came. So, I told him to go into the room and he joined the party,"

Faadumo narrated the first part of the story exactly the way it happened, but the ending was her own interpretation. She thought that Maana was an escort who was being offered to the young chocolate-brown fellow. She was unaware that Axmed had left the disgraced scene in an amnesiac rage.

With disappointment, the two women looked at each other.

"Where are they now?" asked Leyla, as though angry with Faadumo.

"When you enter the house, it's the room to your right. They were in the corner. Oh, I'm late now," added Faadumo fearfully.

"OK. Faadumo, get in there and go about your business, sweetie," said Xaawo.

"OK, bye."

"If the madam asks about us, tell her that we left, and don't let anybody else know about us," said Leyla.

"OK," Faadumo said and walked away.

Once Faadumo left them, the two put their heads together.

"What can we do now?" each asked the other. Dejected and discouraged, Leyla deemed that what she heard was damaging, and suggested that she burst in, cause a chaotic melee, snatch her sister, and drag her out of there. But Xaawo, who was a bit older and wiser and who possessed a calmer demeanor, said, "If you whip this crowd into a frenzy at this late hour, it will only disgrace you. The commotion you stir up will attract outsiders who will spread the news that you too were here. 'What business brought her here?' would be the question. So just wait for her. I am going in there, and I will find a way to get her out safely."

Xaawo knocked on the door briefly and walked in without permission. Reeking of alcohol, the smoke-clogged room and polluted air stifled her. Forcing herself to breathe, she ran her eyes over all who were there. She could have put up with the smoke and the stench of alcohol, but the scene of young women with older men, devoid of decency and shame, appalled her. Deplorably, she heard words that the sane and sage would never dare to say.

The scene was so disheartening. Maana-faay was lying on the floor on the same spot where she had fallen when Axmed slapped her unconscious. Xaawo, believing that Maana had passed out drunk, turned around and left in haste, shocked.

"My sister, let us leave this Godforsaken place and forget about this young, wasted sister of yours. She is a lost cause," said Xaawo. She went on narrating what she had witnessed inside the house with the green door.

Leyla and Xaawo both rushed out of the scene. Leyla returned to her house with great grief. She believed that she had left her sister Maana dead but not buried.

II

Maana slowly regained consciousness. Gathering strength, she rubbed her eyes with her right hand and looked all around. She was lying on the floor of the party room, surrounded by leftover twigs of *khat*, cigarette butts, used matches, dirty mattresses, burned charcoal, and flasks of sweet Somali tea. "Where am I?" she asked herself and jumped up. She looked at her wristwatch but could not trust the time it told. Confused, she thought: *is it daytime or night? Is she in a house or jail? No clue.* She looked at her wristwatch again and saw it read 4:00. *Is it 4:00 a.m. or p.m.?* She wondered.

She dragged herself out of the room and onto a dead, dark veranda. A sudden beam of light brought her surroundings into focus.

"Hello, Maana." The voice startled her. She turned her head and there she was, the fat old woman standing in a half-opened doorway.

"My 'Niece,' you are awake! Please come back in. Come inside to the room. You need to rest." Stepping out on to the veranda and dragging half of her *guntiino* behind her, Beyddan continued, "You will catch a cold out here."

Once Maana saw who was talking to her, the reality of where she was hit her hard. She was in Beyddan's house! The frightening events of the night flashed through her still foggy mind. Slowly, painfully, the memories became clearer, and then scene by scene she was able to remember the smoke-filled room, the closed door, the mattresses on the floor with couples entangled in compromising positions—all grazing on green vegetation. The final scene was of Axmed bursting into the room; her words "Ah, my sweetheart;" and the slap that knocked her to the floor. "Aaaaaa!" she blurted spontaneously but quickly caught herself. The last memory was of laying eyes on her love; the excitement before the attack; and the disappointment that brought about an overwhelming sadness. Now, assessing the agony at hand, she felt enormous emotional pain. She was shocked, embarrassed, and overpowered by guilt and shame. She let out a wail that awakened the neighbors who quickly began arriving, and the veranda light was turned on.

"You people of God, please help! Please take me out of this place," she cried over and over. But despite all who had dared to come, not one heeded her howling cries for help. They thought she was one of Beyddan's call girls who might have been drunk.

She wanted to run out, but the unknown dangers in the street frightened her. In the dead of night, she neither knew what to do nor where to go. Still, she refused to calm down or go back into Beyddan's room.

Beyddan asked the others to leave. She turned the light off, went back to her room, and closed the door. Maana lay in a fetal position on the now dark veranda.

The only person who remained outside with her was Faadumo, crying.

Faadumo had wanted to come to Maana to wipe away her tears when the crowd of neighbors was there. But she was afraid that Beyddan would berate her in front of all the curious neighbors. She did not really understand why Maana was crying, but she knew about mistreatment, and she knew that no one else was there to care about Maana's pain and sadness. Faadumo felt for her and shed tears for their shared hardship.

The fact that the enemies of good will were united in their mistreatment of the poor and the vulnerable forced Maana and Faadumo to bond. The same people who had caused Maana so much pain and tears, who had turned her family against her and ruined her right to a happy future, were the same kind of people who were exploiting little Faadumo. She toiled to earn mere pennies and had been abused beyond belief for trying to feed herself and her younger siblings.

Enveloped in her threadbare *guntiino*, with its loose hem, she squatted in front of Maana. Hanging her head low and supporting her weight with one hand on the floor, she patted Maana on the back. "Maana, Sister, please don't cry, sweetie," she said with a caring voice.

That angelic voice touched Maana's heart. Maana lifted her head from between her knees, opened her tearful eyes, and looked at the little girl seated beside her on the semi-dark, desolate veranda. She felt comforted by the gentle patting and kind words addressed to her by this dear little angel. There, each felt the other's tender heart. Discounting her own tears, Maana wiped Faadumo's tears away and folded her in her arms like a mother reuniting with her child.

Faadumo and Maana shared this intimate moment on the dark veranda and began to talk. It did not take long to share their stories. Faadumo spoke first. She talked about the hard times she had lived through and detailed the mountains of trouble that her family had faced. She delivered her story with a delicate touch that let Maana know she was not alone in pain.

Maana took her turn to articulate her bereavement and told her tale of love and the recent struggles she had faced. She let it all out to the little girl. She let her know that she was in love with a man; that she had been betrothed to another; that she had run away to her sister's house where she was introduced to a "clothes merchant" who turned out to be the cheat who tricked her into a room full of khat-chewing party goers; and how her long awaited sweetheart had burst in on her in there!

Again, the tears began to flow. Once more the little girl, Faadumo, took on the role of an elder sister, consoling the distressed Maana. Hearing the cause of Maana's tears renewed the feelings of pain she had suffered at the hands of Beyddan.

Faadumo stayed for the few remaining hours of darkness helping Maana to wait for the dawn. At daybreak, Maana kissed Faadumo on both cheeks and walked away. As the sun began to creep over the horizon, she reached the house with the ancient door. Hiding her grief-reddened eyes with her head scarf, she gave the door a hard knock, hoping to awaken her sister to tell her all.

Leyla came to the door but did not bother to allow her sister to speak. Once she laid eyes on her she began to unload her disgust on her.

"I don't want to see your face, you slut, alcoholic, addict. Go back to wherever the hell you came from. I don't want to see you anywhere near me ever again," she fired off, and slammed the door in Maana's face.

Poor, tired Maana sat in front of the closed door and wept. She did not know how long she had been there when a thought finally came to mind. "I could catch Axmed at his home before he goes to work," she whispered to herself. Before arriving at her sister's doorstep, she had hoped that Leyla could mediate and convince Axmed about what had actually transpired during the night. Now that that hope was lost, she could not count on anyone but herself. She advised herself to get on her knees and beg for Axmed's mercy.

III

Throughout the entire night, Axmed did not close his eyes. Fully clothed, he wandered back and forth between his bed and the couch until daybreak. As the morning sun rose, and hours before his usual time to be picked up for work, he left home and walked over to the company van pickup spot.

Seated alone on a bench, he debated with himself about what to do with Maana. One thing had become clear; his memories of her had become more vivid and more deeply entrenched in his brain the harder he tried to forget about her. Suddenly, he looked up and there she was, Maana herself, walking toward him. He shivered as though bolts of electricity were shooting through his body. Goosebumps popped out on him. His larynx locked and his lungs refused to receive needed air. He felt paralyzed but could not tell whether it was excitement, sadness, anger, or fear. He had no idea how to react and had little time to think.

Too many ideas collided in his mind for a second, canceling the other. The love he felt for her in his heart was pulling him one way and pride the other. Love pleaded with him with, *I cannot exist another minute without her. It is a blessing that she has come home to me. I should run to her and envelop her in a much-deserved hug.* But as he motioned to move, he was arrested by his pride. *That same Maana was in the middle of that disgraceful, debauched khat party. I don't want to have anything more to do with her.*

Pride overpowered the bleeding heart of love. As though possessed by the devil, Axmed turned his face, stood up, and walked away.

Maana watched as he turned and walked away from her. Crying out and running after him, she pleaded, "My sweetheart, I beg you to please listen to me for a moment!" The sound of her cry licked his heart like the lurking heat of the sun's rays. Especially piercing was the word "sweetheart." The rest of her plea melted his heart. As the power of words of love began to pull him towards her, the company van arrived.

At the sight of the van, the whimsical wheel of his pride took over and he raced over into the revving beast. But just before stepping in, he turned around and with a feeble voice said, "Don't follow me. I don't know you. Go to Siinay. Find someone who knows you there and have a *khat* party with them! You know that isn't me." With those words, he disappeared into the belly of the van.

Maana was left in a cloud of dust. This, she thought, was the worst moment of her life. She had lost her last ray of hope. She could not shed another tear, and she had no idea what to do next or where to go. Who could she lean on? She was already out of her parents' house. Her sister Leyla had slammed her door in her face that morning. And her love, the man she had sacrificed it all for, including her marriage and her family, had just walked away from her. Painful were the words of war he waged against her. She kept repeating to herself, 'Don't follow me. I don't know you. Go to Siinay. Find someone who knows you there and have a khat party with them. You know that isn't me!"

Minutes later, Maana found herself inside a pharmacy. Her life was over! There was no future.

"Hello, do you sell insecticides?" she asked the pharmacist.

"Yes," he said. Looking back at the shelf, he grabbed an item as she looked around. She realized that she did not have her purse with her. She panicked and ran out before the pharmacist had turned around. She had to find her purse. She hurried back to where she last had it. She remembered that she did not have it when she was with Axmed. She was not sure where she last had it but thought that she might have left it in that hell house she had run out of.

She guessed that Beyddan, with her evil schemes, must have deliberately hidden it. The money to purchase the clothes was in it. Normally, the most valuable thing in her purse was Axmed's picture. At this moment, though, the money was more important. Without money she could not get the poison to end her suffering.

IV

That Thursday morning, when the others in the household awoke earlier, Beyddan slept in. She had gone to bed late, and now it was mid-morning. She rose out of bed, worried. The first question that came into her mind was whether or not Maana was still in her trap. *That bird might have escaped. What if she is gone? What made me oversleep?* She chided herself.

Now fully awake and alert, she tore over to the veranda where she had last seen Maana. She looked all around. Nothing. No one was there. "Hey, Faadumo," she yelled with heightened alarm.

Beyddan recalled that she left a saddened and grieving Maana-faay on the veranda. She had gone to bed with the intent of waking up early in the morning, all the while keeping Maana in her grasp until she could be delivered to her customer. That was the only thing she cared about. She just wanted to execute a promissory transaction. She knew that she had earned every cent she had demanded, and perhaps there was a bonus for her also. *From here on,* she had told herself, *she is going to be his responsibility.*

She ruefully reminded herself that had she been awakened early she would have had enough tricks in her to keep Maana-faay in custody. Now, the young lady for whom she had been laying the trap the entire week was not in her hands. And the man to whom she was to deliver her was due to arrive tonight.

"Hey, Faadumo," she yelled again, "Where is the devil-little-girl with the ugly hips? Where are you?" she shouted, taking her woes out on the innocent child.

"I am here," said Faadumo, coming out of the kitchen.

"Where is that female?"

And though "female" was not a name, Faadumo knew who she was asking about.

"She left," said Faadumo.

"Did you say she left? How could she leave? Who told her to leave? When did she leave?" Beyddan let out. "Where did she go? 'She left; she left' is not the word you should tell me. Why didn't you wake me up? What were you doing, you-the-hungry-cat-look-alike?" she attacked the child.

Why did the little girl deserve all that verbal abuse? She did not know. She had not been told to do a thing about what the courtesan was blaming on her. She neither made Maana leave, nor was she told to notify anybody if and when Maana was to depart. Faadumo, the little girl, debated with herself but did not let Beyddan hear her. She had learned from the past that talking back to her would cost a day's and at times a whole week's wages. So, she swallowed her pain, hung her head low, and pleaded guilty to whatever she was being accused of.

Beyddan remained in a bad mood for the rest of the morning. She knew the blame did not lie with Faadumo, yet she could not help but berate her. She felt dreadful that the prized young lady had slipped through her fingers. She worried about how to tell Jaamac-dhegey that the plan had been aborted. *Where am I going to find Maana-faay? She is probably at her sister Leyla's house, the same Leyla who came to know all about me last night*, she thought. *Forget about going to Leyla's place. I'll be lucky if her whole clan doesn't show up at my doorstep to beat me up*, she said to herself.

Beyddan felt that the red house had become an object of associative guilt. She was acutely aware of both her culpability and her incapability: culpability because of how she had lured Maana into her trap; incapability because she had failed to deliver Maana-faay to Jaamac-dhegey. The information he was going to seek from her, as well as the trouble she was in with Maana's family, gnawed at her equally. So, she ran out of her house again to hide in a neighbor's home. She left Faadumo with detailed instructions that she should tell no one where she had gone. She further instructed her to say nothing either on the telephone or in person. If any other business should develop, Faadumo was to report to her. She needed time to think about the failed promised goods to her client Jaamac.

The only hope she had in hand was that Maana-faay's purse was with her, and she took that with her.

Secluded at her neighbor's house who was harassing her with useless chatter, Beyddan saw Faadumo walk in a few minutes later.

"Hey, you, why are you here? Has something happened?" she asked the little girl with her usual stern stare.

"The young lady is back and..."

"Say what? She is back? Are you sure?" Beyydan interrupted with excitement.

"Yes, for sure," she said...

"What did she say?"

"She said, 'Ask Beyddan if she has seen my purse'."

"Who is with her?"

"No one."

Nothing was more important to Beyddan than hearing that "no one" was with her. She collected herself and rushed out of the door.

She found Maana waiting on the veranda. Beyydan began trying to sweet-talk her. "Hello, my sweet 'niece'. I am so sorry about what happened last night. What I don't like about your generation is that they don't take the time to think things over. Unfortunately, I was not here when the young man walked in. I had taken a walk with a guest, but our paths did cross on his way out. He was so mad that you would think he was possessed by the devil. He would not talk to me. I said to him, 'Don't be childish, calm down and listen to me. Don't defame that angelic young lady. Everyone here would attest to her decency. Don't defame her. You have been mistaken.'

"He finally said, 'I am so out of it today that I'm unable to hear a thing you say. Come and see me at my office tomorrow. We can talk then.' So, I am going to see him as we speak. I am going to convince him that he was wrong. I am going to scold him, letting him know that he should do right by you and buy you gold. Or else I will have nothing to do with him! He usually hears me out. He owes me, for I did a lot of favors for him. I can promise you that tonight or this afternoon he will be here trying to right his wrong. You, on the other hand, should rest, have a cold drink, and eat some lunch. You will not be disturbed. You understand? And if I stand up for... Hey you-the-little-one, bring sweets and cold drinks to my baby here. Woe is me, woe is me! See how tired you look. See how …"

"Listen to me," Maan-faay interrupted her, "I don't need your lunch or your cold drinks, I will never again set foot in your house. I've had enough. Just do me a favor, give me my purse, nothing else." At the beginning she had let Beyydan chatter on, although she was practically burning inside, especially when Beyydan talked about Axmed. Finally, when Beyydan tried to sweet-talk her, Maana cut her off.

"No, my daughter, you misunderstand me. I just want to wash off what happened to you last night and deliver that young man into your hands."

"No, no, I don't want to be at your house. You put me through enough already. You cost me my sister, who threw me out of her home, though I did nothing to deserve it."

Her sister throws her out and she is homeless out there for you? How great is that? thought Beyydan. But aloud she went on to say in a sincere-sounding voice, "My daughter, don't be childish. I am going to trouble myself for your well-being. There is no one I would like to see succeed more than you. What happened last night was an unfortunate accident. You came to me only to purchase some new clothing. The problems now have all but passed. Don't worry. Say your prayers to shoo Satan away. I have saved the clothes for you and will give you a big discount to right the wrong. Don't worry. I promise you that I will bring both your sister and the young man into your hands today. They will both apologize to you when they realize that they were wrong. Their perception was wrong, and I will correct them. I also saved your purse for you. I feared it was going to be stolen. If you don't like this noisy house, I can take you to my niece's place to rest. She is great. She lives alone, and you will see no one else. Your eyes will appreciate the beautiful villa and the lush gardens surrounding it. Once you meet my niece, you won't want to leave. You can wait for me there until I bring you news from your sister and that young man. My niece will take care of all your needs: breakfast, lunch, and music that will erase all your worries. Just take a seat here for a minute, drink some Fanta while I get your purse. I am going to call your sister, too," Beyydan ordered.

Maana dropped her exhausted body down onto a nearby chair. She thought she needed to rest to sort out all the misery that Beyydan had put her through. She was worried and knew she had nowhere to go. She was angry at Beyydan and disgusted with the intemperate behavior of her group, but still could not figure out how she had been tricked into participating in last night's charade.

Beyydan scurried into her room to make an immediate phone call to Jaamac-dhegey. Her fingers quickly flew over the numbers. At the other end of the line, Jaamac was in his office ranting and raving at some of his employees. He could hear the phone ringing but did not bother to attend to it. Irritated, he finally picked up the receiver with an exaggerated air while still carrying on his tirade.

"Hello," he said with agitation. He briefly listened to the caller on the other end, then surprised the people around him when he changed his tone.

"How are you, Beyydan? Wait a second," he interrupted himself, covering the receiver with his hand, "Could you do this for me? I have too many things that need my immediate attention now. Come back in an hour," he said to the others around him. "Shut the door behind you, and don't let anybody in," he ordered his secretary. He quickly returned to his call.

"Please excuse me. I was trying to finish up with a group here. I am glad you called. Give me the good news, Ma'am. I was just thinking to pick up the phone. I wanted to call you about tonight's plan and where you are with things. But then I have the utmost confidence that whatever Beyydan takes on will be executed in time. I just wanted to know what time I should arrive. So, tell me, you are doing fine, right?"

"Listen, let's get right down to business," said Beyydan, riffling through a notepad. "The plan is on."

"Tell me. I knew it was going to happen, but how did you do it?"

"The strategy was successful. All was executed according to the plan."

"*Bravo* to you!"

"The boy she was in love with, the one I told you about, took his suitcase with him last night. In other words, I got him out of the way. That dazzling young lady is out there for you to claim."

"Do you swear she is in your hands?" asked Jaamac-dhegey excitedly.

"She is in my house at this very minute. I am whispering so that she cannot hear us."

"I would have shaken your hand if I were with you. I can attest to the fact that you are one tough lady."

"She is in our corral. And I also severed the relationship between her and her sister. Her sister threw her out. God forgive us! I want you to have a small, secluded, secret 'wedding'. Then she is yours until you get your fill of that energizing vitamin—Maana-faay."

'Feri, gud [very good], Feri gud, it's what I expected of you."

"I told you, I will do as I promise. I have been working for you all along. I would not have done this for anyone else. I swear, even if it meant I would lose my first-born," Beyydan claimed.

Jaamac, laughing, almost said, *how unfortunate your first-born would be, if he only existed for your swearing!*

He did not say it aloud, of course, but he went on in the same hypocritical way, "You don't have to swear, Ma'am. I know, and I have been waiting for you. I will compensate you accordingly. Let me hear the details of the 'wedding' plans again."

"Is the Green Villa ready for us?" she asked.

"Several green villas are ready for us."

"My plan for you is to have your little 'wedding' there!" Beyydan said.

"That part is finalized," confirmed Jaamac.

"Now, there are two tiny issues that need your attention. Leave the rest to me: labor and expenses," she said.

"Labor and expenses? Tell me what you need. I am ready," he responded.

"I am not going to bother you with the little details. I am aware that one has to be easy on a 'groom-to-be' because his major task will be waiting for him later in bed…"

They both laughed.

"All teasing aside, you need to order the Green Villa employees to be on standby. Call them, tell them to welcome the lady who will be arriving and to prepare a good lunch for her."

"Don't worry, I will do that."

"I told her that she was going to have lunch with my niece. So, my plan is to send one of my girls ahead of her to welcome her as though she is my niece. That same one will entertain Maana until she feels safe and at ease. She is sad and frightened. After all, she is very young. You understand me, right?"

"Yes, I do."

"You and one of your friends should stay inside the villa, but don't show yourself until sunset. We will plan the rest together. I can't tell you all over the phone, but I will come by your office shortly. Now call the villa. Oh, and I need a car to pick me up," Beyydan said.

"OK."

"Hand some tip over to the driver for me so that I can care for the working girls' needs, and leave the rest of the cost to me."

"Sure. You take care of the rest," he let pass through his lips. *What other cost is she referring to? She is going to bankrupt me. And why is she lying about the poor young ladies? I know they will never receive a penny of whatever she makes off me. Nevermind. Go for it, for I am in your trap today,* he said to himself.

While Beyydan was on the phone, Faadumo was lurking in the next room, leaning on the wall that separates the two rooms. Word for word, she overheard all that Beyydan had said. When she left, Faadumo came out of hiding.

Every word she had heard pained her like an open sore. Earlier she had been confused about what exactly Beyydan was intending to do with Maana. Now she had just heard the whole plot. It became clear to her that Maana-faay was in grave danger.

It occurred to her that whatever happened last night that had caused Maana so much grief was nothing in comparison to what was in the plan. *Someone should warn the poor creature about the Green Villa. She needs to be warned. She should be told to cut her losses and run. I should do that before the madam comes back out,* Faadumo thought.

Faadumo looked around, then dashed out like a thief running for her life after her first heist. But before she reached Maana-faay, she heard the voice she hated behind her.

"You, Faadumo."

Faadumo froze. A bullet would have been much easier to bear than Beyydan's voice. It seemed like she was reading her mind. She expected her to say, "I know where you're going and why you're going."

How did she know my secret thoughts? She felt dizzy, the earth spun around her, and she almost fainted. She expected Beyydan to say, "You lurked around in order to take my secret out and share it? I should slit your throat!"

"You, go and get me some items from the corner store," she heard her say. Faadumo sighed with relief.

Walking to the corner store, she began to think about a way to warn Maana. She hoped to gain a little time while Beyydan was busy organizing the Green Villa for the man she was talking to and the young lady who was going to be sent ahead of Maana.

The plan would have worked had Faadumo gotten back in time. But the corner store was farther than she thought. She had to walk a bit longer than she had calculated. While she was away, the car came, took Beyydan, picked up Saynab from a neighboring house, and then returned for Maana. When Faadumo got back home they were all gone.

On their way to the Green Villa, Beyydan cozied up to Maana-faay, leaned on her shoulder, and began to pat her back and sweet-talk her.

V

That Tuesday and Wednesday, Sahra Yuusuf was busy, correcting a pile of exam papers. She did not have time to think about Maana-faay or anyone else. On Thursday after breakfast, she decided to find out about her friend, who she hoped would soon be her cousin-in-law. She picked up the telephone and called Leyla for an update.

"Good morning. May I speak to Nurse Leyla Xaaji Muumin, please?" asked Sahra.

"Sister, she is in surgery assisting a physician and can't be reached."

"Ok," she said and hung up. She picked up the receiver again and dialed another.

"Good morning. Is this the Glass Factory? Could you please tell me if Axmed the Engineer is back from Jilib?"

"Yes, Sister. He came back yesterday, but today he wasn't feeling well. He took the rest of the day off!" said the voice on the other end of the phone.

"Thanks," said Sahra and hung up.

She was glad that Axmed was back. She hoped that he could take the load of responsibility off her. She reached an immediate decision on her own. *I have to do a lot this afternoon. I should see both Maana and Axmed, about their marriage plans, and bring him up to speed. The whole matter should be expedited. There should be no more delays. We should introduce Maana to Axmed's family. My uncle will be pleased with her personal value and beauty. From today on, she should be known as a Jaamc-dhegey family member. Her parents will eventually come around. Love will conquer all.* All day long Sahra worked on that plan, adding and subtracting.

****

At four in the afternoon, Axmed was awakened by a persistent knocking on the door. The banging bothered him, for he did not plan to see a soul. He neither wanted to see nor talk to anybody. He left his work earlier for that reason. As a matter of fact, he did not make a single stop on his way home, not even for lunch, but came straight home just to be alone. The sadness he was wallowing in, the sleepless night that followed his horrific encounter with Maana, the agonizing dawn, and the arguing back and forth with himself had taken a toll on his well-being and killed his appetite. He felt lightheaded and dizzy.

He was in bed, but he had been unable to sleep for the past two days when he heard the knocking at the door. His heart pounding in his chest, he rose from the bed.

It must be her. She is back, he thought. Anxiety took over him and his heart beat faster. He felt light like a feather as though his spirit were returning. *What do I do? Why didn't I think about this before she arrived? I was not expecting her,* his thoughts ran fast. The knocking intensified.

"Axmed, it's me, your sister," a female voice called out.

Nevermind. It is not her. It's Sahra Yuusuf. What does she want from me?

He felt gloom gathering but had no place to hide. He forced himself to open the door. She walked in, hugged him, and kissed him on the cheeks.

"Hi, Axmed. How are you? I am happy for your safe return," she went on with genuine excitement. She pulled her shawl and her purse off her and took a seat. As she began to talk, she sensed that Axmed did not share her lightheartedness. She took a careful look at him. His facial expression was flat, and his eyes were red and buried deep within. She suddenly felt sad for him.

"Brother, Axmed, are you sick?" she asked, concerned.

"I am not well," he warned.

"In God's name, what happened to you? Oh, I am so slow! I called your office and was told that you had left," she said. "What is the matter, brother? Have you seen a doctor?"

"I am not sure what else to tell you, Sahra, but I am not well."

When he realized that she would just keep on questioning him, he thought it better to calm her down.

"No, sweetie. It isn't that type of illness. It is fatigue from the trip and all. How about just telling me about yourself?"

"I am well. My only problem was brought about by your absence. Now that you are here, all is going to be well. The minute you left, a bit of trouble arose. It wasn't the right time for you to leave."

"What happened?" he asked.

"Did you see Maana last night?" she asked.

Axmed hesitated, cupped his hands to his face, paused, and finally said, "Listen, Sahra, if you value me as your cousin, you won't mention that lady's name again. Don't let me hear it."

Sahra put her hand on her mouth and said, "What is this, my cousin? What happened? Maana's issue is what I came to see you for. What is the matter, tell me!"

"I am not going into it. You are the one who brought her to me before you made sure you knew who she was. You hung her around my neck. You brought about the problem I am dealing with. If you keep on talking about her, I am going to leave," he warned.

The biting incrimination angered Sahra.

"Just tell me what is up with you? What did I hang around your neck? You were crazy about her! And you are paying me back by saying that I brought a problem to you? What is the problem that I hung around your neck?"

"What problem is bigger..." he jumped in, defensive, "than lying here blinded by love? Why do I have to be tethered to a woman who uses *khat* and parties with men all night long?"

"What are you talking about? Are you saying that the Maana Xaaji Muumin that I know chews *khat* with men?" she asked, incredulous.

"Who else do you think that I am talking about?"

"Did the useless street people have you believing that nonsense?"

"The street people have me believing nothing. I am talking to you about what I have seen with my own eyes."

"What have you seen with your own eyes?"

"I saw the saintly woman you are talking about sitting in the midst of a *khat*-chewing party with men. As a matter of fact, they were feeding her when I walked in on them. And she had some in her hands. Is that enough proof for you?" he asked.

In disbelief, she put her hands over her mouth again and looked at him as though trying to make sure that the person talking to her was her cousin Axmed Jaamac. "Woe is me. Our boy has lost his mind! Brother, are you psychotic, or sane? You are right. You are sick! You are out of it. Let me take you to the mental health service," said Sahra, taking her hands off her mouth.

"We will find out which one of us is sick. Now do me a favor and stop reminding me of her."

She knew better than to shut him off. And though she knew that he was not one to lie, she made him tell her what had happened step by step, starting with Kulmiye's report, then to Ciise's phone call. He told her about the fat woman who had come to see him in his office with "the news"; the directions she gave him to get to her brothel; what he did when he got there and what he did when he came to his place in the morning. Finally, he told her about encountering Maana at the brothel and what her reaction was when she saw him and how he cold-heartedly rejected her.

Befuddled, Sahra alternated putting her hands over her face and on her head. Silent, she weighed all parts of the alarming story she had just heard. She could not fathom the faults he listed and could not map any of this out to a logical end.

Suddenly, she clapped her hands and said, "No, Axmed. That couldn't have happened. Never. Tell me anything else. I am not saying your story isn't true, but there has to be something else at work here. This matter needs thorough examination!"

"You are telling me that I am psychotic, right?" asked Axmed, incredulously. "Trusting a young lady of today and giving her my heart was a mistake. I had been warned about women and their schemes, but I did not heed the advice. I deserved whatever happened to me. I have to admit that Kulmiye has more experience than I have. He was right when he said, 'Don't give your heart to the young ladies of today. You just sleep with them for two nights and then tell them to take a walk.'"

"I am so disappointed in you. You allowed Kulmiye and his kind to tell you how to treat young women and you accepted that as a life lesson?" asked Sahra in disbelief.

"His 'lies' were closer to the truth than the rhapsody of virtues that you read to me when you introduced me to her. Before you begin preaching to me, don't you see how wrong you are?"

"I am still in disbelief," Sahra said.

"What is so hard to believe?"

"That Maana cheated on you and that she did what you purported that she did," she responded.

"Whether you believe it or not, that was what she did. So, I have had no choice but to revisit Kulmiye's teachings that I had refused to put to use: that I should not trust women and that I should cross out any plans of ever wedding a decent one! If the same Maana that I had thought was an angel turned out to be this cheat, would another angel drop from the sky?"

"Listen to me," Sahra said with deliberate intonation, "You are wrong reaching such a hasty conclusion. Last night you reacted fast, this morning you acted like a child, and now you are irrational! You need to calm down. Anything can be said by many. But you need to verify the facts before you take it all at face value. I know Maana well," she went on, "I know what is possible of her and what isn't. If there is anything wrong, it's because she gave herself to you, Axmed. She isn't able to see anything else, let alone cheat on you or date another. If you leave her, I am quite certain that she will have no desire to live. You will regret your decision later."

"Just last week she did what no peers of hers would have dared to do. It is the reason why I came to talk to you this afternoon. But you are delaying us with your floodgates of fictional issues."

"What did she do?" Axmed asked.

Sahra went on to tell him about the weddings that had been planned in Xamar-weyne and were now ruined because of him. She told him all that had happened while he was away: the fight between Maana and her family; the other wedding that was tied to hers that had also been canceled; that Maana herself had been disowned by her parents; that she had been looking all over for him; and that Leyla fought with her; now Maana was all alone, crying for him.

"Now my brother, I swear to God," Sahra continued, "all that I have told you about her, where she has been and what she has been doing in your absence, inch by inch, step by step and hour by hour is true. Well, except for last night and the night before. How can I believe that she was at a *geerashayn*? When and how did she find the time and desire? Are you telling me that she became a different person overnight? That does not make sense. Something else is going on that we need to get to the bottom of," Sahra concluded.

She quieted down and looked at him. She was trying to read his face, wondering if anything she had said was having any effect on him. When it occurred to her that he was thinking about it, she went on. "Did you ask yourself, who the hell is this woman who gave you all this information? Did you ask yourself, 'How could you trust a woman that you did not know?' Did you ask yourself what was in it for her when she paid for a taxi to see you? Was she doing this out of the goodness of her heart? How did she know what was going to happen that night if she had not planned it herself ahead of time?"

Axmed tried not to answer her questions and looked away. He began debating with himself, though he pretended not to hear. In fact, he did hear. He was fully aware of what he saw last night, and he was too angry. He was trying to answer to himself first. The news puzzled him, and like colliding ocean waves, it confused him. The hardest of all was that the weddings in Xamar-weyne had been brought to a halt. The questions about Beyydan that Sahra addressed to him confused him. Half of him wanted to indict Maana, and the other half wanted to defend her. Half of him accused himself of rushing to judgement, and the other half supported his decisive act. He began to regret that he hadn't posed these questions to Maana.

Sahra surmised that he was trying to sieve the facts from the fog of fiction.

Now it's best to prepare for what's next, Sahra said softly to herself. But the responsibility she had sworn to bear was vexing her. She had to use her time well. She looked at Axmed, then at her wristwatch. "I am going to leave now, and I want you to know where I am going. I am going to find Maana. And when I find..."

"Are you going to find her for me?" Axmed interrupted her, "I know you aren't for me."

"Wait, hear me out. Don't be childish!" Sahra berated him. "I am going to her sister Leyla's house. I hope she is there. I am going to talk to her, and I will do my own fact-finding. I am going to get to the bottom of this, then I will come back to you. Just promise me one thing: that I will find you home when I get back."

"That I will do for you," he responded nonchalantly.

"OK. See you later," she said but was already out the door.

Outside, she hailed a taxi. "Please take me to Boondheere."

CHAPTER ELEVEN

I

A t 5:35 p.m. Ciise-dheere and his wife, Leyla, were standing in the middle of their bedroom. Leyla, who wanted her husband to look his best, was busily engaged in helping him dress. She was dusting off his shirt with her open hand, although there was nothing on it. She looked him over to see if she had left a button undone and then straightened his collar as well as the sleeves on his shirt one more time. She checked his shoes again, the same shoes she herself had already polished; groomed the same hair she had already combed; and sprayed a touch more cologne onto him. When she was sure that nothing had been left undone, she admired him with an affectionate smile.

Ciise thought that her message meant, "Honey, I am done adorning you." Smiling back at her, he said, "Thanks, honey." He kissed her below the ear. Looking at each other with admiration, Leyla bent down closer. She buried herself in his chest and whispered into his neck, "I love you, honey." As though they were newlyweds, their lips met, and electricity surged through their bodies.

A few moments later, Leyla gently pulled away and renewed her inspection of his attire. When that was complete, Ciise opened the door. Husband and wife walked out of the bedroom together. Today was a day of leisure for both. On the days when Ciise was not at work, when Leyla did not assign him household chores, he usually would go downtown to socialize with his friends. But not today.

Taking a few steps out the door, Ciise was missing something. He paused, turned around, looked at his wife, and asked, "Hey, Honey, where is Maana? I have not seen her around all afternoon!"

The question startled her. For one, she did not want to hear Maana's name. Second, she did not want her husband to know about what a "disgrace" her sister had become. But lying to him was not an option.

"I don't want to hear or talk about that dirty young lady," she snapped.

"What happened? Where did she go?" Ciise asked suspiciously. He walked back to his wife.

"That one is a loss," she tried to deflect his concerns but knew that she was not convincing.

Ciise had come home late last night, gone to work early in the morning, returned late in the afternoon for lunch, and then took his afternoon siesta. So, he had only noticed now that he had not seen his sister-in-law around the house. He turned back to the house and called his wife to update him.

Leyla, who needed little cajoling, poured out all she knew. What she reported puzzled him. It angered him too that she had thrown her own sister out into the street.

"Leyla, I thought you were wiser and more patient than that!"

"What is the matter with you? Do you want me to let her in when she has been sleeping around with men, chewing khat? I will not have that kind of woman in my house. Let her get lost..."

"No, Leyla," Ciise countered, "Honey, your mistakes are piling up as we speak. First of all, why was that courtesan in our house? Second, it was wrong of you to send Maana alone to that woman's house. You should have told the woman to bring whatever she was selling here."

"Did I know who that woman was and what business she was in? I was only told about her last night...!" Leyla interjected.

"And then you left her in that house. That was the third and biggest mistake of all, a major mistake. The last straw was when you turned her away this morning. Turning a young girl out onto the streets is the worst blunder a parent can make. Putting a young lady in jeopardy by leaving her to the mercy of the streets because of a brief lapse in judgment would destroy her self-worth. Isn't that the cruelest act of all? Where is she now?"

"I don't know," Leyla said. "Maybe she is at Sahra's place. She doesn't have anywhere else to go."

"That could be the one place. She doesn't know anywhere else to go," Ciise agreed. You need to find her, Leyla. If nothing else, it would have been wise this morning to ask her what happened to her last night instead of throwing her out. By the way, Axmed Jaamac is back. I spoke with him on the phone yesterday, and he is probably on his way to our house right now. What are we going to tell him?" Ciise asked.

"That is the worst part. She disgraced us in front of a decent, respectable guy. I know he is back. He was here last night, too. He came here thinking that there was a respectable woman waiting for him. And now you are telling me that he is on his way here tonight again. What am I going to tell him? That young lady is disgracing us, but most of all she is disgracing the... "

Before she could finish, they heard a knock on the door and a voice called out, "Permission to enter?"

"Granted," Leyla responded and walked over to the door. Sahra stepped in from the veranda. Seeing Sahra made Leyla angrier. She felt she should lunge at her with, "that loser has sent you to sweet-talk me. I suppose she is waiting outside. It would have been better if she had come in herself." But then she forced herself to say, "Hello, Sahra, are you well?"

"I am. What about you?"

"We are fine." Walking into the living room, Leyla pointed to the couch and said, "Please take a seat."

Ciise walked into the room, too, greeted Sahra, and joined them. As he and Sahra began idly chatting, Leyla went to the kitchen to fetch cool drinks.

"Sahra, we have not seen you in a while. Why? What brings you here today?

"It's that-one-who-sent-you-to-sweet-talk me, right? She sent you?" Leyla asked, returning from the kitchen.

"Who is That-one?"

"That-one is the so-called Maana!"

"I have not seen Maana. Did you send her to me?" Sahra asked. "Maybe we passed each other on the way, but I haven't seen her."

"Are you serious? She didn't come looking for you?" Leyla asked, now worried.

"No. I haven't seen her. The day before yesterday to be exact was when I last saw her. Was she supposed to be at my place?" she asked, looking at Leyla and Ciise.

Leyla and Ciise looked at each other. "Well, where in the world is she?" Ciise asked.

"I don't know, maybe she is with Axmed," responded Leyla in a hushed tone, trying not to let Sahra hear her.

"No," Sahra, who heard her, said. "She isn't with Axmed. I just came from his place."

"What? She isn't with Axmed either?" she looked at Ciise.

Ciise reacted, "Why are you looking at me? You are the one to be blamed! You gave her no choice but to be out on the streets!"

"What is going on?" asked a puzzled Sahra.

Ciise pinched Leyla under the table between them. Leyla thought that he was asking her not to say a thing about the "disgraceful" person Maana had turned into. After all, Sahra was Axmed's cousin.

"Not much, but Leyla fought with Maana this morning," he said to Sahra.

A light went on for Sahra. She made the connection between Axmed's argument with her and Leyla's fight with Maana. She sensed that both Leyla and Ciise were holding something back. *I have to share what I know with them, and they have to tell me what they know. So, the truth is out,* thought Sahra.

"What brought about the fight? Was it what was said about last night?" asked Sahra, trying to slightly raise the veil and hoping they would reveal the rest.

As she expected, Leyla jumped in with, "You mean, what was said to have happened?" She did not look surprised posing the question. She figured that what she was trying to hide was not much of a secret after all.

"The news that Maana was found in a house of disrepute in Boondheere. Is there anything else?" Sahra asked.

With that, Leyla began to recount all she knew. She thought that she had to come clean with Sahra to preserve the trust between them. Secondly, she wanted to shift the blame away from herself. So, she let it all out. She started from the first night that Beyydan Shabeel had come to her house and snared them with her clothes-for-sale scam. She went on to tell them how the next night she had allowed Maana to go unaccompanied to Beyydan's house, and that when Maana did not return, she went out to retrieve her. It was while she was in search of Beyydan's house that she ran into Xaawo, who knew of Beyydan and her reputation. Xaawo knew that Beyydan was a madam who owned a brothel. She agreed to take Leyla to the brothel, where they found Maana among a group of *khat*-chewing men and young women. Finally, she related how, in her anger, she thought that Maana was drunk and left her there, and when Maana returned in the morning, she had refused to let her in her house.

Quite disturbed, Sahra began to share what Axmed had told her. "I think what Axmed told me this morning is true. He said, 'Anything is possible about a human being.' But Maana, after all, might not have done all of what she is being accused of...."

"So, what have you heard, Sahra?" Leyla interrupted her.

"I saw Axmed, who said that he had gone to Boondheere and found her in that house."

"What? At Beyydan's?" Leyla shouted in dismay.

But before Sahra could respond, Ciise jumped in, "How did he know to go there in the first place?"

"He told me that yesterday a heavy-set woman had come to his office and told him about how Maana had been lost to the streets. She told him that if he wanted to verify what she was telling him about Maana he should come to see it for himself. He did not believe her at first. But when he could not find Maana, he went to the place he was told she would be and found her in that disgraceful place: the brothel. He also said that Maana came to his place this morning, possibly after leaving the brothel and he too like Leyla, had turned her away."

"Yes," said Ciise, shaking his head. "I understand the chess game being played here! I understand the whole thing now. It's all a plot that Beyydan Shabeel concocted."

"Yeeeeeeeeeeeeeeees," jumped in Leyla, as though awakened from sleep. "I get it, I get it. Why, I recall a night ago that the same woman, Beyydan, tried to turn Maana against Axmed. When that didn't work, she switched to making up stories and lies."

"Ha-ha, so she is the same person who gave Axmed the directions to her brothel," said Sahra.

"Who else? None other than Beyydan Shabeel!" followed Ciise. "The whole thing is a chain that she linked together."

"She should be in hell," Leyla let out.

"Look how poor Maana has been wronged," Sahra bewailed.

"But if she were so innocent, what was she doing in the middle of a group of people drinking alcohol and chewing khat?" Leyla asked, trying to deflect blame from herself.

"We can't fault poor Maana unless we figure out what happened!" Ciise said. "She is the only one who can tell us what happened, but you fought with her before asking her a single question. Anything is possible. She could have been deceived, she could have been drugged, which is a common trick that those filthy women employ to break young ladies. She could have been lying there unconscious after being drugged or forced to drink alcohol, but you left her with predators. And when she came to you for help, you turned her away."

"My God! How can I find her now?" Leyla cried out.

"'How can I find her now? How can I find her?'" Ciise mocked her.

"I don't know where to find her. I just need to lay my eyes on her. I am afraid Maana may not be alive by now! Even if she is, there is no doubt she is not safe. Woe is me, woe is me!" wailed Leyla, attacked all at once with guilt, worry and regret. Changing her tune, she began to bawl.

"Look, now she is crying!" Ciise said.

"When Axmed finds out about all of this, he is going to be in worse shape than Leyla. What exactly was that old woman trying to gain with this elaborate scheme?" wondered Sahra.

"It is an age-old trick that women of her kind use. When they see a young couple in a loving relationship, it's an affront to their line of work. So, when they come upon a beautiful single young woman, they try to snare her, selling her off to an older man. They first have to demean and destroy her honor in order to bring her out into the street life. Many times they are successful. It is a lucrative business for them. Those are the telltale signs of..."

A knock on the door interrupted Ciise. "Come in!" he responded.

A haggard little girl wearing a threadbare *guntiino*, two different flip-flops for the same foot, and no shawl hurried in. With a worried look, Leyla ran to her. The little girl was covered in soot, sweating and panting, and trying to catch her breath. At first Ciise thought that she was running from an angry parent's corporal cruelty. Leyla looked at her, thinking, *where have I seen this dark, sinewy little girl before?* She was sure she had run into her somewhere.

"Hello, my child. What is going on?" Leyla asked.

Still panting and now with six eyes fixed on her, the little girl looked at each person and asked, "Who is Leyla Xaaji Muumin?"

"It is I," Leyla responded panicked.

"Do you have a sister by the name of Maana?" the little girl asked.

"Yes," blurted out Leyla, further alarmed.

Sahra jumped up from her seat and said, "Woe is me, my little girl, where is she?"

Leyla was extremely worried about what this girl might say next. *Maana what? She's dead? She was run over by a car? She was kidnapped by criminals? Why on earth did I turn her away this morning?* All these questions flashed through her mind in a second.

Ciise, who was emotionally in a better position than the others, took over.

"Come closer, my child," he began. "Sit down. Tell me, where did you see Maana?"

"That poor girl is going to be in trouble tonight. Some people are planning to gang up on her. If you care about her, you better be quick to rescue her!"

"Wow," sighed Leyla with relief. "Thank God, she is alive…!"

"Wait, Leyla," Ciise interrupted her. "What is your name, dear?"

"Faadumo, The-little-one."

"Faadumo who?"

"Faadumo Aw-Madoobe."

"Sure. So where did you run from? Do you live in the neighborhood?"

"I work for a madam named Beyydan Shabeel."

Hearing the name Beyydan Shabeel sent shivers through their spines. They looked at each other.

"I hope she burns in hell," said Sahra.

"Yes, I recognize you now," let out Leyla. "You are the smart little girl who helped us last night. Faadumo, right?"

"Yes," said the little girl.

"Go on, tell us what is happening," urged Leyla.

After eavesdropping on Beyydan's telephone conversation, Faadumo had been wondering how she could warn Maana about the danger she was going to be in. But she had not found an opportunity to tell her so. Beyydan had busied her with chores.

When she last saw Beyydan putting Maana into a car, she knew what the plan was and where she was taking her. Worried and fearful for her, she decided that she had to find Maana's sister and tell her all that she knew.

Again, after darkness had descended, Beyydan sent her out to pick up dinner for her. That became an opportunity the little girl did not want wasted.

She told them all she had heard. She responded to their questions and filled them in. Suddenly, they had answers to their questions of why Maana was in the middle of a group abusing *khat* and alcohol. How she got there and how Axmed found himself there became clear. They knew now why Maana was lying there when Xaawa saw her last night. They understood what Beyydan wanted to gain.

Sahra Yuusuf got a clear answer to the question of "What was the old lady trying to gain from her Axmed's encounter?" that she had asked Ciise. Faadumo had just made that crystal-clear.

There was only one puzzle left to unravel. Who was that mysterious man of means who had devised the scheme with Beyydan to snare Maana? To glean some identifying clues, they addressed more questions to Faadumo.

Faadumo told them that she heard Beyydan's side of the telephone conversation, but she could not hear his voice, nor had she seen him. She did think that the man of means owned a villa, that he loaned Beyydan a car, and of course, that he must have financed the whole scheme. She went on to say that she had overheard something about the Green Villa and that she thought that she had been there before on other nights for parties which Beyydan had organized. Beyydan Shabeel took her there to help her serve clients. She stated that she saw a man with a belly issuing orders that were to be obeyed. She thought it was probably the same man as the one who was on the telephone with Beyydan.

When she was asked where the villa was located and how to get there, she could not articulate the exact route. They asked her to go with them to show them where she thought the Green Villa was.

"I am sure she is not going to let me out again!" said Faadumo, scared. But when they all begged and pleaded with her, she said, "I am going to see if there is any chance." She ran back to Beyydan's house.

The group doubted Beyydan was going to let her have the slightest opportunity to leave.

When Faadumo jumped onto her feet, Sahra did the same. She got into the waiting taxi and headed out to find her cousin Axmed Jaamac. Axmed needed to hear the latest news!

CHAPTER TWELVE

I

If you ever happen to be in north Mogadishu, go to Hawl-wadaag Road, cross Jidka Soddonka, and take Daraawish Road. There you will come to an open space. To your left you will see a hilltop covered in lush greenery during the daytime and at night blanketed in a darkness that would breathe fear into your heart. The Green Villa rests on the tip of that hilltop, and like a ship floating in the middle of an ocean at night, radiates a light brighter than all the neighbors'. This imposing villa, a regal palace, was built with government funds under the pretext that it would be used as a residence for foreign experts, contracted to work on the project directed by Jaamac-dhegey, as he claimed. All requests to gain occupancy were held at bay. The reason was rumored to be that the executive director, Jaamac-dhegey, and his friends used it for pleasure.

The villa was divided into large apartments. Each room had its own veranda, using the latest tile. Each apartment also included its own kitchen and baths. The roof was festooned with elaborate, artistic designs. It was fenced in with an adobe terrace, adorned with native flowers, and surrounded by a manicured lawn and pruned trees. The branches of these trees leaned on each other and seemed to share their shadows. This lush surrounding was the inspiration for the name Green Villa.

That night the palace was filled to capacity. Servants had made sure that cold drinks and food to feast on were ready. Jaamac was in the middle of it all, salivating. Maana, the most desired dessert, was on his menu. Unaware of the plot brewing against her, Maana was seated on a chair at the front of one of the verandas. The pattern of this malicious scheme had been played out before on many young ladies, including very young schoolgirls. Many lives had been ruined here.

Fortunately, Maana was no longer a clueless victim. She knew that if dusk descended on her, she would be in danger, maybe not clueless but a victim nevertheless. Several times she had considered leaving but was too confused to do so. She did not know where she was or where to go or how. And she was not left alone long enough to cull fact from fiction. She felt as though she was on a ride on an unknown route, or a bag of groceries handed back and forth between Beyydan and Saynab, her other handler. Time and again she would ask Saynab why Beyydan was so late and when she was expected to arrive.

II

Earlier that morning, long before they had arrived at Green Villa, Beyydan had convinced Maana to get into Jaamac-dhegey's car on the pretext of re-uniting her with Axmed. She had then driven her north to this unknown estate. As they arrived at the gate of the huge villa, an amiable young lady, Saynab, greeted her warmly and escorted her to a room in the west wing of the villa. Maana was impressed with how beautifully the place was furnished and warmed up to the ingratiating, queen-like attention she received!

Maana was advised to take a shower. She was offered new clothes and makeup of the latest brands. All kinds of food and drink followed. While Maana was being entertained with stories that brought a slight smile to her face, Beyydan slipped out of her hideout on the pretext that she was going to fetch Maana's boyfriend. The same Maana who earlier in the morning had thought about overdosing herself now looked amused. She was made to somewhat forget her misery and even joined in the chatter, sharing her own jokes. It did not take long, though, for nervous jitters to return and gnaw at her.

Suddenly, she interrupted the idle conversation with, "Sister, I am not sure why the madam is not here."

"Don't be in a rush," Saynab deceptively reassured her, "The madam is working on your behalf. She will soon be here with the young man you love." Saynab was not alone in the ruse. There also was a server from Jaamac-dhegey with them.

Shortly after 5:00 p.m. Saynab took a thermos of sweet tea and some batteries for a record player outside to an adobe bench.

"Hey, Sister, let us sit outside for a bit of fresh air," she said to Maana-faay. Maana went along and joined her on the bench. Both Maana and Saynab watched as a middle-aged heavyset man, wearing his sleeping pajamas, came out of the east wing and took a seat on the closest bench.

There were adobe benches throughout the villa's gardens. Scattered amongst the gardens were small, beautifully landscaped private seating areas. It was here that Maana and Saynab now sat with their thermos and cups of sweet tea.

The man in the pajamas was about twenty feet away. With his back to them, he began brushing his teeth with a twig. He pretended that he was not aware of their presence but threw a furtive look at Saynab, casting a subliminal message her way. She knew that he was asking: *Why have you not begun the game we planned: snaring Maana?*

To initiate the charade, Saynab addressed Jaamac with, "Jaamac, when you were out at work, the building contractor came by. He said that they were running out of cement!"

Jaamac-dhegey, who was waiting for the bait, walked over to the young ladies and with an exaggerated interest asked, "What else did he say, Saynab?" He took the seat opposite the young ladies. Saynab repeated the rusty story.

While Saynab poured a cup of tea for him, his eyes scanned Maana. As though he did not know who she was, he quickly asked, "Is this girl who has graced us with her visit your sister?"

"This young lady is like a sister to me. Her name is Maana-faay," responded Saynab. "Maana, this boy's name is Jaamac. He is our neighbor, and he is an important man. He is rich and owns half of Mogadishu. Whenever we are financially squeezed, he is the one who bails us out," she said looking at Maana. Saynab went on and said, "But we owe him no gratitude. He has so much money that when he tries to make himself light, some loose change finds its way to our side." Saynab and Jaamac both laughed. It was not apparent whether they were laughing at the clever way Saynab delivered the jab or the meaning embedded in it. And just because they laughed, Maana faked laughing too.

I don't give a damn how rich he is. Maana thought, *good for him, why would I care? Did she dare to call him a boy? He is older than my dad! How audacious of her to call him a boy! Hah, how crass is that?* Maana repeated to herself.

"Hello, Maana-faay. Nice to meet you," said Jaamac-dhegey, looking at her with lust. "It's an honor that you have paid us a visit. In our culture, you know people say, 'Visitors are a good omen, announcing the arrival of angels.' Today that omen is real, because you are real."

"Don't commit blasphemy. I am not an angel," said Maana with uncomfortable shyness.

"No, I am as innocent as a child. I am too young for the angels to indict me. And please don't jump to conclusions because of my silver hair. I am not that old," Jaamac ended with a nervous giggle, tapping into his own insecurity. Saynab faked a slight laugh with him, and Maana tried a little giggle.

"But look," he continued, "are you aware of the crime you have committed?"

"What crime?" Maana asked, suspicious.

"If you alone own all this beauty, what is left for the rest of the young ladies? Now you should be aware that if those young women sue you, I am going to be a cooperative witness. I am going to be on their side testifying to the fact that you robbed them of all their beauty. Perhaps you should compromise and return some of that beauty so they can divide it among themselves. Or you could at least give back one of your two names. Choose either Maana or Faay," Jaamac teased Maana to soothe her.

"What would one do with the name that I gave away?" Maana asked.

"I will take the one you did not choose and will give it to my yet-unborn daughter."

"I read you well," Maana said. "You are telling me that I have committed a crime. Now you are the one whose crime is known: a crime against me. You are trying to take my name away for your unborn daughter."

"Give me your hand. You just stopped me cold and rightfully so," he stated. "But having this much excess beauty could be a problem for you," he continued. "You are going to attract so many men that you will not be able to handle them all. Some will be much older than you and some will be as ugly as I am. What if someone fat like me is attracted to you and wants you? What would you do?"

"That will be his problem," Maana said with a serious tone. Consulting her women's intuition, she examined where he was going with his tasteless attempt to flirt. She judged that he was a sleazy old man but waited to hear where he was going with his contorted comments.

"Excuse me for a minute. I have to attend to a matter that needs my attention," said Jaamac with pretentious self-importance. Minutes later, the well-dressed Jaamac-dhegey got into his sizable luxury car, and off he went.

Saynab and Maana remained seated and continued to converse quietly while sipping their now-lukewarm tea.

III

At about 7:00 p.m. a large, luxurious sedan arrived back at the villa with three corpulent occupants, two males and a female. The car came to a halt in front of the gate. Cawaale, one of the two males, alighted. With two bottles of whisky in one hand and a carton of cigarettes in the other, he walked through the gate, leaving Beyydan Shabeel, the female, and Jaamac-dhegey in the car. Beyydan knew that Jaamac probably still did not trust her. But with Maana currently in her snare and being guarded by Saynab, it was time for her to make her move and shake some more notes off him.

"Of course, with my expertise in such matters, I have corralled her," Beyydan began to brag. "I made you a prince and I made her a Cinderella. She is laughing and enjoying herself. I tell you, she is ripe for your picking. You saw how jovial she was with you this afternoon. When you two are alone tonight, you will taste her through your bones."

"I knew you would come through," said Jaamac. "Please go on."

"The game will proceed as planned. The most beautiful garden unit will be furnished for you tonight. Two others will join you. There the four of you will chat. Music will be playing in the background, lights will be dimmed, all of which will make for a very favorable ambiance. You know your game," she said.

"Good," he responded with self-assured pride. "You did your part, and you did it well. Go on."

"While the other two are still with you, she will be shy. She is still a young girl, you know. But once that first phase is over and Cawaale and Saynab are gone, you two will be alone. It is then that the game begins. Handle her like ripened fruit and feast on her. But I must warn you, if you aren't going to perform up to expectations, don't put yourself in the line of fire," she warned teasingly.

"Let me handle that, let me handle that myself," Jaamac said. He was already focused on what he thought was going to happen that night.

"Have a nice but short 'wedding,'" Beyydan said. "I don't want to sour your good time or delay you a minute longer, but could you provide me with a driver to take me back? Also, I am indebted to a grocer for all the delicacies I have prepared for tonight. Would you get the debtor off my back and pay him off?" Beyydan slid in.

Ha-ha, her time to squeeze me has arrived, Jaamac whispered to himself. To shut her up, he said,

"We will pay off that debt, but we should talk about it tomorrow…"

"Tomorrow? Tomorrow?" she interrupted, "There is no tomorrow, 'Cousin.' He is sitting at my house as we speak. If I don't have his money with me, I won't be able to enter my house. He is a hell of an obsessed and nettlesome man. But he is in the right, because I promised that I was going to pay him off in a few hours. You know that you put me in charge of a major mission yesterday and I executed it flawlessly. So, every time I ran out of money, I had to run to him with excuses of 'I forgot the combination to my safe. Can you loan me this and that amount: a hundred, two, five?' He trusted me and I trusted you. I don't like borrowing money and being in debt, but I was on a mission to deliver a 'wedding' to you. I did not want a thing to distract either of us from planning your day of fun. So, I didn't come to ask you when I was short. I have no idea what you have done to me, but I have not worked this hard for anyone else."

Jaamac was very close to saying aloud: s*top pretending that you did all this from the goodness of your heart. You were trying to make money off me. Don't patronize me. Forget about the debt that you incurred. The money that I have already doled out to you should not only cover all expenses for tonight but should last you for months.* Yet at the same time, he was lustfully savoring the images of what was to come.

"Everything will be taken care of, Beyydan. We will pay the man off and whoever else you owe money. Don't worry. But I really thought that you had taken care of all the expenses yesterday, so I don't have much today. However, take whatever this is today and let us deal with the rest tomorrow." He handed her a small wad of notes.

Beyydan was angry. Looking at the money, she knew he had more stashed away. She knew the game well. The two were sizing each other up. Each was trying to outmaneuver the other. Jaamac did not want to spend a penny more but was trying to deescalate the tension, at least for tonight, and get on with his agenda without any distraction.

Through experience, Beyydan had learned that during the early excitement she could milk men for all they were worth. But she was also fearful that within the next few hours Jaamac was going to trip over the mirage of lies that she had devised and discover that Maana was not as docile as he had been told. She was calculating how the web of deceit that she had spun could dissolve. She did not think that messages of gratitude would be forthcoming tomorrow.

Now the co-conspirators sat staring at each other, having reached an impasse. Niceties and pretentious politeness had faded away. An argument had erupted, and words had soured their earlier elation. It looked like no further payments were heading her way, so she threw the first stone.

"I have wasted my time sweating on your behalf. You are the most undeserving, stingiest person I know."

Jaamac tried to bite his tongue. He needed to be patient with her. Then he heard her say, "You are the most undeserving, stingiest person I know." Suddenly, he could not hold back. It burned him that yesterday this same woman had eagerly grabbed hold of handfuls of his ready cash. Now she was accusing him of being stingy. He blew up.

"You are ungrateful, courtesan."

Beyddan reacted to this epithet with a threat to take back the young lady.

"Get out! I dare you to set foot in my house again. Do you own these young ladies? Are they your children?" Jaamac reacted furiously, trying to fend her off.

"Are you denying me and throwing me out of the house after I spent the whole day cleaning and decorating for you yesterday?" she asked. "Do you know who you are challenging? I will light up this whole house with trouble the like of which has not been seen before," she added.

As Jaamac was about to get out of the car, a new idea dawned on Beyydan. She thought it best to levy her revenge on him with, "It will be all-out war between us. If you don't regret what you have just said, my name isn't Beyydan Shabeel."

"Go ahead. Do whatever the hell you want. But if I ever see you again, you alone will be responsible for whatever happens to you," Jaamac warned.

He had taken her threat to mean that she was either not going to further pursue the transactions with him, or she was going to turn the young ladies in the Green Villa against him. *If I need a female companion, I don't have to beg Beyydan. And if I need a courtesan, there are others with more reasonable prices. To hell with her. Maana, the-light-one, is in my hands. I don't care about anything tomorrow, but tonight is very important. The only thing Beyydan could do is come back and ruin the fun for me tonight. For that, I will make sure that security handles her if she returns,"* Jaamac thought. He got back into his car and drove through the compound gate. Had he known where Beyydan was heading with her threat, he would have stayed and bargained with her. As a matter of fact, he would have paid whatever price she was asking.

IV

Cambaro Cali Dhoof, Jaamac's wife, had sent her children to the Nasar Cinema. On Thursday nights, the older children would usually go out to see movies or plays, as the next day is the Muslim weekend holiday. Last Thursday they had chosen to see a play performed by the Banaadir Artist Troupe at the National Theatre. Cambaro did not care much about plays, but while the children were away, she rested or visited other neighbor friends. It was also the neighborhood housewives' night to catch up with their weeklong gossip. Thursday nights were chosen because there was no school the next day and no work for their husbands. With the children at the movies and the husbands at tea shops, the housewives were free.

Around 7:45 p.m., almost all the neighborhood women, with their *gambarro* and mats ready for an evening of friendly gossip, gathered in an open space between Jaamac-dhegey's house and the next building. Some knitted, some weaved, but the pregnant ones brought their pillows and propped them up against the wall, letting the ocean breeze breathe on them. Doling out one story after the other, they were having a good time. Every now and then they would all talk at the same time. At times one could not tell who was talking to whom or who was listening to whom, but they were all happy competing to tell their stories.

When it was Cambaro Cali Dhoof's turn to share her neighborhood news, she began to deliver it so well that the rest were forced to pay attention. Suddenly, a voice she did not recognize interrupted.

"Where is the daughter of Cali Dhoof?" said the thunderous, female voice. "You have been wrongly blaming me for things that I had nothing to do with." With difficulty Cambaro recognized Beyydan Shabeel as the latter plunged in the crowd, shouting, "Let me ask you, do you know where your husband is tonight? When does he come home? I don't think he will return tonight because he is out fooling around with another woman. So, don't say that he is just chewing *khat* at Beyydan Shabeel's place. He isn't at my place tonight. Don't accuse me tomorrow."

The neighborhood's joyous housewives' gathering came to a hushed halt. Some zipped their lips tight, others turned their hearing off, and some simply looked away. As though an electrical current had shot through the group, the chatter and laughter ceased all at once.

Soon though, the temptation to reap more from the gossip mill overtook the silent souls. Some of those with their elbows on the pillows perked up their ears for more, those who were weaving paid greater attention, and those who had gone inside their houses returned to join. In minutes, those who remained inside their houses were now sticking their heads out of the windows to cash in on some scandal. The children who had not gone out to the movies but were busy playing gathered to hear it, too. All came and watched, waiting to see how Cambaro would respond, and with what. Beyydan stood still and Cambaro remained silent, staring.

No one was more tongue-tied or shocked than Cambaro. She was not a confrontational type to begin with. She was a quiet, caring wife and mother. Lately, though, she had been dubious about Jaamac-dhegey's behavior. He had been coming home late and would stagger into bed, and at times he even dared to spend the whole night out. "I have been in a meeting that took too long or went out of state for another," he would offer as an excuse.

At first, she wanted to believe him but as rumors grew, her suspicion grew, "Don't come by with your indictment. It isn't an issue of mine. Whoever commits such a crime will answer to his Creator," she would respond when other women tried to lure her into talking about her husband's shenanigans.

But day after day she grew more and more disturbed as rumors became more frequent. She heard that he had hired both courtesans and pimps. Beyydan Shabeel was one of the names she had heard. A friend of hers who was there with her that night knew who Beyydan was. This friend was a woman known to have a short fuse who had long suspected her husband of being in league with Jaamac-dhegey. The same friend whipped Cambaro into action when yesterday, news arrived that Jaamac was at Beyydan Shabeel's place. Cambaro and her friend had then confronted Beyydan at her place and warned her "to stay away from our husbands." That was what Beyydan was referring to when she said that she had been wrongly blamed.

This Thursday evening, Jaamac had called his wife to tell her that he was going to take a delegation of foreign experts to tour the Lower Shabeele region.

"I did not want to trouble myself with their responsibility, but my associate got sick. Now, I have to take them. So don't count on me for lunch or dinner," he had said to his wife.

"How long will you be away?" she asked.

"No one knows, but I am sure I'll be gone at least for one night. It's even possible it could take three to four days. The state is large, and we have to show them the farms and a lot of the area's natural resources."

"Well, be safe and please bring some fruit back with you," said Cambaro.

"Will do," he followed and hung up the phone. He smiled thinking, *yes, I will bring fruit, but not from Shabeele! I will tell the driver to pick some up from the Xamar-weyne market here in the capital. How nice it is to use that as an alibi.*

Beyydan's question "Do you know where your husband is now?" reminded Cambaro of the conversation she had had with her husband that morning.

Cambaro was shocked by Beyydan's news. Thousands of thoughts battled in her mind. She didn't know much about this woman, Beyydan Shabeel, and didn't want to listen to her. It was painful to be the recipient of an all-out assault for all to hear. It bothered her that other women who had ill-will towards her husband would hear it, too. Yet she did not doubt the validity of her news. She was burning inside with dishonor.

And though her thoughts engaged a battle in her, she remained silent. But when she felt all eyes on her, waiting for her to respond in kind, she managed to hide her turmoil within, prop herself up, and assume a defensive posture.

"Listen, you," she began, addressing Beyydan, "what business do you have putting yourself in between my husband and me? Don't you know he can do whatever he chooses? By the way, I have no issue with that. Are you satisfied now?"

Cambaro's response elicited whispers around her. "Sisters, can you see what an ingrate she is?" one woman said.

"She is making a case against the woman who just warned her! Some human beings are never grateful," said another.

"Good. She gave her a well-deserved answer. She is tough. What business is it of hers to come between a husband and wife," said another, who supported Cambaro.

"She learned her lesson. See how her eyes are blinking now," said another.

"Where on earth is she from? She isn't from our neighborhood," followed another.

"It's all on Cambaro and her cluelessness," said the one suspicious of her own husband. "Using the information provided, she should have jumped on it. Instead, she is cutting off the flow of information. If this were about my husband, I would have kissed that woman's feet."

"My sister, adding fuel to the fire is not virtuous," said one next to her.

"Don't tell me that," jumped in the one who was suspicious of her husband. "He is cheating on his wife. If he were my husband, I would hope someone would tell me about it. Why does he deserve Cambaro? Why is she tethered to the house when he is out doing what he wants with other women?"

"But Jaamac-dhegey is a man of integrity and a leader. I don't think he would do such a thing. This woman is after something else," said an older lady.

"Integrity, integrity. The men nowadays—my cousins—are neither decent nor ethical. Anything is possible. They are faithless and faceless."

"My sister, the women themselves aren't that innocent. I know many whose husbands are faithful but it's the wife who is cheating."

"The proverb goes, 'Don't do any favors and you will reap no evil,'" Beyydan said aloud, bringing the rampant whispers to a halt. "It's because of you and your childlike minds that you are not heeding my good intentions. I brought you this news, for I as a woman felt sorry for you. I thought that if you witnessed your husband's behavior with your own eyes, you would be able to rein him in. I thought it was wrong of him to horse around with a new woman every night while you were alone on your bed. Again, lending 'poor-you' a hand so that you no longer had to rely on hearsay was my intent. But you seem to be deaf to my alarm, so all that I said about your husband, you can try to wish it away. Goodbye," Beyydan said, and pretended to walk away.

"Come back, come back. Wait a minute," called Cambaro's friend, the one with the hot temper. Another, who did not want it to end joined in too, calling after her.

Beyydan, who was not that serious about leaving anyway, stopped. If they had not called after her, she was going to hurl a word to follow it up as though she wanted to finish her point. She knew that her self-interest outweighed any adversity she was going to face. Going back to Green Villa meant much to her.

Beyydan had initially wanted a minute to pull Cambaro aside, away from the others, to tell her about her husband's philandering. But she ruled that out when she saw the crowd of gossips huddled together. It was then that she wanted to maximize Jaamac-dhegey's disgrace, exposing him to as many people as possible.

Beyydan came back and talked, the neighbors crowded around her, noise rose, and Cambaro got confused. Her lucidity tipped and she was lured into a quarrel. "Where have you seen the man you are talking about and his women?" Cambaro asked.

That is the question that needed to be asked, Beyydan thought. "I am the only one who knows where I saw him. Nevermind, though. You want your husband to have a good time and just have him home when the others are done with him."

"No, no, woman, listen," began Cambaro's friend, "Forget about what my sister said here. She did not mean it. Just tell me where we can find him."

"It's at her place, where else?" said Cambaro, looking at Beyydan.

"Wait, Cambaro; let us listen to her," continued the woman to keep the flames burning.

Beyydan recapped it all, adding more spice.

It did not take long for Cambaro to reach her tolerance threshold. She stood up and interrupted Beyydan with, "Can you take me to that hell-house you are talking about?"

"Well, though I have better things to do, there is a taxi waiting for me outside. I only came here out of the goodness of my heart. Yes, I can take you there."

"OK, let us go," said Cambaro.

Now some of the women felt the urge to intervene. They thought it better to let the situation cool down. So, they began to berate Beyydan Shabeel for inciting an unnecessary brawl.

"Hey, you-woman, smother the flames you have ignited with your allegations. Leave our neighborhood in peace. Why on earth are you disturbing the order we have worked so hard to achieve here? What is in it for you? What are you going to gain pitting one Muslim woman against another?" one asked. Others converged on Cambaro to calm her down but to no avail. Still others kept fanning the flames.

Cambaro lashed out at the one who had tried to bring order back while ensconcing herself deep inside the taxi. Once the car door shut, she lost control and began weeping.

But Beyydan had joyfully followed behind, getting into the taxi and closing the door, winking to herself. The idling red taxi roared off, leaving clouds of smoke and dust behind. Using their own language that no one else was able to decipher, the neighborhood children chased them with: "Finish it, decrease."

"One."

"Finish it, decrease it."

"Two, Escape..."

The children's hide-and-seek chant continued, followed by another, unintelligible chorus. The fastest ones latched onto the back bumper for a short but exhilarating ride. Once the taxi was out of sight the children returned to their mothers. The neighborhood women were now left wondering what or who Cambaro and her companion were going to find, and what or who they were going to bring back.

V

"It's 7:20 p.m. That little girl has been gone too long," said Ciise, looking at his wristwatch.

"Is it possible that she has stood us up? We should call the police," said Leyla, whose worries had risen to high heaven.

"Let us wait a while," said Sahra.

"How long ago did she leave?" asked Axmed.

"About an hour ago."

"It would have been nice had you insisted on asking her to show you where to go first, then let her go to deliver the dinner."

"She would not agree, and we were waiting for you as well."

"Guys, let's go look for the place before it's too late," said Axmed. He jumped like a lion that has lost a cub.

"Let's just wait a few minutes more, Axmed," Ciise tried to soothe him. "Without her we don't even know where to start looking."

"Did she give you any directions?"

"As I might have mentioned a while ago, she isn't able to give directions well," Ciise answered.

"I am afraid that the damn man will get away from me," said Axmed, pacing back and forth. "Either he, the man who snared my Maana, is going to die today or I am!"

"Leave the abominable courtesan to me. She is responsible for all of this," Leyla followed.

"Whatever we do to them will never be equal to the tragedy these two have already caused," Sahra added.

"The madam is the vessel used but the main culprit is the man. He is the one who deployed the weapon: money and a car. No shame whatsoever," said Ciise.

"As we can glean from what the little girl said, he is a man of means, that much we know," Axmed added. "He is one of those who think themselves so high and mighty while corrosively eating away at the core of decency in this society. Fingers are pointed at the youth, but the older men are the worst offenders. I am telling you that man is about the same age as my father. You will see."

"My uncle warned me about unethical older men with cars and looted money hunting young ladies," said Sahra.

"That's what the little girl said — that the villa where Maana was taken to, is owned by a corpulent man who was issuing the orders when she was once forced to serve him and his team. And I bet it's the same older man who is also after Maana," Ciise said.

"He is the type that Axmed talked about. The kind of man who has gotten fat off the blood and sweat of the rest of us. He is taking advantage of a plague of poverty that is the result of corporate theft and greed," said Leyla.

"Where are this almighty condemned man's wife and kids?" asked Sahra.

"He cares neither about children nor his wife. But I am sure he has both. I hope I don't die before I lay eyes on him. I promise I will force him to throw up all the crimes he has committed against us tonight, and I will do the same to that fat hippo courtesan of his," said Axmed.

"Brother, I am begging you, please leave the madam to me. I am going to make her pay. I will beat her up with my own shoes." Sahra said. "You know, if all men were as faithful as your father, the world would be a better place," Sahra added. She had no idea that her uncle, Axmed's father, was the predator they were going after.

"I have a lot of faith in my father's 'piety.' What I do know is that he makes a mountain out of minor issues. And he wants to take control of me as though I am a little girl, *maqabiyad*," Axmed said.

Sahra, as though she had remembered something said, "But Axmed, if your father knew about this mess, he would have been appalled."

"Yeah. I would have said to him, 'Listen, you were blaming us. Come and do something about your peers who are hunting from our marriage pool,'" lamented Axmed.

The other three let out a nervous giggle, but Leyla seemed to sense Axmed's vulnerability. She looked at him, and warned, "Axmed, please don't tell your father about this."

Axmed read her well. He knew that she was worried about airing her sister's disgrace to her future father-in-law. "No, Leyla. I am just venting but I dare not talk about such a vile subject."

"Here she comes, the-little-Faadumo," Sahra interrupted the group.

"Great, Faadumo!" Ciise greeted a panting Faadumo.

"Let's go now. We have no time to waste," said Axmed, who had already motioned to leave.

VI

As they got into the waiting taxi heading to Jidka Soddonka, Faadumo took on the responsibility of giving directions that she hoped would take them to Green Villa. They turned on Daraawish Road. Here Faadumo hesitated, then soldiered on. She told them to turn right on a dusty road. When the dusty road came to a cul-de-sac, she got confused. When she hesitated, the team showed a bit of apprehension. As they turned left, another car drove toward them. It slowed and then came to a sudden stop alongside them. The group's driver leaned out his window and shouted at him, "Hey, you-man, where is the *khat* you promised me?"

"Cousin, I have not broken my promise, but I have been engaged by a raving lunatic. She is using all my time," yelled the other driver.

"Who is the raving lunatic you are talking about? Is she the same woman you were occupied with earlier, what's-her-name, Beyydan?" asked the group's driver.

"Yes, the same one; she is fanning a fire tonight. She has been arguing with a man over some business matter between them…"

"Hey, don't tell me tales now," interrupted the group's taxi driver. "I have passengers with me."

The driver threw a bundle of *khat* to him. Grabbing it, and no longer interested in the story about the raving woman, he shifted the car into gear.

Hearing Beyydan's name mentioned, his passengers perked up their ears and looked at each other. They wanted to hear more about her and the man she was arguing with.

"We aren't in a hurry. Please keep on talking," said Ciise.

"Were the man and woman fighting over money?" asked Sahra.

"Yes, they were fighting over money. By the way, the woman went to the man's house, and we picked up his wife from there. It took a long time for her to convince the wife to leave because I waited for over an hour. We picked up the wife and brought her to the same villa where I had seen her introducing the young lady and the old man."

"Aw my God! Woe is me! She brought the wife to the man while he was with another woman?" cried Sahra.

"Great! He deserves it," said Leyla.

"When we were close to the villa, she asked me to stop the car. The wife got out. As she rushed in, Beyydan said to me, 'Let us watch it from the terrace.' When we got to a back wall of the terrace, we saw a man and young lady engaged in a struggle. Was the man attempting to force himself on the young lady? I couldn't tell. I heard the young lady yelling. The man was holding her against her will, it seemed. She was fighting him off with all her strength. She was grabbing items around her, shoes, sticks, and whatever her hands could hold, and was throwing them at him. Suddenly his wife, too, was upon him. She hurled flying fists, shoes, and spittle on him," said the taxi driver.

"Great! He deserves it," Leyla said again.

"Well deserved," followed Sahra.

"She was crying, wasn't she?" asked Leyla.

"Well, when I left, they were still at it," the taxi driver said.

"Where is the madam now?" asked Axmed.

"She was watching from the same place I had dropped her: behind the terrace wall, laughing. My God, she has no heart. She was enjoying it like she was watching a movie."

"So did you sneak out?"

"No, she asked me to come back for her in a half an hour."

"Can you tell us where that villa is?"

"You, Mr. Taxi Driver, please make sure you have the right directions to get back there," said Leyla.

"Let us go, let us go," said Axmed.

Once the taxi began to roll, they addressed the matter more and were glad that the man of means was disgraced and enjoyed the fact that

Maana and his wife had fought with him. They appreciated that he had been attacked but were worried about Maana.

VII

The speeding taxi came to a halt right in front of the Green Villa. Like an army on the attack, the occupants scrambled out. Axmed, who was almost out before the taxi came to a full stop, took the lead, storming the gate. Sahra and Leyla were not far behind. Ciise followed but was prepared to take on a conciliatory role.

As the others poured out of the taxi, Faadumo-the-little-one, was heard to say, "Leyla, I am going to be late. Can the taxi drop me off?"

"No, Faadumo, no," said Leyla. "You are not leaving. You will not go back to that evil woman. Don't worry, I will take care of you."

As luck would have it, the outside gate was open and the guard in charge was nowhere in sight. Once he had heard the commotion, he had run into a dark alley where he could watch the action from afar. He could have broken up the fight but had to follow a policy that he was not to get involved in any kind of wrangling between guests in the villa.

The invading army moved in. Axmed was running so fast that he was yards ahead of the rest. And though he did not see anybody at first, they let their ears lead them to a wailing, moaning, and swearing female voice. The invading army pushed on, trampling the flowers and lawn. Sahra, on the offensive, took off her shoes to beat the enemy with, and Axmed threw off his shirt. Just before him, he could make out silhouetted figures: two people pulling and pushing. As he approached, he saw a male and female in a tug of war. The female was holding the male by the collar of his shirt, and he was trying to fend off the blows as well as working hard to get himself loose. Unable to pull away, he begged and pleaded with her to let him go.

"Leave me alone if you are a woman of faith in Islam," he kept repeating.

"You are the one who left Islam. At this advanced age, you began to fornicate and cheat," the woman was saying.

"Don't cause me to punch your teeth out," the man threatened.

"You can do that, I tell you, and you can slit my throat too, for all I care. I can't live with the dishonor and the disgrace you have brought on me anyway. I swear, one of us is going to be buried tonight. Grant me my divorce right now!" she wailed.

"Your place is in your house. Why are you into my business? You made it your business to follow me around. I am telling you; you are going to regret it if you don't go back home. Why…"

"What home? I have no home anymore. You have destroyed it, haven't you?"

Axmed rushed forward. The clearer the voices became, the slower he paced himself. Soon, he sensed something wrong and stopped. *What am I hearing? Am I familiar with the voices I am hearing? No, it's not possible. I am losing my mind!* Such were the thoughts that raced through his mind.

He took tentative steps and got closer to the fight. A minute later he locked eyes with a woman, his own mother! In shock, he averted his gaze and turned to the man. This was a nightmare. There before him was his own father, too!

Nauseated with confusion, Axmed felt dizzy. As he was about to faint, he steadied himself, leaning on a tree trunk to support himself. His legs wobbled. He closed his eyes to wish it all away.

He heard Sahra running close behind him. She caught up with him but thought he had been shot, so she froze. "Axmed, what happened to you?" she pleaded. When he did not respond, she wailed, "Woe is me! What has happened to my cousin?"

Not that far behind, Leyla and Ciise came sprinting. Ciise ran up to the two engaged in combat. The nightmare halted his speed. It occurred to him that the man was his own boss, Jaamac-dhegey. His eyes refused to believe what he was looking at, and he turned away now looking at the woman. There was Cambaro, his friend's mother and his boss's wife, locked in battle. Ciise was shocked but quickly shook it off and pressed on. He pushed through and placed himself between the two, separating them, while trying to calm them down.

Realizing that they were no longer alone, Jaamac-dhegey thought the muscular man who separated him, and his wife was his friend Cawaale, who must have heard the commotion in his room and come out. As a matter of fact, neither he nor his female companion had come out. Actually, the light was off in their room. They were hiding inside, fearing that their complicity in the whole scandal would be discovered.

Panting with exhaustion, Jaamac managed to look into the face of the man who had peeled him off his wife. In disbelief, he blinked and blinked again trying to clear his vision. As he attempted to steady his gaze, he realized that the man standing before him was Ciise, one of his young employees to whom he had been selling the fake "integrity" package. Now that same young man was a witness to his shame and sham. He knew that this scandalous news was no longer going to remain on the back pages. His employees and his colleagues would feast on his dishonor, and Green Villa proved to be right in the middle of it. Everyone would soon know how the public property was being used.

Jaamac-dhegey was not the type of a man who would soldier on regardless of the glaring gaze of guilt and disgrace. He preferred to keep his immoral and unethical failures hidden beneath the surface and away from public scrutiny. He used to try his best to keep his dignified appearance. So, to hold his shenanigans secret, he had gone far away from the city to the suburban area where he thought his secret would be safe—to the secluded Green Villa.

While the others were preoccupied (Axmed in a daze, Sahra attending to him, Ciise busy separating the entangled husband and wife), Leyla Xaaji Muumin had one thing in mind, to find her sister. She ran past the melee yelling, "Maana, Maana, where are you? Woe is me! Is she not alive?" she wailed.

VIII

Earlier that day, Maana had been lured into the villa with Beyydan's deceptive promise. But it did not take long for her to grow suspicious and sense the impending danger, yet she did not know how to extricate herself.

She also maintained that faint hope that the promise Beyydan had made of bringing Axmed to her might materialize. She did not know that Beyydan had planned all that had happened to her last night. One thing became quite clear to her, however: that Beyydan was a courtesan and that this was a troubled house, a brothel. Had she been her old self, she would have figured out the cabal too and would have never gotten into a car with her to the Green Villa. The hurdles she had gone through in the last 24 hours had almost paralyzed the normal functioning of her mental system.

"Where is that old lady?" Maana asked Saynab as her anxiety increased. "Tell you what, if that half-witted old lady isn't coming, can you take me to where I can catch a taxi, please?"

But her handler swore, as much as Beyydan did, that Beyydan was on her way with Maana's lover, just to calm her down.

But when two unknown men arrived, Maana became scared. *I need to get out of here. What are these guys doing here?* These thoughts raced through her mind. Her hunch was proven right as the two men and Saynab began joking about copulation. But she didn't make a move to leave. She questioned her fears and decided that they were all just teasing each other.

Despite her uncertainty, she began to think that she was not going to be left alone with Jaamac-dhegey. In fact, she convinced herself that this encounter was going to be like what she experienced at Jungal, just eating out at night. But all that changed at dawn when she realized that she was alone with Jamaac-dhegey. She had no doubt about her predicament now. When Saynab, under the pretense that she was going to get something out of her room, abruptly left the dinner party, she knew. And shortly thereafter, Cawaale also left, saying that he was going to the bathroom.

Once Saynab and Cawaale had left, Jaamac-dhegey made his move. He sidled in closer, looked at Maana with lustful eyes, and began assaulting her with sexually suggestive language. When he attempted to grab her hand, Maana had had enough. She jumped to her feet and with fear in her voice cried, "I have to leave."

Jaamac-dhegey tried his best to stop her, but to little avail. His pretentious sweet-talk whipped her into a brawl. Maana snatched up her belongings and pulled away. "Leave me alone, leave me alone," she kept repeating.

Jaamac-dhegey was counting his losses. The man could not think beyond the money and the countless hours he had spent preparing for his seductive coup, and she was now rejecting him. Beyydan, it seemed, had disappeared along with the others, so she could be of no help. He could not take all that loss. *With all the trouble I have been through, how could this little rascal of a young lady reject me? I don't care what it's going to cost me. I must get my way. If she does not relent, I have to use muscle on her,* he thought.

It was at that exact moment that his wife Cambaro barged in. Instantly, she was shocked by the sight of her husband struggling with a young lady in an attempt to rape her. Soon, however, she lunged at him with both fists and verbal salvos.

Cambaro's surprise attack gave Maana the opportunity to slip away and run for the gate. Just outside the room, she realized that, again, she had left her purse behind. She hesitated, but knew she needed money for the taxi fare. So, she turned around and tiptoed back into the room. She grabbed her purse and made another dash for the gate when she heard the commotion outside. People were getting out of a car and running into the compound. *These are his friends who will side with him*, she thought. She turned around and ran to the back gate, which was located in the high wall that surrounded the villa on the dark side of the garden. When she found it locked, she tried to pull herself up on the wall to jump free to the other side, she slipped, risking both life and limb. Suddenly, she heard a familiar female voice call "Maana! Maana, where are you?"

That is Leyla's voice, she thought. She let go and slid back down the wall, tearing clothing and skin, and started hurrying through prickly brush. Drops of blood dripping to the ground, she kept running toward the sound of Leyla's voice. Later, she would learn the injuries she had sustained.

"My sister, Leyla, Leyla, my sister," she screamed.

Axmed, whose heart was already weakened by the disgraceful scuffle between his parents, heard Maana's voice and took it hard. His parents heard it, too. Hearing Maana's voice disoriented him. He could not tell where it was coming from. *My sister, Leyla, Leyla, my sister,* echoed through his mind. *Where is it coming from, where is the voice coming from? From the left, or right? Is it a dream or is it real?*

He looked to his left, then to his right, and then he turned around. "Maana!" he yelled and frantically rushed about, turned, and turned again. Then he ran. He did not know that she was so close.

When she was about ten feet away, dream-like elation and waves of electricity shot through her body, forcing her feet to buckle under her. For a split second, she closed her eyes and wondered whether she would be able to see correctly again. When she opened her eyes, her gaze met his.

Their passion-filled eyes locked. Arrows of affection seemed to be aiming at both of their hearts. Maana was virtually paralyzed. She could not move a muscle. Axmed flew at her, lifted her up, then returned her to the ground. Once more they locked eyes and became lost in each other's arms. The wounds of love lamented. Maana let her tears flow freely. And Axmed softly whispered the most valued word in his vocabulary,

"Maana, Maana." Gently, Axmed wiped away her tears, repeating, "Maana."

The melody of hearing him say her name melted her heart. She held him tight to her body, whispering, "My sweetheart, Axmed."

The two lovebirds blended their passions into a single one. Each held the other in a tight embrace, then they would let go, but grab again. They kissed, moaned, and hugged. Happiness rolled over them. "Honey" and "sweetie" were the shared words of love. *Axmed, my sweetheart,* were the words Maana repeated. Her tears dampened his shirt.

Axmed began to plead: "Maana, please forgive me. I belong to you for the rest of my life. I love you, Maana. I love you more than anything on earth. There is nothing I would choose over you. I will have no life if I can't share it with you. You are a part of my heart. My jealous love took over and made me suspicious and blind. You didn't deserve that. If you can bring yourself to forgive me, I promise you that no doubt will ever come between us. All that has happened should be a lesson for us that will last a lifetime."

Every word that passed his lips inflamed Maana's passion. Tears of happiness flowed from her eyes. She felt as though the key of life had just been handed back to her.

IX

Sahra ran past Maana and Axmed, lost in each other's embrace, but came upon Ciise, who had just separated the couple locked in battle. She felt angry at him, thinking, *why doesn't he let them fight it out?* She thought the fighting was between Beyydan and her male client. Getting a closer look, she realized she was wrong.

"What! Oh my goodness, it's Cambaro," she let out. She looked at the male. "Oh my gosh! It's my uncle, Jaamac!" *Woe is me, is it my uncle who abducted the future wife of his own son! Where can I hide myself?*"

There was nowhere to hide. She fell to the ground and wallowed in the grass.

All of this took place in the span of a minute. A minute when Ciise-dheere and Jaamac-dhegey came face to face; when Jaamac tried to turn away and came face to face with his niece, Sahra. An arrow of shame pierced his heart. He turned in all directions trying to find a hole in which to hide. *Where is there a hole to hide in? Disgrace! Failure. I hope that is not her. Is that my niece? Why is she here? What brought her? Why did I do this? What did she say? My sister's daughter. What daughter? What sister? What son, Axmed? That is a lie. My God, please make it a lie. Is the other young lady my son's fiancée?*

The fatal blow that smashed the face of Jaama-dhegey was yet to come. He was struck dumb when the passionate sight of Maana and Axmed came into view. The sight of a couple overwhelmed with love. He couldn't believe what he was seeing. He tried to avert his gaze from what was now reality. His heart seemed to explode. and he fell to the ground.

Ciise, who was the closest to him, sat down beside him, lifted Jaamac's head into his lap, and tried to feel for a pulse. He could not tell whether he was breathing or if his fingers were even on the right spot! The others were immediately by his side offering to help. The situation escalated into an emergency.

"He is breathing. No, he is not," were echoed.

"Leave him be," Ciise yelled. "Leave it to me, please! Let him have some air. Give him a space, so he can get some fresh air. He is in shock and may soon come out of it!"

"Is he alive?" Cambaro asked, worried. Once he fell to the ground, all her anger faded. She was now quite concerned for his life.

"Yes, he is. Don't worry, he is going to be fine," said Ciise, trying to calm her. "I am going to take him to the hospital. You guys take care of all the other issues. He will regain consciousness."

Medically, Ciise had no clue about Jaamac-dhegey's condition but was simply trying to restore some order to console the others, particularly Cambaro. He did not let on that he, like everyone else, was worried. He was not sure which side, the shadow of death or the sign of consciousness, Jaamac-dhegey was closest to. But he was leaning to the side of death. He was worried for all the others who he thought were now too weak to withstand another blow. He was worried that if Jaamac would succumb, other wounded hearts were in danger too. So, he took on the responsibility to keep the rest of the group safe, dispensing instructions.

"Go bring your taxi here!" he told the driver. "Come over and help me pick him up!" he directed the guard who was now on the scene. "You guys, stay out of the way," he barked at Axmed and Sahra when they rushed over to help lift Jaamac-dhegey into the taxi.

"I am going to take him myself to the hospital and will update you minute by minute," Ciise assured them. Ciise would not let anyone handle Jaamac-dhegey but himself, including the nurse, Leyla. He did not want anything else to contribute to the chaos.

"It's payback time. He is being punished for his crimes," said Cambaro once her husband was hauled away. She said that to show the others how mad she was, but she was actually worried sick about his condition. "God, please help care for him," she whispered to herself.

"Let whatever happened be in the past. What we need now is prayer," Leyla said. Of course, she had not heard what Cambaro whispered.

X

That was the first time Cambaro and Leyla had met. When the smoke had settled from all the pushing and shoving, Sahra introduced the two women to each other. Each was surprised by what the other shared. Leyla and Sahra told Cambaro about the plot to ensnare Maana, laying the blame solely at Beyydan's feet. By so doing, they were trying to lessen Jaamac-dhegey's part in the crime.

Cambaro felt heartbroken and embarrassed when she learned that Maana was the girl chosen by her son to perhaps be her future daughter-in-law. She shrank with shame and began to wail, putting all the blame on her husband. Leyla responded with compassion and comforting words.

As the reality sank in that the man who had attempted to rape her was Axmed's father and the woman he was fighting was her mother-in-law-to-be, Maana descended into a deep emotional haze. Again, she began to cry on Axmed's shoulder, moistening his shirt, seeking solace in his soothing words and careful caresses. When she caught her breath, Maana ran over to Cambaro, put her hands around her neck, kissed her in respect on the forehead, and began to plead with her, "Mama, Mama, Mama!" as though saying, *you have been disgraced on my behalf. I am so sorry!*

Cambaro tried to dry her tears. The ache of sadness and shame needed the gift of motherly care.

"It's my good fortune that my son found someone like you," she responded. "With God's mercy, I am hopeful that you will have each other as husband and wife, and I am going to do everything possible to make that happen for the two of you."

Once those words passed through Cambaro's lips, Maana jumped, bent over, and kissed her feet in a mixture of respect and joy.

"Where is Axmed?" continued Cambaro. "My son, I have been praying to God to bless you with a good woman. She is here before me today. Please, my son, don't let your carelessness call you away. Keep her safe from further cruelties like what she has just endured. I know that it was never your intention to have her suffer such dangers."

"Mistakes have been made," Sahra commented. "Had Axmed returned a day earlier and brought Maana home to be introduced to his family, all would have been avoided. I had been urging him to arrange for all of you to meet, but he kept saying to wait."

"I made a mountain of mistakes both last night and this morning," responded Axmed. "My jealousy got the best of me. I handed my sweetheart over to an enemy that I was not aware of. Had I been patient enough to gather facts, the problem would have been mitigated. If Faadumo had not saved the day, my losses would have been greater," he added. As soon as these words had left his mouth, his gaze fell on Maana holding Faadumo-the-little-one in her lap. Looking at them with great affection, he added, "Faadumo, I owe you a lot, my dear. I promise I will pay you back. And let me tell you, you are a part of us now, you aren't going back to Beyydan's den. No more. You should never see that hellhole again."

Hearing Axmed utter such kind, compassionate words caused Maana's heart to shiver with fondness. She hung her head in tears. As one hand wiped her eyes with her shawl, her other hand held Faadumo tightly. She looked at her and, filled with compassion, said "You saved my life, sweetie. Thank you."

"My brother, we all made major mistakes," said Sahra, picking up on Axmed's self-criticism, "but all those problems came about because of this ancient, outdated culture in our society."

"What do you mean by 'outdated culture?'" asked Cambaro, surprising the younger generation.

"I mean this ancient and rigid culture where parents force their young daughters into arranged marriages, where no one takes the young ladies' choice into account," explained Sahra.

"My daughter, that is the parents' responsibility." Cambaro disagreed, "If they don't guide the young, they could dig holes of trouble for themselves. Because of age and experience, parents are able to see the road ahead better."

Leyla could not hold herself back. The discussion irritated her. She remembered what she had been through with her parents. She sided with Sahra and said, "My aunt, Sahra is right. Look, if my father would have considered Maana-faay's choice, this problem would have been avoided. What has he gained now? We are all losers. Sahra is right. My father regrets how he had treated our oldest sister, Iisha. Are we going to live a life of regrets forever?"

"You are right," added Maana, whose fresh wounds compelled her to join in.

Leyla walked over to Maana, held her like her own child, and softly said, "My sister, please forgive me!"

"That is right," Sahra said in support.

But Leyla interrupted: "My sister Sahra, I myself committed a crime and should be blamed," she volunteered. "I had a colossal lapse of judgment. I sent my sister away when she came to me for help. I threw her into the lion's den where she was about to be disgraced by her own future father-in-law. I should have listened and weighed the danger, should I not?" Leyla moved closer to Maana, kissed her on both cheeks, and said, "Please, my sister, forgive me. You aren't the only one at fault."

"My sister," said Maana crying, "I have to accept my share of the blame, too. I was easily fooled. I am angry at myself, though most of the blame lies with Beyydan Shabeel. That wicked witch planned to destroy me, all for money."

Indicting Beyydan, Maana reminded Axmed of the severity of the courtesan's crime.

"By the way, where the hell is she?" he suddenly asked, looking around. "I totally forgot about her. Remember, the taxi driver told us that she was around enjoying her setup from afar." With that, Axmed got up and set out to find the woman behind all the madness.

Yelling and shouting, the women also got up and began the hunt to find Beyydan. Each grabbed whatever she could get her hands on—a rock from the yard, sticks, and even shoes, but Maana took off for the kitchen and came back with a knife.

"I am begging you, leave her to me." She was beyond rage and capable of who knew what!

Outside the gate, Beyydan was waiting for her taxi. She heard the commotion coming from inside the compound and realized that an impending attack was upon her. Huffing and puffing and blown up like a porcupine, down the road toward the city, she marched. The invading army approached, coming quickly around the wall. Axmed, in the lead, was the first to spot her. Running parallel to her along the shoulder of the road, he was able to catch up with her and cut her off. In a voice filled with rage, he screamed, "Stop! There is nowhere for you to hide tonight!"

The female crew trailing behind him began to shout, "Get hold of the whore! Don't let her get away! She is not going to get away, not tonight, not tonight."

XI

Beyydan, who realized that she was not going to outrun Axmed and his army, stopped, and with her feet spread apart, she stood her ground firmly and said, "Listen!"

No one did. Axmed planted himself in her path.

When the group of women caught up with them, each aimed her weapon at her, short of the knife, and began swinging. Axmed had to cover her with his body to protect her from the raining blows.

"Don't harm her. She has to answer for her crime in a court of law," he pleaded.

Beyydan, however, was not able to keep her mouth shut.

"You people need to come back down to earth," she began. "Someone should tell you that you won't be able to do anything to Beyydan Shabeel. If you harm me, you will only be making it worse for yourselves. If you take me to the court you are clamoring about, you will not gain anything except shame that will cling to you for the rest of your lives. By the way, I know how the court system works. And win or lose, I am going to have the upper hand."

"OK, allow me to ask you one simple question. Why? Why are you doing this?" asked Axmed. The others stopped to hear her response.

"*You* made me do it; you are responsible for it!"

"Who are the *we*?"

"You well-off ones, your class system, your selfish mentalities, your arrogance, your society, all of you."

"How?"

"By your misuse of the means and the power which…!"

What means and power do I have? She seems to be mixing me up with my father! Should someone tell her that I am an ordinary man with an ordinary job? Axmed was asking himself.

"Because if you hold the money, you hold the power, and with those two things in your possession, you also believe that you are the only ones who earned the right to live with dignity, denying the rights of disadvantaged citizens. Am I not a citizen of this country with rights too?" she said, flailing her arms and getting into Axmed's face.

"OK, OK," Axmed responded calmly.

"Where are my rights in this country?" she yelled repeatedly. "Your mother and I are the same age. She has everything and I have nothing. She has a husband, a house, children, family, and prestige. People stand up in respect wherever she enters, giving up their seats for her. But me, people would murmur curses about me. Do I deserve that? Where are my rights? Where is my husband? Where are my children? Where is my dignity? Where is the fruit of my sacrifice for the future of this country? Where is my beauty? Where is my youth? Where? Where? Where are they?" she screamed, beating her thigh, tearing at her shawl and walking over to the women to face them. Surprised, they backed off.

"Don't I as a citizen have the rights to all that I have said?"

"You should, but who has denied you these things?" asked Axmed calmly.

"*You* did! *You* denied me. You wronged me. You are responsible for whatever wrongdoing you accuse me of. That's why I will do no favor for anyone. I will keep pulling the rug out from under whomever I can, just as they keep pulling it out from under me. You cannot damage me any further by dishonoring me. You have already shunned me and treated me like an outcast. So now I have sworn to be an enemy of those who have it all. I will destroy your loved ones as you've destroyed me. I respect no law, no culture, and no religion of yours …!"

Engineer Axmed Jaamac and the others with him were startled. This was not the same "predator" of young women they had faced in Boondheere and at Green Villa. Her protestation about the societal chasm between the haves and have-nots garnered her some guarded attention, particularly with Axmed, who now felt irked by his social conscience.

"Can you tell us about the rights that have been taken away from you?" he asked.

"Sure. Why would I not be able to tell you? If you really want to know. I was born and raised in the countryside. When I was sixteen years old, a drought wiped out all our livestock. There was nothing left. So, I ran away and came to Mogadishu. This all happened during the colonial era. The colonial administration had no use for me. I had no education and no skills other than caring for the herd. Unskilled in the city, I could find no job, and therefore I had no way to support myself. I was in dire circumstances when a young lady I met told me about a job opening.

Some Italian men running my country were looking for a maid. I went to see them, asked for a job, and I was hired." She paused and drew on her cigarette. "Soon rumors began to swell that I was their mistress. It did not take long for my community to make me an outcast. My own family would have nothing to do with me. 'There she is, the one the infidels mated with' became the battle-cry I heard on the street. But I had nothing to do with those foreigners except to clean up after them and their friends. Don't get me wrong. I was beautiful in those days, and they were relentlessly hitting on me. But I did not succumb to their pressure.

"Yet the rumors and innuendos continued until my reputation had been dragged through the mud and dirt. I was too young and helpless to fight back against such social disdain, and eventually I gave up.

"Later I found out that all the girls like myself who worked for the officials of the colonial administration were sabotaged. They were prevented from ever earning respect and a decent living in the society, so we accepted work as their domestic servants. The men we worked for knew that if we worked in their homes and offices we would be shunned by our society and would be accused of all kinds of disreputable dirt. They had planned the whole scheme, knowing that they would turn our people against us, thus forcing us to lose the ability to resist their overtures," said Beyydan bitterly before pausing.

"Are you saying the colonial officials had planned all that?" asked Sahra.

"Yes, and that was exactly what happened," continued Beyydan, "and once they had lost their political power in this country and were preparing to leave, they threw us out. We told them that we had nowhere to go. Our families would not take us in. And with our reputations so tainted, where could we go? Their response was that they were going to help us with finding another source of income. They gave us distinct identification cards and rented us separate housing. 'There you are, use your beauty and your bodies to make a living.'"

"Is that how you got involved in this kind of business?" asked Leyla, rattled by her story.

Beyydan did not respond to her but went on, "So I thought we could put up with the indignities for a while, just to wait for the dawn of Freedom Day: the day the colonial powers would be replaced by ours. I thought Somalia's independence would bring back jobs and lost honor. I wanted to be a part of the effort to build a future and had become a member of the Somali Youth League, known as SYL, the leading movement for independence. I became an informer, spying on the Italians. I had even sold my jewelry, necklaces, bangles, and earrings to aid the party financially." She stopped and lit another cigarette.

"So, what happened?" asked Axmed.

"Somalis inherited the offices from the white Italians who had denied me a decent job. Now I had to start job-hunting all over again. Unfortunately, each officer I approached reacted as though my body was what I was selling. Nothing else. Where was my fair share of the fruits of freedom I had fought for? All of my hopes for a decent life once our national flag was hoisted were dashed.

"It so happened that those who were sleeping in their houses when many were dying for their freedom, some of whom were supporters of colonial rule, got hold of the reins of power and milked it. Yes, those of us who sold our jewelry were kept at bay. Where should we find justice then? I can tell you, nowhere.

"Once more a revolution arrived, and we welcomed it. Again, we thought it was our time, time for due justice to arrive. I believed the sweet words that radios and Reorientation Centers disseminated: 'We will uproot corruption, we will bury clannism, and justice will prevail. The poor and neglected will get their fair share.' I was overjoyed and was at the forefront of those women who, in celebration, volunteered to work day and night on government construction projects in return for nothing, with the hope that I will be rewarded one day. Was it worth of my sweat? What did I gain? The same treatment as before from those sitting in luxurious offices!" She began choking back her tears.

"Aha, then what?" asked Maana-faay in a sad voice.

"What do you mean by 'then what?'" answered Beyydan. "The new regime disappointed me again. I became an alien in my own country. So, you can see with your own eyes what I have become and what I am forced to do for a living."

She shook her head and bit at her forefinger, wailing, "My, my; am I going to get my full citizenship rights in the hereafter?" She paused, casting her gaze down.

"Then what did you do?" asked Leyla.

"I should not trouble you with my woes," continued Beyydan, "but nothing has changed. The only thing that those who got fat on my behalf helped me with was to make a living off my body. Once my beauty withered, they helped to snare young beauties. So, I have been doing that. I have to live, you know. I don't care if I cheated them out of a lifetime of happiness, self-worth, and the love of family. I lost all of mine, why shouldn't they?

"I don't care if their daughters lost their prospective marriages. Let them be damaged and doomed. Again, I lost mine, so they should."

As she began to sob, she pulled out her handkerchief and wiped her tears.

"But Beyydan, you are wrong," Axmed interjected. "Those young girls whose lives you are ruining have nothing to do with your losses or suffering. They are like you. Most of them are on the same stage that you were on in the 1950s you just told us about. The same type of men who had committed a crime against you are now using you to do the same. You are siding with criminals, so that they can use their muscle on the vulnerable, just as they did to you. Don't you see that?" asked Axmed.

"The young ladies have committed no crime against you." Sahra asserted. "They too are living in poverty and most likely are hoping to find a place in society where they can earn self-respect. You are making them powerless and turning yourself into the kind of person that you abhorred."

"My child, my heart has been drained of compassion. From what I've seem, there is no innocent soul left," said Beyydan.

Suddenly, she saw Faadumo at the far end and could not control her impulses. "Hey, you the-little-one, why are you here? Who brought you here? You with your ugly face. Do you see that one? I am training her, too. In a few months I am going to adorn her and initiate her into the business. She will soon be ready for male customers who would love to party with the likes of her."

"To hell with your 'party with,'" whispered Faadumo.

"If you were offered a decent job now, would you take it?" asked Axmed, ignoring her crass behavior.

"Who me, Beyydan Shabeel? My son, I learned only one line of work," she responded, implying that that was it for her.

"OK," said Axmed. "You are free to go. We will not go after you."

"Thanks," she said, relieved.

The women with him were incensed. Each tried to stop her. Maana-faay, who had been waiting all along, was the first to protest Axmed's move.

"What do you mean by letting her go? This woman who has burned down Mecca and Madina [two of Islam's holiest cities] with her crimes?" she asked

"Maana, whatever she is now, she was forced to be," said Axmed "I am sure if she had a choice, she would have chosen a self-respecting life over degradation. You have heard her story."

"She chose to commit crimes against so many, no matter what she claims," said Sahra. "Do you think it's right to let her go free after all the social destruction she has sowed, so that she can continue her plunder?" she asked.

"Let me ask you this, what would be the right thing for us to do now?" asked Axmed.

"I think the right thing to do is to take this woman to jail, in order to save the society she is tainting," said Sahra, "She should be banished from the community. Bacteria needs to be isolated so that it doesn't infect the rest of the healthy body. Right, Leyla? You are the one with medical knowledge!"

"You are right. A tumor or bacteria should be removed, I agree," supported Leyla.

"But one can only be saved with the removal of a tumor if the rest of the body is healthy," Axmed argued, "If the tumor has metastasized, the rest of the body is already infected. Removal of the tumor in one place will not bring about a cure, and pain and misery will continue."

"You may be right, but are we just going to fold our hands and do nothing?" asked Leyla.

"No, Leyla. The whole body should be cured. To treat one festering wound would not do the job. The solution is to remove all of the infected parts," said Axmed.

"What is all this talk about tumors and bacteria?" asked Maana, who seemed to be confused. "We were talking about Beyydan and what she did. All I want to know is what we are going to do with the woman who tried to ruin me? If you are sympathizing with her, I am not. I will go to her house and stab her," Maana threatened.

Axmed forced a smile, moved over to Maana, put his hands back on her neck, and said, "Honey, nothing can change who Beyydan Shabeel is. She is so far gone. What I meant was that whether we take her to prison or beat her up, we aren't going to gain anything. And because of her age, not much can be taught. On the other hand, there are hundreds of women just like her in the society. But we can focus on Faadumo-the-little-one, others like her, and many to come after to save them from this kind of abusive life. You just heard Beyydan's plan for Faadumo and the generation to follow. If the poor and weak aren't cared for they will be forced to live a life like Beyydan's."

"Please, don't portend that for Faadumo-the-little-one," said Cambaro with a maternal plea. "In the name of God, don't let her hear that. From this night on, she is one of my children. Tomorrow I will take her to the Quranic School and introduce her to learning." Looking down at Faadumo, she added, "Isn't that right, my daughter?"

Faadumo, however, did not jump at the opportunity. She took her time as though thinking about what to say. The question was repeated, but she would not say a thing.

"What is on your mind, Faadumo? Don't you want to be free from Beyydan's grip? Don't you want an education and better life?" asked Axmed.

With tears now running down her cheeks and choking on her words, she stammered, "I would love that but, but…" She hesitated.

"But what?" asked Leyla?

"Who is going to support my younger siblings?" Faadumo asked with a sad voice.

Stunned, the rest looked at each other. Sadness descended on the group.

It occurred to Axmed's mind that this was a child whose responsibility for caring for her brothers had sent her foraging through Beyydan's leftovers at night while the rest of humanity was sleeping and keeping her in indentured servitude in a brothel. It was a heart-breaking reminder of how reckless and corrupt the society had become.

Sahra's mind too was silently disturbed by the complexity of the situation. *Raising one child would be reasonable, but to take on the responsibility of an entire sibling group is something else altogether. How many families like Faadumo's are living in Mogadishu?* Sahra asked herself.

"Faadumo is right," Axmed finally said. "Her problems are much greater than what we can see. The solution isn't that simple. But she placed herself in grave danger to save Maana, and she deserves to be rewarded. We must care for her somehow. Also, she is right that something needs to be done to save her siblings. The problem that afflicted Faadumo and her family still remains in society. Hundreds of Beyydans are in the making, and there are hundreds or thousands of Faadumo's who need to be saved," Axmed added.

"What is the solution, then?" asked Leyla.

"Well, the solution is a social makeover. All those ancient social ills that are impediments to progress should be uprooted," said Axmed

"What do you mean by social ills?" asked Cambaro.

"Mom, I mean there are diseases like cancer and the likes, right?"

"Sure."

"As those diseases debilitate the body, there are social ills that do the same to society," Axmed explained.

"What are they?" asked Maana.

"For example, first is the ancient illness of clannism. Others include nepotism, injustice, and corruption, which were the factors behind Beyydan's misery and her wrongdoing."

"But whose responsibility is it to come up with how to create social change?" asked Sahra.

"That is a problem waiting for all of us, the younger generation," responded Axmed.

"I know, Somali's younger generation. Everyone whispers about national responsibility, but when it comes to action, we all cede it to others," argued Sahra.

"No, Sahra, don't be so pessimistic. Though I have to admit that feeling is mutual. What we really need is some faith in the future and a vision to help this country to find its moral compass," said Axmed.

XII

"Why is Ciise not back? It is getting so late! Maybe the old man is still in a coma," said Cambro, who was no longer following the debate. She was so worried about her husband, wondering whether he had survived or passed away. Words of concern were said here and there about Jaamac-dhegey. Maana-faay, who was furious with him, thought to herself, *I hope he dies.*

She thought that if he survived, he would be an embarrassment as well as an obstacle to her desired marriage to Axmed.

At that same moment, Axmed had arrived at a stage where he needed to clear his mind of the debate on the burning social issues.

Axmed's mind slipped back into a morass of the twists and turns of all that he had been through. He thought of how to wrestle his future away from the wreckage. The hardest part was how he was going to mitigate his family's diminished social status by marrying the same woman who had unmasked his father's disgrace! He asked himself what it was going to be like if his father survived. His worries surged as he thought about Xaaji Muumin and his family's problems. One thing remained quite clear, though; he was determined to marry Maana, no matter what. Where and how he should start repairing his family's stature in the community were also the issues that disturbed his mind.

After a while, he turned to Leyla, who was standing not far from him, and said, "Leyla, I appreciate that you supported Maana and me. We will pay you back one day, but we still need you, sister. My request is that you go to your family and plead with them on our behalf without revealing all of the mishap. Say to your father …"

"My God! I forgot to tell you some good news!" Leyla interrupted him.

"What?!" asked both Axmed and Maana simultaneously.

"My father sent for me this morning. So, I went to see him. A lot of people talked, people of goodwill. He was advised, 'You Aw-Muumin, the young man you wanted for your daughter has lost her already. Bury the past. If you don't allow your daughter to make her own choice, you are going to lose her the same way you had lost Iisha. Let her marry the one she loves. Who knows who is good for her? You let her sister Leyla marry her choice after they had eloped. Look how well she turned out.'

"So, my father answered that he was going to think it over. He later asked me to bring Maana with me. I did not tell him what had happened.

"I will take Maana with me tomorrow. I will let her apologize to her father and bow before him. Let's hope for the best," she concluded.

"Thanks, my sweet sister," said Maana with tears of happiness, kissing Leyla all over.

"Many thanks, Leyla," seconded Axmed.

Oblivious to all around them, Axmed and Maana sank into each other's arms.

Afterword

The first time that I ever heard the name 'Maana-faay' was being called it myself; "Is this Maana-faay?" my father's friends would say, looking down at me with a knowing smile in my childhood living room, as I shyly stood by the door, gathering the courage to greet these giants as they smiled warmly back at me. "Yes, this is my girl, Maana-faay," my father would reply, proudly. I knew my name was really Muna, but Maana-faay was another name that people would call me, and I knew that it had something to do with a famous book that my father had written. It always stood somewhere on a bookshelf in our home, and on the rare occasions that I would grab it, nonchalantly off the shelf, it would only be to look at the picture of the author, my father, and point at it to childhood friends, who showed little interest, as the words were foreign to them, and the book had no other pictures. Soon, I lost interest too.

As I entered my teenage years, I would google my father, reading the Wikipedia page with a detached fascination, noting the word 'exiled'. Why was he exiled from Somalia? I wondered. Something to do with the government, it seemed. It all sounded complicated. I never thought to ask my father directly. I could have called him anytime, and he would have answered with detail and vivid recounts of the adventures of his youth, delighted that I had shown interest in discovering more about him.

I sat with him once, in a coffee shop, as I was transitioning from childhood, into a teenager, still too young for coffee. I'd clutched the hot chocolate that he had bought me and asked him a question, in passing, about his childhood. He replied with long, interesting tales about growing up in a village near Galkayo. He told me how he had once been chased by a lion, and I listened, wide-eyed, almost in disbelief. We could have spoken for hours, and I could tell that I was just glimpsing the tip of the iceberg that was his life before me and my siblings were born. "You could write my life story," he had said to me, with a smile that said that he trusted me with his legacy, that I never really understood at the time. "That would be interesting," I replied, although deep down, it seemed like a long, difficult task that I could do in the future, there would be more time, I thought. I had already forgotten most of the things that he had told me by the time that I got home, and sadly still do not remember, as much as I try to think back. "You could bring a pen next time and make notes," he had said, as he wrapped up his childhood tales. I nodded enthusiastically, but I never did, and we never really spoke about it again.

Flash forward to 2019, I was an adult now, with my own responsibilities and future to pursue. My father was my father, and what that meant to me was someone who I would go to if I had problems or needed financial support planning my future. It pains me to say that, although I loved him deep down to my very bones, as I had grown through the years, so had my disinterest with his projects and work in Somalia and Djibouti. My father, perhaps sensing this disinterest, kept his important work and responsibilities to himself. Instead, we spoke about his health, and what was happening in *my* life. Until one day, he told me that he was translating Maana-faay into English, and that he wanted me to look at the first few chapters. I did, although I dragged it out, busy with teaching and things that I deemed more important. Nonetheless, he sent me a long email, praising me in a way that only a parent would, proudly claiming that I was talented, even included me in his acknowledgments, something that I only found out very recently.

Fast forward again and it was now September 2021, and I was aware that the English translation of Maana-faay was coming out soon, and I was looking forward to finally being about to read his famous book, that I had been named after as a child. Although Covid had kept us apart for a long time, my father was coming back to London, and we could finally have a proper catch-up. Then, just two days into his mandatory isolation period, with just 8 days until our reunion, I entered a nightmare. My mother gently woke me and, as I stared at her, blurry-eyed, she told me that my beloved father had suffered a major stroke. After the worst two and a half weeks of my life, on the 9th of October 2021, my father, Dr Maxamed Daahir Afrax, passed away.

Suddenly, I realised that there was no more time. If I wanted to find out more about my father, I could not ask him anymore. I had to work for it. I received countless calls about how much he had done for Somalia. I had lost him, but so had my country. My father and I had always bonded over creative writing. Since I was six years old, I had wanted to become a writer, and he had always kept the stories that I had clumsily written from childhood, up until I was in university. I found them on his laptop after he had passed away. "That one inherited my creativity, she will be a writer too," he had often proudly remarked to my mother. I was going to make him proud one day. He had been working through the last stages of editing and publishing the Maana-Faay English translation, alongside all his other many responsibilities, up until he became ill. I damped his hospital gown with my tears, praying that he could hear me through his coma; "I promise you that I will make you proud, I will write everyday like you always told me to. Don't worry about Maana-faay, I will take care of all of that for you, I will take on all of those responsibilities, I promise, you just rest now Baaba."

And so, the work began. I contacted the publisher, and Professor Ali Ahmed, who was unfailingly helpful, going above and beyond to support me. I sat in the same coffee shop that I had sat in with my father, now old enough for coffee, and spent my days carefully reading through and proofreading and copyediting Maana-faay. I had never felt closer to my father, as I read his words, hearing his narrative voice as a young man in the early 1970s, highlighting the social issues of a time and place that I had never been. I had expected the story to be outdated, with themes which were no longer relevant, alien to me as a young woman who had grown up in London England, but his words transcended time and space, they were timeless. I finally understood why he had been exiled from Somalia. He had held up a mirror up to the government, the corruption and the misogyny present in the society that he had perceived around him, and they had not liked what had been reflected back at them. I looked around at where I was living, the society today, and was saddened to see that, although my father was gone, the wrongs that he had highlighted had not gone away. Reputable, powerful men, who were protected by the industries or institutions which they represented, were still hypocritically abusing their power, whether that was to use women, girls, or for their own financial gain. Living one way of life but preaching another. I saw it in 21st century Western society, just as my father had seen it in 20th century Somalia and he had bravely and beautifully woven his criticisms into his novel Maana-faay, regardless of the consequences.

I watched my father give his life to his country, sacrificing his family time, sleep and health until the end to continue to work to make his country great. He had been working with the government to write a new constitution for Somalia, now with a new enemy, terrorism, and he still got into his bulletproof car and continued to do what he felt was right, regardless of the consequences. The least that I can do is to ensure that I keep my promise. So, this is for you Baaba.

Muna Maxamed Daahir Afrax